Amy Cross is the author of more than 100 horror, paranormal, fantasy and thriller novels.

OTHER TITLES
BY AMY CROSS INCLUDE

American Coven
Annie's Room
The Ash House
Asylum
B&B
Better the Devil
The Bride of Ashbyrn House
The Camera Man
The Curse of Wetherley House
The Devil, the Witch and the Whore
Devil's Briar
The Dog
Eli's Town
The Farm
The Ghost of Molly Holt
The Ghosts of Lakeforth Hotel
The Girl Who Never Came Back
Haunted
The Haunting of Blackwych Grange
The Haunting of Marshall Heights
Like Stones on a Crow's Back
The Night Girl
Perfect Little Monsters & Other Stories
Stephen
The Shades
The Soul Auction
Tenderling
Ward Z

Days 46 to 53

AMY CROSS

First published by Dark Season Books,
United Kingdom, 2018

Copyright © 2018 Amy Cross

First published in November 2013 as *Mass Extinction Event:
The Complete Third Series*. This edition originally published
in August 2018

ISBN: 9781718170087

Also available in e-book format.

www.amycross.com

CONTENTS

DAY 46
PAGE 13

DAY 47
PAGE 71

DAY 48
PAGE 125

DAY 49
PAGE 195

DAY 50
PAGE 241

DAY 51
PAGE 295

DAY 52
PAGE 349

DAY 53
PAGE 397

DAYS
46 TO 53

DAY 46

ELIZABETH

SHE'S MAKING NOISES AGAIN, but I can't go to her, not yet. It's too early.

I'm sitting at the kitchen table, watching as rain falls gently but persistently against the window, and somehow I feel as if the whole world has just stopped. It's been more than a month now since I arrived at the farmhouse, and over the past few weeks I've managed to force myself into some kind of routine: I get up with the sun and attend to Rachel, and then I plan what we're all going to eat for the day, and then I usually wash myself before getting on with any household chores that need doing. It's mind-numbing, but that's the point: I *need* something to numb my mind, because if I actually sit back and think about what's happening, I think I'll start crying and never stop.

Meanwhile, Toad comes and goes like a ghost, rarely saying much. It's almost as if he resents my presence. By sundown, we're both too tired to do anything, but at least Rachel almost never cries. She makes lots of faint gurgling sounds, but she barely cries at all.

Is that what babies are supposed to be like?

In movies, they cry a lot.

I wish this was a movie.

At the same time, I can't help feeling that she knows I'm not her real mother. I'm an interloper. I don't have a clue how to look after a baby. All I can do is hold her, clean her, and try to entertain her. I even sing to her sometimes, when I'm certain that Toad can't hear, but she doesn't smile much. Most of the time, she seems to have this perpetual frown on her face, and the only noises she makes are occasional gurgles and coughs. Right now, I'm trying to give her a little tough love; I don't want her to get too used to the idea that I'm looking after her, and I guess that deep down I'm worried that she might eventually start to see me as her real mother.

I'm really not sure that I'm ready for that responsibility.

The truth is, although I always wanted to have kids of my own one day, I figured I had at least ten years before I needed to worry. Now, suddenly, someone else's child has been thrust into my arms. I should be able to rise to the occasion. I should have maternal instincts that kick in and help me to cope.

But I don't.

I'm failing at this.

Hearing footsteps near the window, I look over at the door just in time to see Toad heading inside. He pushes the door open with so much force, it bangs against the wall and the windows rattle, and then he makes his way over to the table with a large box of potatoes in his arms. Setting them down in front of me, he mutters something that I can't make out as he picks up a few of the potatoes and examines them. I want to say something, to ask how things are going, but I know I wouldn't get much of an answer.

"What's it like out there?" I ask eventually, figuring that I *have* to at least try.

"Fine," he mutters.

"I was going to take Rachel outside," I continue, "but I guess the weather's not too good right now. Maybe I should just..." My voice trails off as I realize that there's no point continuing. I'm just trying to make idle conversation, which is probably the worst way to get Toad to talk to me.

He smiles faintly, but it's clear that he doesn't give a damn about anything I have to say. He's worried, too, but there's no chance he'll ever tell me what's on his mind.

Finally, he seems to lose interest in the

potatoes altogether. He wanders over to the counter, pours himself a glass of water, and then he heads back outside, not even bothering to glance back at me.

I sit silently at the table for a moment.

"Okay," I say finally, "sure, I'll see what I can do with these, then."

The truth is, I don't remember when I last heard Toad's voice. He seems to have become so insular and sullen since he recovered from his injuries. He gets up before I'm awake, and he usually works until after I've gone to bed. I hear him at night sometimes, stomping about the house. I guess it's good that he keeps busy, but there's definitely a part of me that worries he's losing his mind. On the very few occasions when he says anything at all, he just seems to mutter under his breath, and I can barely make out any words at all. He sure as hell doesn't seem to want to talk to me, or even to have a conversation. I can't work out if he hates me, or he sees me as irrelevant, or if he's just too exhausted to do anything more than work.

One thing's for certain. He barely even looks at me these days. There was a time, a while ago, when he seemed to like me. And then he just seemed to turn cold, almost overnight.

Leaning over to peer into the box of potatoes, I can't help but grimace at the sight of the damn things. They sure as hell don't look like any potatoes I ever saw in the store; instead, they seem weedy and thin, twisted a little as if they've been tortured to the point of mutation. In the old days, I'd have shoved them straight into the bin, but somehow I have to turn them into a meal. Toad always just assumes that I'll do the cooking, which I guess is fair enough since he works outside all day. Still, as I reach out and pick up a particularly freakish potato, I can't help but wonder if something is seriously wrong with the crops. Every vegetable Toad brings inside these days seems to be twisted and 'wrong', and I'm worried that the soil all around the farm just seems to be giving up on us.

I guess the potatoes are a metaphor. They're getting worse and worse, and so are we. If I didn't know better, I'd start to believe God's trying to tell us that we can't live like this for much longer. Food's getting harder and harder to come by, and each day feels a little more difficult than the last. I've been ignoring this realization for a few days now, but finally it's front and center in my mind and I feel as if something has to change.

Suddenly the door opens again. Toad stomps through and tosses something onto the table, before turning and leaving again. Shocked, I stare at what turns out to be a dead rabbit, its eyes bulging out of their sockets. There's still part of a wire trap wrapped tight around its neck, and its mouth is slightly open. I guess I'm going to have to work out how the hell to skin and prepare something like this. There'll be a lot of blood, and plenty of misplaced fur, but I'm pretty sure I can at least get *some* meat out of the endeavor.

Hauling myself up from the chair, I carry the rabbit over to the counter and place it in the small tin bath I use whenever I have to cut up anything that used to be alive. Maybe I'm squeamish, but I still haven't got used to the sight of blood. Still, I figure my first step has to be to separate the rabbit's head from the rest of its body, so I grab the large meat cleaver and take a deep breath as I prepare to make the cut. Damn it, after a month, I should be better at things like this. I've killed several chickens, but killing a rabbit somehow feels more daunting. Finally, figuring that I need to toughen up, I force myself to keep my eyes open as I slam the cleaver down as hard as I can, severing the rabbit's head in one go.

Upstairs, Rachel lets out a brief cough.

THOMAS

"COME ON, YOU GODDAMN LITTLE -"

Kneeling on the ground, I desperately dig through the soil, trying to catch the damn thing. I saw it a moment ago, glistening in the dirt, but it managed to wriggle away. I've learned how to get them, though, and finally I push my fingers as far down as I can and I bring up a huge bundle of soil, which I immediately toss onto the ground a few feet away. I start sorting through the remains, and after a moment I spot him: the biggest, juiciest worm I've ever seen in my life.

Picking him up by his tail, I blow on him to get rid of any chunks of soil, and I admire him for a moment. Goddammit, if circumstances were different, I'd keep him as a pet. Unfortunately, I don't have that luxury, so I just stare at him for a moment longer and then I dangle him in my mouth. I bite him in half and immediately swallow the front half, before doing the same with the rear. I don't like the taste of the damn things, but I'm kind of paranoid about swallowing them when they're alive.

"Sorry," I mutter, hoping that if the worm had a soul, it might still be close enough to hear.

Looking down at the pile of soil again, I spot two more worms. Once I've pulled them loose and eaten them, I double-check that there are no more and then I get to my feet. Back in the old days, I could damn near eat half a hock of lamb, but these days three worms feel like a pretty good meal. There's a bitter after-taste in my mouth, but my mother always told me that beggars can't be choosers, and I'm finally starting to understand what she meant.

Everyone's a beggar now.

Wiping the sweat from my brow, I turn and make my way back toward the truck. It's a warm day, although there are dark clouds in the distance and they seem to be moving this way, which means I should be able to top up on water before evening comes. Climbing up onto the back of the truck, I unzip one of the hold-alls and take out an energy bar. I've got a system these days: if I want to eat something normal, first I have to find something from the land, which usually means worms. With trembling hands, I unwrap the bar and start to eat.

"You'd hate this," I mutter between mouthfuls, imagining a conversation with my brother. I've been doing this for a few days now, and part of me thinks I'm losing my mind, but the rest of me doesn't give a damn.

I sit in silence for a moment. Sometimes, as well as talking to Joe out loud, I imagine his replies and I even pretend I can hear them. I know it's not exactly healthy, but it makes me feel less alone.

"I mean, where are we going?" I continue. "Are we just driving 'til the last of the fuel runs out?"

"What's the alternative, worm boy?" he'd reply. "You know, I used to call you that when you were a kid, but for a different reason. Anyway, what's the plan? You wanna turn and drive straight into the nearest brick wall?"

"Maybe," I say out loud. "At least it'd be quick."

"If you want quick," he'd say, "you might as well put a shotgun in your mouth and blow your head off. But even that isn't foolproof. I read about this guy once who somehow managed to fucking miss his own brain. Must've been the size of a walnut. I mean, God, imagine waking up in hospital and being told you couldn't even kill yourself with a shotgun."

"So what would you do?" I ask.

"How would I kill myself?"

"How would you stay alive?"

"Why do you wanna know?"

"You were smart. If it wasn't for that accident, you'd have survived. I need to work out what you'd have done, and then I need to do the same."

"Me?" I imagine him pausing for a moment. "I'd go for broke. I'd make sure that if I go out, I go out screaming and take some of those bastards with me. But that's just me, Thomas. You're different. You've always been more of a thinker. You can't really take care of yourself in a difficult situation."

"Yes I can," I mutter.

Now he's laughing. Sometimes I find it hard to make his voice fade from my mind, but finally I manage to get rid of him.

"I can," I say again. "I can do this. I'm not dead yet."

"When the shit hits the fan," he'd continue, "you fuck things up. You panic and you make mistakes. All you're doing now is sitting around, waiting for one of those mistakes to finish you off. Deep down, you know it's true. After all, it's not really me you're talking to, is it? It's yourself, you fucking psycho."

It's been a month since I saw another person, and I'm starting to wonder if I'm the last person left in the whole goddamn world. I've driven through countless small towns, although I avoided St. Louis completely since I was worried that there might be more of those creatures. Sometimes I stop off at gas stations and steal as much as I can, but the last one was a week ago and now I've only got enough gas to last another few days. At least I haven't seen any more of the creatures. I kind of keep expecting a bunch of them to come marauding over the horizon, ready to finish me off, and to be honest I don't reckon I've got much chance of defending myself.

Still, I have to keep going. I figure I must be in Illinois by now, which means that the dark smudge in the distance is almost certainly Chicago. If things don't pick up soon, I'm gonna go straight into the heart of the city. If there are creatures, then that's something I'll have to deal with when I get there. I sure as hell can't survive much longer out here, living off worms. Maybe Chicago can be my brick wall.

"You're angry," I imagine Joe saying. "How are you gonna let that anger out, huh?"

As soon as I've finished the energy bar, I climb down and head around to the front of the truck. I have to keep moving. If I stay still for too long, I might just keel over and die.

ELIZABETH

"I WASN'T REALLY SURE what to do with it," I explain as I place two plates of fried rabbit and boiled potato on the table, "so I just got as much meat off the bones as possible and fried some of it up. There should be enough left over for two more days."

Without saying anything, he immediately starts eating. I don't know why I keep trying to strike up conversations with him, when it's clear that he's retreated into his own little world. There was a time when we talked, and he even kissed me once, but now I feel as if he barely even notices that I'm around. The worst part is, I've come to realize that we're all probably going to die soon, in which case Toad is my last and only chance for real human contact. It'd be funny, if it wasn't so tragic.

"How long do you think we've got?" I ask eventually.

He glances at me, but he's too busy eating to reply.

"We're going to die here," I continue, feeling as if I can't hold my thoughts back any longer. "We are, aren't we? This whole thing, trying to keep going, it's not working."

He doesn't say anything.

In the room above, Rachel lets out a brief gurgle, but at least she's not crying.

"So how long have we got?" I ask.

He carries on eating, but at least I seem to have got his attention.

"What are we supposed to do?" I continue, trying not to sound desperate. "Are we just going to sit around here and wait until we run out of everything, and then starve to death? Is that your plan?"

He pauses.

"Have you thought about maybe trying something else?" I ask. "I mean, I don't know what to do, but -"

"We need to hit the road," he says suddenly.

I stare at him.

"You're right," he adds. "Sitting around here won't do any good."

"I..." Pausing, I try to work out what to say next. "Where? I mean, what are our options?"

"I've been thinking about it for a while," he continues, coughing for a moment as if to clear his throat, "and we need to get out of here. I worked for years to get this place ready in case I needed to survive here, but things aren't working out as I'd hoped. We're running low on supplies and I don't know how much longer I'll be able to find fresh meat out in the forest."

"Why didn't you say something sooner?" I ask.

"Why didn't *you*?"

"I was waiting for you," I tell him.

"Why? Because I'm the boss?" He pauses. "You're not a kid, Elizabeth, so you need to stop thinking like one. I could tell you were worried, and I kept waiting for you to say something. Eventually I realized you were slipping into a subordinate role, and that's not gonna work, not anymore." He pauses. "I need you to believe that you're an equal here, not that you're a kid who has to wait to be told what to do. I figured I needed to wait for you to speak up."

"So this was a test?" I ask.

"I've been preparing for a journey," he tells me. "I didn't need to warn you in advance, so I decided to wait and see if you'd ask about what I'm thinking. You can't sit around, expecting me to be the adult here. If you've got something to say, you need to say it, instead of waiting quietly and trying to work out what I'm thinking just by watching me."

I pause for a moment, genuinely shocked by what he's saying. I thought Toad was becoming more insular, but now it seems he was testing me all along. Suddenly I feel like an idiot, and as I look down at my plate of food, I have to fight the urge to get up and leave the room. I actually thought I was doing pretty well; I've been keeping the house in good order, and I'm always able to get some kind of meal on the table. Hell, back in the old days, I barely even knew how to use a can-opener, and now I'm starting to think I might actually be a damn good cook. I thought Toad appreciated all of this, and that we'd fallen into complimentary roles, but now it's clear that he thinks I'm just a dumb kid.

"You're right," he continues, his voice sounding harsh and tired. "The crops are failing. I don't know what's wrong with the land, but ever since that big rainstorm, everything's been dying. There used to be so many rabbits in the forest, you'd damn near trip over one if you weren't careful. Now it's getting harder and harder to find them, and the few that are left seem diseased and sick. I don't know where it's coming from, but something's playing havoc with the world around us. I go out there every day and I do my best, but it's clear that this isn't working. The land isn't going to keep us alive."

"Okay," I mutter, surprised that he's finally

talking to me. "Sure, but where can we go?"

"The truck's no good," he replies, "so we'll have to go by foot. The kid'll slow us down, so we need to be realistic about our options. Pittsburgh should be within our range, so if we prepare properly we can set out tomorrow." He pauses. "If you're worried about the creatures, I think it'll be okay. We haven't seen any for weeks. I was expecting more of them to start showing up, but so far it's almost as if they're dying off. Either that, or they're avoiding us."

"What about disease?" I ask. "There must be thousands of dead bodies in the city."

"We'll take precautions," he continues. "There are no risk-free options here, Elizabeth."

I watch for a moment as he finishes his food.

"How are your shoes?" he asks eventually.

"My shoes?"

"You need to make sure they're sturdy enough for the journey," he continues. "If they're not, you'll have to fix them up."

"How?"

"Work it out for yourself," he replies. "I'm not here to do everything for you. There are some old shoes kicking about too from other people, so you might be able to adapt some of them and make yourself a spare pair. This is the kind of thing you need to be able to sort out without always looking to me for help, okay? If you can't think laterally and work with your hands, you're going to be a drain, and that's the kind of person who's really not going to last long."

I nod, but the truth is, I feel as if I'm about to start crying. I'm sure Toad would be very impressed if that happened, so I force myself to start eating, hoping that I'll be able to hold back the tears.

"This isn't a game," he continues. "If you fuck something up, you don't get to go back to the start of the level. If you don't have proper shoes for the journey, you'll end up with broken skin on the soles of your feet. Eventually you'll get an infection, and then you'll probably end up with blood poisoning and you'll die. There are a million other little things that you need to think about, and you can't rely on me to look after us both. I'm sorry if I seem harsh, but I need you to grow up, Elizabeth."

"Okay," I reply, taking a deep breath.

"And you need to -"

"Okay," I say firmly, interrupting him. "I get it. Just... I get it."

"I hope so," he replies, finishing his food before getting to his feet. "At least you finally told me about your concerns. I was starting to think you were gonna just sit around and wait for me to make the decision. We'll set out tomorrow. Until then, we need to start getting ready, and you need to work out how to keep that baby alive on the journey."

"Sure," I reply as he heads to the door. "I'll

do it."

"There's another reason I haven't said much lately," he continues, turning back to look at me. "This farm was supposed to be a hold-out in case things went to hell. I spent a lot of time and money getting it ready, and it's barely lasted more than a month. It's a failure, which means *I'm* a failure, and..." He pauses. "Don't go relying on me to save your life," he adds finally. "You need to make your own decisions, Elizabeth. The walk to Pittsburgh is gonna be tough, and there's a good chance we won't make it. We're equals here. I'm not in charge. The sooner you realize that, the better chance we'll have."

"Okay," I reply, my voice trembling a little.

"To start with," he continues, "have you done what I asked about the pit?"

I shake my head.

"Why are you delaying?"

I take a deep breath.

"Get out there and do it today," he adds. "The damn thing's probably rotted away by now anyway. If you want to prove that you're not a kid, go and do a man's job for once."

With that, he heads through to the next room, leaving me sitting in stunned silence at the kitchen table. I know that Toad's right, but at the same time I'm shocked by the fact that he seemed so aggressive. It's almost as if he's disappointed in me, even though I feel as if I've been doing a pretty good job. Either that, or the guy's a massive asshole. Could that be what's happened? Have I been stranded at the end of the world with a misanthropic, self-absorbed misogynist?

Upstairs, Rachel lets out a few more brief gurgles.

THOMAS

CLIMBING OUT OF THE TRUCK, I push the door shut before turning and looking over at the gas station. It looks peaceful and completely undisturbed, which suggests that not only has it escaped the creatures, but it also hasn't been ransacked by anyone else.

Still, I know I have to be careful. One wrong move could be fatal.

"Watch out," I imagine Joe saying. "There could be zombies all over the fucking place."

"Shut up," I whisper.

"Shut me up," he'd reply. "It's your imagination, asshole."

Heading around to the back of the truck, I grab a spade before starting to make my way across the gas station's forecourt. There's a part of me that's desperate to just go right ahead and break through the window. After all, there should still be plenty of food in there, enough to last me at least another month, but at the same time I have to be absolutely certain that there are none of those creatures around. I have no idea if they're smart enough to set up a trap, but I'm going to hold back until I'm certain.

Spotting something around the side of the building, I make my way over and find that there's a car parked next to one of the pumps. It's an old convertible with the roof down, and I immediately start to worry. If the car's here, it means someone drove it to the station and then didn't leave, which means they have to be around here somewhere. I raise the spade, ready to defend myself at the first sign of movement, and I make my way around the side of the car, keeping a good distance back so that nothing can attack me.

So far, there's no sign of anyone.

"It's a trap," Joe would probably be saying right about now. "They're smart, those zombies."

I complete a full circuit of the gas station, making sure that there's absolutely no way anything or anyone can get a jump on me. Once I'm back around at the forecourt, I stop for a moment and listen out for any sign of movement, and finally I start to cautiously approach the building. Putting my foot in the way to make sure nothing can burst through the door, I peer through the glass and see nothing inside but rows and rows of food. There's a fresh fruit stand nearby, covered in mold, but a little further inside there seems to be plenty of tinned food, as well as candy and some bottled water. Given the way things have been lately, this is almost like winning the lottery, but I still can't relax.

There's a car here.

Which means there's at least one person here.

"Nice set of wheels," Joe's voice says in my head. "I wouldn't mind a car like this."

"You're dead," I reply.

"A man can still dream, can't he?"

Taking a step back, I pull on the door and find that it's unlocked. I open it all the way and lean forward, although the smell from the moldy fruit is pretty horrific. The lights are off so the interior of the gas station is pretty gloomy, but at least I can see that there definitely isn't anything hiding nearby. I step inside and pause for a moment, waiting to see if there's any hint of movement. After a few seconds, I make my way past the ends of the aisles, while constantly looking around to see if there's anyone nearby. I head along the far wall, with the spade still raised in case I need to defend myself, but eventually I get to the cash register and find that it's deserted.

There's no-one here.

"Hello?" I call out.

I wait.

Nothing.

Once I've taken another circuit of the room and confirmed that I'm alone, I finally dare to put the spade down so that I can fill a sack with tinned food. It doesn't take too long before I have to hurry out to the truck and toss my haul into the back, before grabbing another sack and making my way back into the gas station for some more supplies. I swear to God, I've been dreaming about a moment like this for weeks. All the other gas stations I've found have provided slim pickings, but this one is like Christmas and Easter rolled into one. Hell, I'm gonna be able to have a feast tonight, and my days of eating worms are long gone.

"Well, this is a turnaround," Joe would be saying right about now. "Remember when I robbed a store like this? You were so goddamn appalled, and yet now here you are, doing the exact same thing."

"This is different," I whisper.

"You think?"

"This is about survival," I point out. "Back then, we didn't know what was happening. You were just looting booze and cigarettes. I'm leaving that stuff behind."

"Damn shame," he'd say. "Why not grab a bottle of whiskey? Go on, save it up for when things are really bad. Trust me, there are times in a man's life when he really needs to take his mind of things."

"I don't drink," I reply.

"And therein lies half your fucking problem," he'd continue. "God damn it, Thomas, you need to relax a little. I mean, fuck, I know everyone thought I went crazy on the stuff, but it's not like I had much else to do, sitting around that stinking farm all day. I think maybe I had the right idea."

"And yet you're the one who's dead."

"That's just bad luck," he'd say, "and thanks for throwing shit like that back in my face. Asshole."

Finally, after nearly half an hour, I've managed to more or less clean the entire place out. There are a few other items that I'd like to take, but I'm worried that I've already weighed the truck down enough, so I decide to head out and get as much gas as possible out of the machines. First, though, I walk around to the cash register and try to get it open. I know old-fashioned cash isn't really much use at the moment, but I still figure I might as well grab what I can. With the power off, I can't get the register to open properly, so I take a step back and smash the front with the spade. I don't really know what I'm doing, but finally I'm able to break through the top of the terminal with enough force to expose the drawer underneath.

I start pulling out the notes and coins, but that's when I hear it.

I pause.

There's a faint sound coming from somewhere nearby, like a kind of scratching and clicking noise. I look over at the door that leads through to the office. Earlier, I checked and made sure that it was locked, but now there's definitely something moving about in there. I keep telling myself that it's probably just a rat, but after a moment I realize that I can hear something breathing on the other side of the door, just a few feet away. I take a step closer, trying to work out if it's actually a person.

Silence.

Then a clicking sound that seems strangely familiar.

"Thomas," I imagine Joe's voice saying, "get the fuck down."

At the last moment, I suddenly realize what I can hear. I step out of the way just as a shotgun round blows the door apart. Fragments of shattered wood are sent spinning across the room, and one of the pieces catches my face and cuts the skin, but all I can do is back into the corner and wait as the dust settles. After a few seconds, with dust still filling the air, I realize I can hear someone still moving about in the next room.

ELIZABETH

IT'S BEEN A COUPLE of weeks now since Toad told me to come out here and get this job done, but I've been putting it off. He probably thinks I'm being squeamish, but the truth is that I've been hoping the job would kind of take care of itself. After all, it's been almost a month since either of us came to check on the creature in the pit, and I figure it must have rotted away by now.

Setting the can of gas down on the ground, I stare at the top of the pit and wait for some hint of movement from down below. Hearing nothing, I lean down and open the can before tilting it and dousing some rags. My heart is pounding and I can't help glancing around every few seconds, just in case there's anything else out here. It's been a long time since we saw any of the creatures, but I know that one could appear at any moment. Finally, figuring that I just need to get this done, I grab the can and head over to the edge of the pit. Along the way, I catch my foot on something, and I feel a sharp pain in my right ankle.

Taking a look, I see that I've cut myself on an old piece of barbed wire. It doesn't look too bad, so I figure I can clean it up later.

When I look down into the pit, I see that the creature's body is little more than a husk now. It's strange to think that just a few weeks ago, Patricia was planning to keep the damn thing alive so she could carry out experiments. Sometimes those days feel as if they happened a million years ago, to someone else in another life. Holding the can up, I start pouring gasoline down into the pit, making sure to cover the creature's body as much as possible. Maybe I'm getting hardened to this kind of thing, but now that I'm finally out here, there's definitely a part of me that's looking forward to watching the damn thing burn. After all, if these creatures had never appeared, a whole lot of people would still be alive.

I'd still have my parents, and my brother, and a future.

Once the gas can is empty, I set it aside and grab the rags. Reaching into my pocket, I pull out the old cigarette lighter I found in Patricia's room. It feels good to be finally getting this job done, and

I'm starting to think that in some ways Toad was right. I tend to spend far too much of my time sitting around, waiting for things to happen, when really all that I need to do is get off my ass and start working. I know Toad thinks I'm too passive, but I'm determined to show him that I can step up to the plate. Sure, things might be looking pretty bleak right now, but I'm damn well not going to just sit down and wait to die. At least one member of the Marter family is going to make it out of this nightmare alive.

Hearing a creaking noise from the pit, I glance down, not really expecting to see anything. After a moment, however, I realize that the creature's head seems to have moved slightly. I stare, trying to stay calm while reminding myself that this is probably all just in my head. After a moment, however, there's more movement, as the creature very slowly turns to look at me, even though its shriveled eyes look as if there's no way they can see anything at all.

I stare back down at it, but to my surprise I realize that I'm not scared. I'm angry.

"Have you been conscious down there all this time?" I ask.

There's no reply. Judging from the state of the creature's emaciated face, I'm not sure it's even capable of talking anymore. Most of its skin has rotted away, exposing part of the skull, and the jawbone looks to be hanging loose from one side. Between its rows of stained teeth, however, I can see something moving, and finally I realize that the tongue is twitching. I guess the creature might be trying to say something after all.

"I was supposed to come and kill you a long time ago," I continue, feeling strangely bold and calm. "I figured I'd let you suffer, though. I hope it hurt as you were wasting away down here. I hope you felt every second of pain as your body broke down."

Slowly, the creature tilts its head a little, almost like a dog that doesn't understand a command.

"Can you even feel anything anymore?" I ask. "I knew someone who was going to carry out a load of experiments on you. She wanted to test you and poke you, and try to work out exactly what you are." I pause for a moment. "Part of me wishes she'd had the chance. She was very focused on her work, so I doubt she'd have spent much time worrying about your well-being. She'd probably have tortured you, just to get a better understanding of how you work. I'd have been horrified, but maybe I'd have come to enjoy it after a while. Still, she went kind of crazy in the end. She was trying to work out which one of us had been infected in the house, and she went overboard. She was probably a nice person before this madness started, though. That's the worst thing. You're making us become different people, just so we can survive."

The creature shifts its position a little, almost as if it's trying to get up. It clearly has no chance of moving very much, though, since most of its muscle mass is gone. I watch as it keeps trying, and finally its entire jawbone comes loose, dropping down onto its ribs before falling to the ground. The creature continues to stare at me, and now I can see its tongue rising up from the back of its throat, flicking in different directions as a faint gurgle emerges. The damn thing looks ridiculous.

"I'm not even scared of you," I continue, staring at the shriveled brown orbs that were once a pair of eyes. "Not now. You might look like some kind of zombie, but you're not, are you? You're a living, breathing thing, or at least you used to be. We thought you were going to overrun us and rip us to pieces, but we haven't seen any more of you for weeks. What happened? Did you all just wither away like this? I don't know what the hell you've been planning, but right now you don't look so scary. In fact, you look pretty goddamn weak. I could probably just leave you down there and you'd rot away by the weekend, or I could climb down and throttle you with my bare hands."

Pausing for a moment, I realize that it actually feels better to be saying these things. For the past few weeks, I've lived in constant fear of these creatures showing up again, but now I'm starting to think that the threat might be over. After all, if they've all started to rot away, there's a chance that nature might just have taken care of the problem. Then again, there's probably an element of wishful thinking about this scenario, and I try to focus on the fact that things can't be so easy.

"This is for my brother," I say finally, holding the rag up and lighting the gasoline-soaked bottom half. "It's also for the other people who've died since all of this began, but mainly it's for Henry, and for my parents, because I miss them and because I'm never going to get them back. I don't know how many other people have also died over the past few weeks, but I'm sure it's a lot, and it's all your fault."

The creature stares up at me. For a moment - just a moment - I almost feel sorry for it, but then I remember some of the things it said when we spoke last time, and I realize that even this quick death is too merciful.

"Go to hell," I add, before dropping the rag. The gasoline at the bottom of the pit immediately ignites, and I have to take a step back as the heat becomes unbearable. Staring into the flames, I try to imagine the creature's body being burned to ash, and I can't help but hope that there's still enough of its mind left to allow it to feel real pain. This is a whole new side to me, but I swear to God I want every damn one of those things to die in the most agonizing manner possible. I don't care if that makes me a bad person.

After a moment, I realize I can hear a noise in the distance. Turning and looking back at the house, I'm surprised by the fact that suddenly Rachel seems to be crying. More than crying, maybe; it's almost as if she's screaming.

THOMAS

"I CAN HEAR YOU!" the man shouts from the next room. "Don't think you can keep down and trick me! I know you're there! I saw your skinny ass ducking out the way! What's up? Did I get you?"

Squeezed into the corner behind the cash register, I try to work out how to get away from here as fast as possible. The problem is, I have no way of knowing if this madman has another shot ready to fire off, and I'm pretty sure he wouldn't have much trouble blowing a hole through the wall if he thought he had a chance of hitting me; there's also the fact that he could lean out through the hole at any moment, so I need to be careful. Wiping some blood from my cheek, I look up at the counter and try to work out of I could jump over and get to the door.

"It's been a while since one of your lot was here," the man continues, "but I blew the other bastards away and I'll finish you too!"

Pausing, I realize that he thinks I'm one of the creatures. I want to call out to him and tell him he's wrong, but I might just end up helping him get a better shot at me. All I can think about is that I have to get the hell out of here, but I'm terrified to make a move in case he catches sight of me and fires again.

"What's wrong?" he asks. "No more gloating? You lot normally have a hell of a lot to say, even when you're in a bad way. Aren't you gonna tell me all about how I'm gonna get picked off eventually? That's what you usually do, isn't it? I've lost track of the number of your lot I've taken down, and I'm still here! I was starting to think you'd given up on me. Frankly, I was feeling a little insulted."

"I'm not one of them!" I shout, although I immediately regret the outburst.

"Bullshit!" he shouts.

"I'm not!" Taking a deep breath, I figure that now I've started talking to him, I'd be crazy to stop. "I'm just passing through! I thought this place was deserted!"

"I'm onto you!" he replies. "I know what you're like! You're trying to trick me!"

"I'm not!" I shout back at him. "I swear, I'm

just looking for food! I'll put it all back, I promise!"

"And how the hell am I supposed to believe you?" he asks. "For all I know, you're probably lying your goddamn rotten mouth off!"

"I've seen them," I reply. "The creatures, I've seen them, but not in the past few weeks. I've been driving, I'm trying to find other people, or..." I pause as I realize that I'm not really sure *why* I'm driving, except that I keep hoping I'll somehow stumble across something that helps all of this chaos make sense. "I'm like you," I continue, "or at least I think I am. How do I know *you're* not one of them?"

"Do I sound like one of them?" he shouts.

"No," I reply. "Do I?"

"That ain't no proof!" he yells. "Maybe the damn things are just getting smarter!"

"No-one can prove anything!" I tell him. "We're in this together. I don't know how many of us are left, but everyone I've met so far has either been dead or they died right after. I don't know what the hell's going on, but I'm just trying to get somewhere safe. Please, you have to believe me. Do I really sound like one of those creatures?"

I wait for an answer, but he seems to have fallen silent.

"I'll get all the stuff I took," I continue, "and I'll put it back. I swear to God. You can come out and keep that damn thing aimed at me the whole time if it makes you feel better, but all I want is to get going."

I wait, but again he seems to have no intention of answering.

"So I'm going to get up now," I say finally, figuring that the guy could probably have shot me through the wall by now if that was his plan. Getting to my feet, I stare at the hole in the door, convinced that at any moment the guy is going to come out.

Silence.

"My name's Thomas," I say after a moment. "Thomas Edgewater. My parents and my brother were both killed by this virus thing, whatever the hell it is, and as far as I know my sister's dead too. I'm just trying to get somewhere safe. I don't know where, but I figure I'm going to head toward Chicago and see if there's any sign of life. I don't know what the creatures are or where they came from, not really; all I know is that I haven't seen one for more than three weeks, but I'm not convinced they're gone just yet."

Silence.

"Two weeks," he says suddenly.

"Two?"

"That's how long it's been since I saw one of 'em," he continues, sounding noticeably less abrasive. "Damn thing was nearly falling apart as it hobbled toward me. Hell, I waited 'til she was right close before I blew her head clear off her body. If you ask me, they're starting to rot and when that happens, they ain't no good at holding together." He pauses. "Okay, Thomas Edgewater, why don't you step into view? Let me get a good look at you and make sure you're not falling apart."

I take a deep breath, staring at the hole in the door.

"I know what you're probably thinking," he adds. "You're thinking you could vault the counter and I probably couldn't get a shot in. You're right. However, I've got a little window here and it gives me a very nice view of that truck of yours, so even though you'd make it to the door, I wouldn't give you much chance of getting away. So if you've really got nothing to hide, why don't you come and let me see you, huh?"

Figuring that this is my best bet, I make my way cautiously toward the door. I'm still worried that this is a trap, that even if this guy isn't one of the creatures, he might still be dangerous. Finally, however, I reach the door and look through, and to my surprise I find myself staring at an old man with a huge white beard, aiming his shotgun straight at me. Damn it, it's like Santa Claus versus the zombies.

"That's right," he mutters. "You just stand there and let me get a *good* look at you. Hold your hands up."

I raise my hands obediently, even though I'm trembling with fear. If I was in the old man's place, I think I'd probably shoot me.

"You don't look like one of 'em to me," he continues. "I swear to God, though... If you so much as look at me wrong, I'll blow your goddamn head off. And if you're thinking I've only got one shot left, you're wrong. I already reloaded and I'm a damn good shot. I don't usually need two goes, and I sure as hell never need three."

"Please," I reply, "I just want to get out of here. I'll put all the food back -"

"No," he says, interrupting me, "you won't be putting nothing back." He pauses. "You got enough gasoline to get to Chicago?"

"I think so, but -"

"The pumps here are dry," he continues, "otherwise I'd have taken off myself. I didn't really have much of a plan, but now fortune seems to have dropped you into my lap so I figure I might as well make use of you. Then again, I'm a fair man, so here's the deal. I don't know if Chicago's a good destination, but I figure it's better than sitting around here. That truck of yours looks pretty decent, so I'll sit out on the back and you can drive. When we get to Chicago, that's where we part ways. Deal?"

I stare at him, and somehow I get the feeling that I don't really have much choice.

"Sure," I reply, "but -"

"Don't think you can try anything, either," he adds. "I can blow your head off through the window in the back of that truck's cab, so you just concentrate on keeping us moving forward. The alternative is that I'll blow your head off right now and take the damn truck anyway. I could do that, you know. I'm being very kind here, letting you live."

"I... okay," I say finally.

"Wise choice," he replies. "The name's George, and that's really all you need to know about me. I'm not intending to become friendly with you, boy, even if you look like a decent type. We're just two people who happen to be going in the same direction, so we might as well help each other out. You're helping me by driving, and I'm helping you by giving you food and by not blowing your head off. One more time, do we have a deal?"

I nod.

"Say it."

"We have a deal," I tell him.

"You'll be walking ahead of me," he adds. "Five paces at all times, and I'll have this gun aimed right at your goddamn back, you understand?"

I nod again, even though I'm desperately trying to think of a way to get away from this guy. It's clear that he's not quite right in the head, and after everything that happened a few weeks ago, I sure as hell don't want to end up being pushed around by yet another madman.

"So what are you waiting for?" he asks, taking a step toward me while keeping the gun aimed at my face. "Move!"

ELIZABETH

"IT'S OKAY," I SAY as I hold Rachel in my arms, "there's no need to cry. Everything's going to be okay."

I've been pacing around the room for the past few minutes, desperately trying to get her to stop screaming. After several weeks of almost preternatural quiet, she seems to have suddenly erupted into a bawling fit that shows no sign of stopping. If I'd perhaps allowed myself to start thinking that I had a natural touch when it came to babies, those beliefs have been completely swept away now that Rachel seems to be turning almost red in the face as she screams. In fact, if she doesn't stop crying soon, I think I might lose my mind.

"Come on," I say, forcing a smile as I walk to the window and look out at the fire burning in the distance. "It's all fine," I continue. "I burned the nasty monster, see? He's gone. We should be happy, not sad."

Looking down at Rachel, I see that her face is screwed up in a fit of absolute despair, and tears are rolling down her cheeks. It's a horrible sight, and I can't help feeling that if her real mother was here things would be very different. Shauna might not have been the most reliable person in the world, but I'm convinced she would have at least known how to look after Rachel. I figure that along with motherhood, there must come some kind of instinctive knowledge when it comes to looking after babies. Plus, Shauna would have been able to provide breast milk, whereas so far Toad and I have been having to feed her water, normal milk and pureed vegetables. I have no idea if we're doing the right thing, but I'm starting to wonder if her diet is the cause of her problems.

"No luck?" a voice asks from nearby.

Turning, I see that Toad is standing in the doorway, watching us.

"She started up a few minutes ago," I tell him, even though Rachel's ear-splitting scream shows no sign of abating. "I don't know what's wrong with her, but it's like all of a sudden she's desperate about something. I don't think she's in pain, at least not from anything I can see. I'm worried it might be something internal."

"Seems a bit unusual," he replies. "Is it normal for babies to change so suddenly?"

"I don't know," I tell him, gently rocking Rachel in an attempt to get her to calm down. "What if we're not giving her the right food? You have to be careful what you feed to babies, don't you? We're probably giving her all the wrong things."

"That noise is driving me crazy," Toad continues. "Maybe you should take her outside or something. It's gonna drive me over the edge if she just keeps on screaming."

I turn to him, and for a moment I actually feel as if I want to hit him.

"What's that look for?" he asks. "Can't you just take her outside for a bit 'til she calms down?"

"*Now* who's making assumptions about roles?" I ask, feeling as if Toad's finding it very easy to put all responsibility for Rachel on my shoulders. "You said I needed to stop thinking like a child," I continue, "and that's fair enough, but *you* need to stop assuming that I automatically know how to look after a baby. I don't have a clue what to do with her. I mean, hell, nothing seems to be working. I've tried singing to her, talking to her, rocking her, leaving her alone... Short of dumping her in the woods, I don't know what else to do."

"Have you checked she's not soiled herself?" he asks.

"Of course," I reply. "I guess she'll calm down eventually. I don't know if maybe she's teething or something like that. She's only a month old, though... I thought things like teething took longer." Looking down at Rachel again, I can't help but wonder how much longer it'll be before she runs out of energy. "I hope she's not sick," I add. "If something's wrong with her, I won't even know where to begin. I know Patricia had some medical books, but still, I'm not a doctor." After a moment, I lean down and kiss Rachel's forehead. "Then again," I mutter, "I guess I'll just have to learn."

"I'm sorry about earlier," he replies.

I look over at him.

"I was trying to make a point," he continues. "It was a valid point, and I'd been thinking about it for a while, but the way I put it across... I acted like an ass, and I'm sorry." He pauses. "You know, I think that's the first time I've properly apologized to anyone for a long time."

I force a faint smile, but I'm sure as hell not going to thank him.

He stays in the doorway, clearly wanting to say something.

"You were right," I tell him eventually. "I *have* been thinking of myself as a child. I have to be more independent. I have to stop waiting for you to make decisions. Before all this started, I just spent my time in Manhattan, arguing with my parents and my brother, trying to have fun. It's hard to believe it's only a month or so since all of this started, and I'm pretty sure I've already changed a lot. I know I've got more to do, though, and I'll get there. I also figure, when we get to wherever we're going, Pittsburgh or whatever, there's no need for us to stick together, not if you don't want to. If we find other people, maybe we'll go different ways."

He stares at me, and it's clear that he wasn't prepared for me to say anything like that.

"Sure," he replies finally. "I mean, totally. It's not like we're..."

I wait for him to continue, but he seems lost for words.

"I'm just guessing," I tell him. "Right now, even getting to Pittsburgh feels like a huge challenge. I don't even know if we'll make it."

"We can try," he replies. "I have maps, and I'm hoping the weather turns in our favor. There's a lot of farmland to the west of here, which hopefully means we don't have to go through a whole load of towns along the way. If we get to Pittsburgh, we'll have to see how things are. There might be other people like us, or there might be no-one. We can't plan ahead too far."

I force myself to smile, even though Rachel's continued crying is starting to drive me crazy. I know it's an awful thing to think, but I can't help wondering if maybe I should just put her on her bed and then go out of the house for a few hours. If there's nothing I can do for her, I might as well just let her keep crying, but at the same time I feel as if that would be a cruel way to treat her. The poor little thing is probably just scared, and I'm convinced she must be able to sense that Toad and I aren't her parents.

"I'll let you get on with it," Toad says finally. "Remember, we're setting off bright and early tomorrow, so we need to be ready."

Once he's gone, I continue to pace the room with Rachel in my arms. After half an hour or so, I happen to pass by the window and see that the fire in the pit has finally begun to go out, probably thanks to the fact that the rain has returned. Still, there can be no doubt that as the last of the flames die down, the creature must have been completely destroyed. I'll go and check later for sure, but I imagine there's nothing left but a pile of charred bones. In a strange way, it feels good to have destroyed that thing.

Suddenly, as if a switch has been flicked, Rachel stops crying.

I look down at her and find that she's staring up at me with a look of wonder in her eyes. I can't help but smile as I realize that somehow, miraculously, her crying fit has come to an end.

"Okay," I say with relief, carrying her across the room and setting her down on the bed, "just for that, I'm going to give you something to eat, okay? Some of that vegetable puree you like so much. Just please, *please* try not to get sick, okay? I have no idea if I'm doing this right, and I know I'm not your Mom, but I'm trying as hard as I can. If you don't like something, try to give me a hint, okay?"

Reaching over to the bedside table, I start pouring out some of the pureed vegetables I prepared earlier. It takes a moment to stir them, but finally I turn back to Rachel and find that she's staring at me with an expression I'm not sure I've ever seen on her face before. Usually, there's a hint of curiosity in her eyes, as if she's trying to understand who and what I am, but this time she seems to be almost frowning. I stare at her, feeling a little disturbed by the look in her eyes, and finally I realize that a faint smile is slowly creeping across her face.

"Rachel?" I say, trying not to panic. "Are you okay?"

The smile lingers for a moment, and then she looks at the cup of puree. I scoop some out with a spoon and feed it to her, and she seems to be back to normal, but for a moment there she definitely had a very different expression. Although I try to tell myself that I mustn't panic, I can't help thinking that I've seen a very similar expression once before, back when I was talking to the creature in the pit. Then again, there's no way a baby could be infected.

The world just can't be that cruel. I'm just imagining things.

I pause for a moment.

"Don't worry," I say finally, giving her another spoonful of puree. "Everything's going to be fine." Telling myself that I'm being paranoid, I focus on feeding Rachel, and I try to put any other worries to the back of my mind.

THOMAS

"CHRIST, BOY," George says as he examines the haul I've managed to collect on the back of the truck, "you're not doing too bad for yourself here, are you?"

"I've been saving," I reply, watching the end of his shotgun carefully and wondering if there's any way I can overpower him. So far, he doesn't seem to be quite as crazy as the old Eads guy, but I still don't like having a gun pointed in my face all the time and I definitely don't want to have a passenger on the drive to Chicago. Then again, right now I don't seem to have much of a choice.

"Wouldn't take much to get a run on him," I imagine Joe saying. "Come on, Thomas. You can't seriously let this old bastard tell you what to do. Wait 'til he's not looking and make sure you finish him with one good blow to the head. There's no room for being sentimental, not with the world ending all around you."

"You can stop with all your plotting," George says with a smile as he opens the bag of energy bars. "I know that's what you're doing every time you fall silent, and it won't work. I don't wanna pull the trigger on you, but I'll do it if that's what's needed. All that matters to me right now is getting to Chicago." He turns to me. "Take a few steps back, boy."

"I just -"

"Take a few steps back," he says again, more firmly this time. "I don't wanna start saying everything twice, you understand?"

Reluctantly, I step away.

"That's better," he replies, before hauling himself up onto the back of the truck. For a fraction of a second, he has to swing the gun away from me, but it's aiming at my face again before I have a chance to contemplate any kind of a move against him. He might be getting on in years, but he sure as hell seems pretty nimble. "So I heard you talking to yourself earlier," he continues. "Are you crazy?"

I shake my head.

"But you hear voices in your head?"

I shake my head again.

"Just a way of passing the time, huh?" He pauses. "I guess I can understand that. We've all gotta do whatever's necessary if we wanna stay sane. I used to think that all the noise of the world was pushing me to the brink of madness, but now it's all suddenly gone..." He wipes his brow on the sleeve of his coat. "Humans are pack animals, aren't they? Some of us like to be alone, but we're the weird ones, we're the..."

I wait for him to continue, but he seems to be just staring at me for a moment, as if he's still not quite sure what to make of me.

"Course, you can always just stay put," he says eventually, with a faint smile. "If you prefer, I'll take the truck and you can hang around here. I'd understand if heading into the heart of the city doesn't really appeal to you."

"It just seems like..." I pause for a moment, trying to find the right word.

"Suicide?" he asks.

"There are probably creatures there," I point out.

"It's quite possible," he replies, "but if I had to put money on it, I'd say something's holding 'em back. And even if there are some of 'em still going, there are probably people too, at least in the city. I figure it's time to take risks. Do you know how long it's been now since all of this started? Have you been keeping track?"

I shake my head.

"This is day forty-six," he continues. "That's

a month and a half. I've been playing it safe, hoping that things would get better, but I'm just about out of patience now. There's no point clinging to life out here, desperately waiting for someone else to ride along and make everything better. I'm fully aware that by going into the city, I'm most likely signing my own death warrant, and maybe the fact that I'm an old man makes that easier to accept. The world has always been divided into two groups: those who go for the safe option, and those who take risks. Only difference now is, the safe option isn't really very safe, and the risks are much bigger."

"I know about risks," I tell him. "I killed my brother."

"Huh. Well, I'm not sure I wanna ask about that right now -"

"He got taken," I continue. "He became one of them, and then he tried to fight back. It didn't work out for him in the end, but he never went for the safe option either."

"Sounds like a good guy."

"He was an asshole," I reply. "I think he would've done better the way things are now, though. Maybe he was better suited to this kind of world. He had, like..." I pause, wondering whether it'd be disloyal to say what I'm really thinking. "He was one of those people who doesn't really have very good morals," I say eventually. "He looked out for himself more than for other people. That's not to say he was a complete bastard, but he definitely focused on himself."

"My daughter's the opposite," he says. "She's always been a good girl, the kind who'd do anything to help a stranger, and..." He pauses. "Well, I have to try, don't I? Even if the odds are a million to one, I have to go and check on her. 'Cause all over the world, there might be people like us, separated from their families, and at least some of 'em have to have a chance of being reunited, don't they? All that's left is family."

"Should I get in the front now?" I ask.

"Hold on a moment," he says. "I want to make this crystal clear, boy. I'm going to Chicago 'cause that's where my daughter and granddaughter are, okay? I need to check that they're okay, and nothing else much matters to me. So you see, I have no real need to keep you alive at all, and it wouldn't make much difference to me if I pulled the trigger right now and took your head clean off your shoulders. However, I like to think of myself as a good man, and for that reason I'm willing to give you a chance. You understand?"

"Sure," I reply, keen to defuse any suspicions he might have.

"Before you go thinking I'm some deluded old fool," he continues, "I want to make it very clear that I know full well how hopeless this is. If things are even half as bad as they look, the odds of finding my family alive aren't good, but I have to try. I don't care what happens to me, but if there's even a chance that I could locate them and help in any way, then I have to give it my best shot." He pauses, and for a moment there seem to be tears in his eyes. "If I find them, we'll have to work out what to do next," he adds finally. "If we *don't* find them, I'll just let you get off on your way."

Without saying anything else, I turn and make my way around to the front of the truck. I'm quite sure that the old guy has got his gun trained on me through the window in the back of the cab, but right now I don't even care. I was planning to go to Chicago anyway, although I was going to turn back at the first sight of any trouble. Now, however, it looks like we're going to go straight into the city, regardless of what we find at the limits. In a way, it feels good that the decision has at least been made, but as I start the engine and ease the truck away from the gas station's forecourt, I can't help thinking that this is most likely going to be my final journey. The creatures have to still be around, and sooner or later they'll catch up to us.

"You're gonna die in Chicago," Joe's voice says. "You know that, right? Maybe it'll be disease that gets you, or maybe it'll be one of those creatures, or maybe it'll even be this crazy old bastard with his shotgun, but you're gonna die there. This is the single dumbest decision you've ever made, and let's be honest, you've made a lot of dumb ones already."

"You're the expert," I whisper, making sure to keep my voice low so that George can't hear me.

"Just make sure it's a decent death," I imagine Joe saying. "My death was fucking horrible. God, I wouldn't wish that on my worst enemy. Can you imagine what it was like under that sheet, waiting for you to smash the spade down? Those final few seconds seemed to unwind like eternity, and then just when it seemed like you maybe weren't gonna go through with it, that goddamn thing came crashing down and split my head in two. I really thought..."

"I did what I had to do," I reply.

"I know you did," he'd say. "Just make sure you go out in style, okay? It used to be that people wanted to live as long as possible, but now I reckon the aim is just to search for a decent way to die. Maybe even noble. Do you think you can do that, Thomas?"

I don't reply, but then again, I don't *need* to reply. The whole conversation is going on in my head anyway, and Joe's voice is just a manifestation of my own thoughts. I know full well that heading to Chicago is suicidal, but even before I met George I was probably headed that way anyway. I don't want to die and I sure as hell don't want to run into any more of those creatures. Still, the old man is definitely right about one thing. It's better to face the risks than to die a slow, lingering death in the margins.

If Chicago's a brick wall, I'm driving straight into it at full speed.

DAY 47

ELIZABETH

"WHAT ARE YOU DOING?" Toad asks as he comes through to the kitchen.

"What does it look like?" I reply, unable to hide a faint smile of satisfaction. "I'm fixing my shoes."

It's a little after sunrise and I've been working for the past hour to patch my shoes together. They started out as an ordinary, slightly weather-worn pair of sneakers, but now they're more like a pair of monster-shoes. I found some old shoes that used to belong to Patricia and the others, and I carefully removed all the soles and then glued them together before adding some stitching and wire. I know I've probably gone overboard, but I figure that's better than not preparing properly, and now I've got shoes that look like they'll last forever.

"Those things are insane," Toad says as he wanders over. He takes one of the shoes from me and examines it more closely. "Maybe we'll make a cobbler of you some day."

"I also cut some tarpaulin down and placed it in layers between the soles," I tell him. "I figured I needed to make them waterproof, but I added some ventilation on the top part, so my feet could breathe. I was worried about getting some kind of fungus or infection if I ended up with too much sweat between my toes."

I pause for a moment, surprised by myself.

"Do you work for hire?" he asks. "These are way better than anything I've got."

"Sorry," I reply, taking the shoe back from him and placing it on the floor. "I don't think I've got time." Slipping my feet into the shoes, I lace them up and then finally I stand, only to find that the extra soles have added a good two or three inches to my height, bringing me almost up to Toad's eye level. I can't help but feel that this is at least a little symbolic.

"Impressive," he says with a smile. "How does it feel to walk on them?"

I turn and make my way across the kitchen, and although the shoes are undeniably a little wobbly, I figure I'll get used to them. It's odd being taller, and I almost walk straight into a set of pans hanging on the wall. Stopping, I turn back to look at

Toad and I can see from his expression that he's genuinely impressed. The truth is, I was determined to show him that I can take care of myself, so I guess it's a job well done.

"The weather's not looking good," he says, turning and heading over to the window. "There's rain coming."

"What does that mean?" I ask.

"It means water will fall from the sky," he replies with a faint smile. "On a more practical level, it means we might have to delay the start of our journey. I know we're going to have to deal with bad weather along the way, but we can at least wait until it clears up before we set off. If it hasn't passed by the middle of the day, we're probably better off waiting until tomorrow." He glances over at me. "It wouldn't hurt to be better-prepared, either. We could fix the bags up a little stronger, maybe rethink the food we're taking. Even the slightest mistake could -"

"You don't have to lecture me again," I reply, interrupting him. "I know we're not just going out for a walk in the country. It's going to be hard, it's going to be tiring, and we might not even make it. Before all of this started, the most I ever walked was from the front door of our building to the bus stop. I'm still a little unfit, but it's not going to hold us back. I can do this."

"I know you can," he replies. "Don't take

this the wrong way, Elizabeth, but if I really thought you were gonna hold me back..."

I wait for him to finish.

"You'd leave me behind?" I ask.

"I'd have to think about it," he replies.

"I'd do the same," I tell him, even though I'm not sure it's true. "It's every man for himself right now."

"So what about that baby?" he asks.

"What about her?"

"She definitely *will* slow us down," he continues. "Do you really think it's a good idea to take her with us?"

"What's the alternative?" I ask. "Leave her here to die?"

"I'm just saying, taking her with us is definitely not a good use of resources." He pauses. "Then again, I guess we need to keep a little bit of our humanity, huh?"

"I'll look after her," I tell him. "I'll do it all, and we'll still be faster than you."

"I went to check the pit this morning," he replies with a smile. "You did a good job out there. There's nothing left but a few burned bones." He pauses for a moment. "So who do you think it was?"

"What do you mean?" I ask.

"If someone in the house was infected," he continues, "who was it? We never found out. I don't think it was Patricia or Erikson, or Shauna, which means it must have been Bridger or Thor. I just wish I knew for certain."

"It doesn't matter now," I point out. "They're all dead."

"But none of them really seemed to be acting differently," he replies. "That's what worries me about the whole thing. I want to believe that I could tell if someone had changed like that, but I don't. I mean, right now, I can't even be sure that it wasn't you, and you can't be sure it wasn't me."

I pause for a moment, wondering whether to mention my concerns about Rachel. I keep replaying that moment over and over in my mind, trying to work out whether the look on her face last night was a sign of something worrying. No matter how hard I try to pretend that I imagined the whole thing, there's a part of me that seems to know there was something else happening behind her eyes. Still, I know that Toad's response would probably be to abandon her, and that's not something I can ever accept, so I need to stay quiet, at least until I'm certain that there's a problem.

"I don't believe for a second that it was you," I tell him. "Like you said, it was probably Thor or Bridger. Either way, whoever it was, they're gone."

"I know," he says with a sigh. "I guess I should stop worrying about every little thing. It's just in my nature to want to dig down and get to the truth every time."

"I should go and check on Rachel," I say finally, bending over to take my new shoes off. There's an awkward moment as I untie the laces, fully aware that Toad is watching me, and finally I place the shoes in the corner of the room before heading over to the door. "I guess we just have to wait for the weather, huh?" I say as I slip past him. "I hope it clears up soon. I want to get going."

"You're doing a good job, Elizabeth," he replies as I make my way to the stairs. "A really good job."

"I know," I reply, not looking back at him. "I don't need you to tell me that."

Smiling, he walks away.

"You're doing a good job too!" I call after him, but he doesn't reply. Still, I think I proved my point.

THOMAS

"STOP!" GEORGE SHOUTS, banging on the glass window in the back of the truck's cab. "Hey! Stop the vehicle!"

Muttering a few expletives under my breath, I park up at the side of the road. We're not even at the city limits yet, and although the scene ahead looks completely deserted, I want to just keep going and get this over with. As George clambers down from the back of the truck, I can't help thinking that he's starting to become an annoying travel companion.

"Floor it," Joe's voice says suddenly. "Get the hell out of here!"

Suddenly I realize that he's right. As George makes his way around to the front of the truck, it occurs to me that I could hit the pedal and just drive away, leaving him stranded here. For a fraction of a second, I actually consider doing it, but finally I realize that there's no point. He's got a gun, and if I'm going into the city, I figure I should at least have him with me. Sighing, I open the door and climb out of the truck, and I force myself to not imagine how Joe would be reacting right now.

"What is it?" I ask as I wander over to George.

"Look at it," he replies, staring at the city up ahead.

"Look at what?" I ask, following his gaze. All I see is a mass of buildings, with skyscrapers rising up in the distance like tall, thin tombstones. It's strange to think that there's probably no-one alive in there, that whatever the hell is happening to the world has been happening not only in smaller towns but also in the biggest cities. Still, now that we're here on the outskirts, I feel more than ever that I want to keep going and get right into the heart of the damn place; I've spent long enough waiting to see what's going to happen, and I'm ready to go take a look for myself.

"Scared?" he asks after a moment.

"No."

"Seriously?"

"Definitely not."

"What kind of an idiot *are* you, then?" he continues, with a faint smile. "Only a fool or a blind man wouldn't be scared right now. I'm damn near soiling myself. God only knows what we're gonna find in there, but I don't see any movement. All things considered, I would say that if you're ever gonna be terrified of anything in your life, this would be a good moment."

Taking a deep breath, I have to admit that

he's right: the city looks completely still, almost as if it's a model. The empty road stretches away ahead of us, but there's no sign of anyone either coming to, or leaving, the city and its surroundings. I can't help thinking about all the people who are supposed to be here. Either they've left, or they're still in there somewhere, rotting and stinking.

"You ever been to Chicago?" George asks after a moment.

"Never."

"It can be a rough place," he replies. "It's like any city, really. There are good parts and bad parts, decent neighborhoods and places you wouldn't send your worst enemy. Two and half million people living and breathing and shitting in close proximity to each other. Mankind just wasn't meant to get so close to his neighbor, that's for damn sure. When my daughter said she was coming here, I was terrified. I thought there was no way she could handle herself living in a place like this, but eventually I realized that she was much more attuned to the way a city works. Some people can handle cities and some people can't. I guess she got it from her mother."

"So you know your way around?" I ask. "I mean, you know which way to go, don't you?"

"I've been coming to the city since I was a boy," he replies, with a hint of pride in his voice. "I never wanted to live here, but I always liked visiting. There was always too much noise and commotion, so after a few days on each trip, I'd feel the need to get out again. I sure as hell wish all those people'd come back right now, though."

"I've never been to a city at all," I tell him.

"We'll go to Melissa's house first," he continues. "That's where she'd have holed herself up if she had a chance. I mean, she's a smart girl, so..." He pauses, and it's clear that he's trying to persuade himself that he might still find his daughter and grand-daughter alive. "She'll be there," he continues after a moment, "and if she's not, she'll have left some kinda note, 'cause she'd know that I'd be coming. She's a..." He pauses, and after a moment he starts coughing. Turning, he has to support himself on the hood of the truck for a moment, and it's clear that this isn't the cough of a healthy man. "She's a smart girl," he gasps, before composing himself and turning to me. "If anyone could get out of this thing alive, it's her."

"Are you sick?" I ask.

"Sick?" he replies with a forced laugh. "Me? Get out of town, boy. Come on, let's get moving."

"You've got blood on your hands," I point out.

He looks down, and as soon as he sees the blood he tries to wipe it off on the legs of his trousers. It's clear that he doesn't want to talk about whatever's wrong with him, and I wouldn't usually press someone, but right now I'm worried that his sickness might have an impact on me.

"Were you sick before all this happened?" I ask, starting to worry that he might be infected after all.

"Anyone ever tell you that you ask too many questions?" he replies, trudging toward the back of the truck. I watch as he climbs up, and it's noticeable that he's barely bothering to keep the gun trained on me anymore. After settling himself back in his old position, he turns to me. "Are you gonna stand there gawping or are you gonna get back behind the wheel? 'Cause I'm telling you, you're only useful to me if you're driving. Asking questions, that ain't something I require."

"You could *easily* overpower him," Joe would say.

He'd be right, too.

"You don't owe anyone," he'd continue. "The way the world is now, you have to look after yourself. Remember that Clyde guy we trusted a while back? Look how that turned out. I'd still be alive if we hadn't tried to be nice."

"No," I'd tell him. "I can't do that."

"Sucker," he'd say, and he'd probably laugh.

Maybe he'd be right about that, too. Maybe I *am* a sucker. Then again, there's not much hope that any of us are going to live much longer, so I figure I might as well at least try to help. I sure as hell don't have anywhere else to go.

"Lung cancer!" George shouts suddenly, clearly frustrated. "There, you happy now? Fucking lung cancer, that's what's wrong with me. Had it diagnosed nearly four months ago, so it's nothing to do with any of the rest of this bullshit. The doctor said I had a good chance of beating it, but now the doctor's gone and I guess there's nothing that can be done, is there? I just wanna find Melissa and make sure she's okay, and then that's me done. I didn't expect anything else out of this life before, and I sure as hell don't now. All you've gotta do is drive, boy, and I figure that's the easiest job outta the two of us. So come on, let's get going. The sooner we get there, the sooner we'll know where we stand."

Figuring that there's no point arguing with him, I get back into the driver's seat and start the engine again. Up ahead, Chicago stands completely still, like a monument to itself. I keep my eyes firmly fixed on the road, convinced that at any moment I'm going to see some sign of life. There's just no way that two million people could have died in the space of a few weeks, and yet the road seems completely clear. I don't even see any sign of people having panicked. It's as if the whole damn city is dead.

ELIZABETH

"IT'S GOING TO BE OKAY," I tell Rachel as I finish wrapping the blanket around her little body. "Everything's going to be fine and we're going to -"

Suddenly I freeze as I realize that she's staring up at me with the most intense gaze I've ever seen from another human being. It's as if she's looking deep into my soul, and maybe even understanding what she finds. All I can do is meet her stare for a moment, as if she's holding me in place. I swear to God, it's almost as if I'm waiting for her to say something.

"Stop that," I say eventually.

She doesn't even flinch. She just continues to stare.

"Are all babies like this?" I ask, looking away for a moment. With fumbling hands, I pretend to be busy with something on the nearby dresser. My hope is that by causing a small distraction, I'll break Rachel's concentration and she'll return to being a perfectly normal baby. I mean, this whole thing is probably just a figment of my imagination. It's insane to think that Rachel, of all people, would have become infected, especially when she's so young. After pointlessly fiddling with some old pots, however, I glance back and see that she's still staring at me.

"What?" I ask. "What do you want?"

She doesn't respond at all. She just keeps staring.

"I've never really been around a baby before," I tell her, trying not to let my fear show, "so I only know about them from movies, and maybe that's why I'm making a lot of mistakes. But there's something about you, I swear to God, that just seems..." My voice trails off as I stare at her. Deep down, I have this dark, bubbling fear, but I don't want to give it a voice, not yet.

Then again, what if I'm right?

But I'm not.

I can't be.

But what if I am?

After looking over at the door to make sure that there's no sign of Toad, I walk toward Rachel and stare down at her once again. I can't even handle the idea that she might be infected, but at the same time, she sure as hell isn't behaving like a normal baby. She's less than a month old, so I figure she should be crying and gurgling and laughing, all the stuff babies do in movies. Sure, she's had a rough upbringing so far, and I know I've made a few mistakes, but it's still hard to believe that I could have caused so much damage in such a short period of time. This weirdness seems to be coming from somewhere inside her, and that's why I'm worried that she might have somehow been struck down by the infection that has already killed so many people.

"Is it you?" I ask eventually, keeping my voice low so that there's no chance of Toad overhearing.

She stares back at me.

"Is it? Are you in there somewhere? Are you so sick and disgusting that you'd take over a child like this? Is that the kind of world we're living in now?"

She blinks a couple of times, and I can't help wondering who is really watching me through those eyes. Is it just the mind of a child, trying to make sense of the world around her? Or is it the mind of that *thing*, of that creature that seems to be able to look through the eyes of every body it infects? It's hard to believe that such a young child could have been affected, but then again, I guess it's perfectly possible. I just really, *really* don't want to believe that it's true.

"So we're going to walk," I tell her, trying to find some semblance of normality in the situation. "It won't be easy, but it's the only option. We have to get the hell - I mean, we have to get out of here." I pause, realizing that I need to watch my language around children. "I don't even know where we're going," I add, "but Toad knows the land, which means we should be okay. I know it's kinda weird to put our lives in some other guy's hands, but he's pretty trustworthy. I've started to get to know him lately, or at least as much as anyone can get to know someone who's so closed off, and I'm comfortable with this decision. I just..."

I wait, desperately hoping that she'll stop staring at me.

"Don't stare at Toad," I tell her. "He's harsher than me. If he thinks something's wrong with you, he won't hesitate to..."

My voice trails off as I try not to imagine precisely what Toad would do to Rachel if he genuinely thought she was infected. I have no doubt that he'd decide it was too great a risk to bring her with us. I can't let that happen, though. As long as there's at least *some* hope, I want to keep this beautiful little girl with us, and to make sure she survives. After everything that has happened over the past month and a half, I need to believe that a new life can grow. It's probably foolish, but I see

Rachel as a symbol of the future. If I can keep her alive, and keep her healthy, and if she can actually grow up and become a proper person... If all of that can happen, then maybe there's some hope for the world after all.

And if she dies...

"So just stop being weird," I say, forcing a smile as I gather Rachel up into my arms and carry her to the door. I know she's still staring at me, but I figure that's just something babies do. Anyway, if she was really infected, surely the creature would try to pretend to be a normal baby? Why would it make its presence so obvious? There are plenty of reasons why I'm probably just worrying over nothing.

I can hear Toad downstairs, getting ready for the journey. My right foot is hurting a little from where I cut it on the barbed wire yesterday, but it's just a scratch. I'll fix it later.

"It's going to be okay," I tell Rachel. "Everything's going to be fine."

Taking a deep breath, I start to carry her down to the kitchen. Every step feels heavy, as if I know that it's a risk to let Toad see Rachel right now. At the same time, I know I need to be brave. Toad wouldn't *actually* do anything to Rachel, even if he suspected she'd become infected. I mean, sure, he's harsh, but he's not a monster. There's no way he'd murder a month-old child just because she's acting a little strange.

It's going to be okay, I keep telling myself. Everything's going to be fine.

THOMAS

"I DON'T THINK THERE'S anyone here," I say as we walk toward the house. "I don't think there's anyone much anywhere these days."

It's been a couple of minutes since we pulled the truck up by the side of the road, and now we're making our way to the house that used to be occupied by George's daughter. All around us, there's nothing but abandoned buildings and abandoned cars, and the only hint of life comes from flies that are buzzing around an open dumpster. I was expecting there to be some sign of looting, maybe some damage, but it's almost as if everyone just vanished.

George has been very quiet since we arrived. I think he knows, deep down, that we're not going to find his family here, but I understand that he has to be certain.

"Do you think many people got out?" I ask.

"And where would they go?" he replies as we cross the lawn and reach the porch of a little white house that looks identical to all the other little while houses on this block. "If the shit goes down, where would they go other than the safety of their own home?"

"Maybe their home wasn't safe?"

"Melissa's a resourceful girl. She'd do anything to keep Katie safe, even..." He pauses. "She'd do anything, that's all I'm saying. She's a good mother."

"So maybe someone organized something," I point out. "Maybe the government took charge."

"I don't think anyone had time to organize anything," he says as he tries the front door, only to find that it's locked. Pausing for a moment, he knocks gently. "Melissa!" he shouts. "It's me! Are you in there?"

"There's -" I start to say.

He turns to me.

"Nothing," I add.

"Melissa!" he shouts again, banging more loudly on the door. "Katie! Are you in there?"

Glancing over my shoulder, I stare at the empty street. I know we haven't see any signs of life since we hit the city, but I'm still worried about attracting attention. It's hard to believe that there isn't someone, or something, close enough to hear us.

"I'm gonna try round the back," George mutters, hurrying down off the porch and making his way around the side of the house.

Figuring that I don't want to be left alone out here, I follow, although I can't help glancing at the windows of the house next door, just in case anything might be watching us. It's been a long time since I saw one of the creatures, and I'm tempted to think that maybe they've all just died off, but there's no way I want to take a risk.

"Jesus!" George says, stopping suddenly.

It takes me a moment to realize what he's seen; there's a dead body in the yard next door, with most of the meat having been eaten away to reveal bone. Flies are buzzing around the carcass, and there's a hint of movement under what's left of the flesh, which I guess means that maggots are at work. I'm no expert, but it's pretty clear that this guy has been dead for quite some time, probably a few weeks.

"Wally Baxendale," George says after a moment. "I recognize the shirt. The most boring man who ever walked the planet, and..." He pauses, staring at the dead body for a moment. "It's a goddamn miracle, isn't it? One man's death has given life to all those flies and bugs. Nothing ain't ever really wasted, is it? I mean, sure, to old Wally, this has been a total disaster, but to the critters that are feeding off him, it's a miracle. When Wally died, he probably thought God had forsaken him. And now those bugs are probably chewing on what's left of him, and thinking how great it is that God gave them such a bountiful harvest."

I force myself to keep looking at the body. Even though it's about twenty yards away, it's still disgusting, and I can't help wondering if that's what's going to happen to all of us eventually; we'll just be left to rot somewhere. Then again, that'd be better than being infected.

"I guess old Wally isn't boring now," George adds, turning to me. "Maybe some other species is gonna benefit from all this shit." Glancing at the house, he seems much more nervous before, which I guess is understandable; until this moment, he's been able to hold out hope that his daughter and grand-daughter might be alive and well, but now there's a chance that we're going to find their bodies.

"I can go look if you want," I say after a moment.

"Huh?" He turns to me, having clearly been lost in thought.

"If you don't wanna look in the house, in case they're..." I pause, my throat suddenly feeling dry. "I just mean, I can look for you, and tell you if I find anything."

"No," he says with a sigh, turning and making his way toward the back door. "I should do this."

"There aren't *that* many bodies," I point out as I follow him. "If everyone had just died, there'd be loads more, wouldn't there? It's like, they all kinda went somewhere else."

"Or they're all in their houses," he replies, trying the back door but finding that it's locked. Without giving me any warning, he takes off one of his shoes and slams the heel against the glass, shattering a small pane. Reaching through, he manages to turn the key from the inside, and finally he pushes the door open. After putting his shoe back on, he steps into the gloomy house.

"Doesn't smell bad," I point out, although I immediately realize that maybe I'm not being very tactful.

"That's a good point," he replies, stopping in the middle of the kitchen. "There's no power, so no air-conditioning. If anything'd been rotting in here for the past month, we'd sure as hell know about it by now."

"That's something, right?" I continue.

"It's something. Doesn't mean they're okay, though."

I watch as he walks over to the kitchen table. He seems to be searching for something, anything that might give him a clue about his family's fate. I guess that if I was in their position, I'd have left some kind of a note, just in case someone happened to come along later; the lack of a note makes it pretty clear that George's daughter didn't have time to plan her departure properly, which in turn makes me think that something pretty awful must have happened to them. Still, I don't want to voice those fears yet.

"Her phone's here," George says suddenly, picking up a cellphone from the counter.

"There's no signal anymore," I point out. "Why would she take it?"

"In case the signal comes back?" He turns to me. "I've still got mine rattling about in my pocket. You never know if the damn things might be useful again. It's instinctive."

"Maybe she didn't want to carry the extra weight?"

"She took this thing everywhere," he continues, turning the phone over in his hands. "She must have been home when everything went to shit. If she'd been out, she'd have had the phone with her."

"That's a good sign, isn't it?" I ask.

He shrugs, and it's clear that he's trying to weigh up the possibilities.

"Isn't there somewhere else she might have gone?" I continue. "It's like... Me and my family, we were out at the farm, so we didn't know what was going on. But someone living in a big city, they'd be able to get information. Someone would've come and told them what to do, or people would've come up with a plan together, or -"

"Or she and Katie walked out the door," he says, interrupting me, "like goddamn zombies."

I want to argue with him, but I can't deny that it's a possibility.

"Then again," he adds, "the doors were locked. Why would they have bothered doing that if they were all zombified, huh? A zombie wouldn't stop to lock the goddamn doors, would it?"

"You shouldn't give up."

"What about you? Where'd you say your family's gone, again?"

"Dead," I reply, feeling my chest tighten a little. "Maybe my sister's alive, but she was out in California. There's no way -"

"So why aren't you headed that way?"

"How the hell would I find her?"

"The same way I'm gonna find Melissa and little Katie," he replies. "By getting on with it, and by hoping that God will have a little mercy."

"I don't believe in God," I tell him. "Not anymore. Not after this."

"I'll believe in anyone and anything if it means I get my family back," he replies, slipping his daughter's phone into his pocket. "They're out there somewhere. I don't know which way they went, but..." He pauses. "I'm an old man. I've got two choices. Either I sit down and wait to die, or I go looking for 'em. I guess the latter would be the best choice, huh? At least that way, there's a chance I might find 'em. I mean, Jesus, I can't give up, can I?" He turns to me. "I don't suppose you wanna either come with me or sell me that truck of yours, do you?"

I open my mouth to reply, but I'm not really sure what to say.

"Where exactly are you going, anyway?"

"I'm just looking for people," I tell him.

"Me too. Specific people, but I figure they'll be going wherever there's others. There has to be some place that everyone's headed, right? Even if only a few stragglers survived, they've obviously set off somewhere. There might well be a whole train of people walking to... Where would you go, if you didn't know what to do?"

I shrug.

"I'd get out of the city," he continues. "That's what I'd do first of all. And then... I guess people go in herds, don't they? Like, they get together and come up with a plan, and then they all go off in one direction. Maybe north, to the lakes, or east to the shore."

"They'd need food," I point out.

"More than they could carry, too," he replies. "So they'd wanna be able to pick up supplies along the way. And they'd need water. These are important considerations, and a mistake could be fatal. You wouldn't want to risk it, would you? You'd pick the direction that was damn near certain to help you stay alive. Melissa was a smart girl, and..."

I wait for him to finish.

"North," he says finally.

"Why?"

"You've got the lakes, and you've got Canada. It's not much, but it's hope, isn't it? I mean, maybe it's bullshit hope, but it's definitely hope, and if that's all you've got, you take it."

"How would people even know which way *is* north?" I ask.

"Well, that's where the old-fashioned methods come into it. Things that kids these days don't remember, like how to work out where you are based on the stars."

"Do you know how to do that?"

"Hell, no. I know how to read a map, though." He turns and heads through to the next room, and when I go through to join him, I find that he's going through the bookshelf.

"Do you really think there's a chance?" I ask after a moment.

Pulling a small book out from one of the shelves, he flicks through the pages until, finally, he finds whatever he's looking for. He holds the page up for me to see what appears to be a map of a city.

"Chicago," he says with a smile. "This is some old book of maps that probably no-one looked at in ten years or more. I'm pretty sure I gave it to her. It's a miracle she didn't throw it out, but here it is, and it's gonna help us find our way north. There's also road signs we can use. It's not much of a chance, but it's better than nothing. How much gas did you say you've got for the truck again?"

"I'm not sure anymore."

"It'll be enough," he replies, looking through the book. "We'll head off there today. If that's okay by you, anyway."

"Sure," I reply. "I mean..." Pausing for a moment, I realize that I've got no better ideas. I think that in some quiet way, I'd already accepted I was going to die. Now, suddenly, there's the faintest possibility that there might be other survivors out there. After all, George and I can't be the only ones.

"There's no point waiting any longer," he says, heading toward the door. "We can take it in turns to drive, so we won't have to have any downtime, and if we keep the pace up, we'll hopefully find people in a day or two, and then we'll -" As he reaches the front door and steps out onto the porch, he suddenly stops speaking, as if he's spotted something.

"What's wrong?" I ask, hurrying after him. As soon as I get outside, however, I realize what's caught his eye.

"People," he says, staring at the thin plume of dark smoke that has suddenly begun to rise up from a part of the city just a few miles away.

"Or just a random fire," I reply.

He shakes his head.

"There are people here," he continues, "and they're alive." He stares at the smoke for a moment, before turning to me. "We have to go find them."

ELIZABETH

"WE'RE GOING TO FOLLOW this route," Toad says, running his finger along a section of the map. "If you look here, you can see that there's a hill just past this point on the river, close to Dan Hodge's old farm, which means we'll get a good lookout as we approach town. If everything goes according to plan, we should be able to scout the entire area."

"And then what?" I ask, trying to make it sound as if I understand the plan. The truth is, I've only got a vague idea; I can't stop thinking about Rachel, and about the fact that this all seems hopeless.

"Then we'll make a more informed decision. We need to know what's going on in the world. If order's being restored, it could be months before anyone gets out to check on people living in remote areas, and I don't think we have time to wait. If there's no sign of civilization, we'll re-evaluate, maybe come back to the farm."

"What about the creatures?"

"I've been thinking about that. They were rotting, right? So even if they were animated, the rotting will have continued. It stands to reason that after a month, they've all fallen apart. I'm not counting on it just yet, but I'm pretty sure that they're out of the picture."

"But you can't be sure of that," I continue. "What if living people have been infected? We still don't know anything about how it spread, or why it infects certain people and not others."

"We just have to go on the evidence in front of us," he replies, folding up the map. "We can sit here all day and all night coming up with theories and ideas, but the best approach is just to get out there, be careful, and trust ourselves to stay smart. For all we know, there could be millions of survivors out there. This thing could be only affecting the United States." He pauses. "Or it could be everywhere, and there might only be a handful of survivors. We won't know until we get out there, so we have to get out there and start coming up with a proper plan."

"Maybe we're the last two people on Earth," I point out.

"We'll have to move fast," he continues. "Of

course, it'd be a lot easier without..."

His voice trails off.

"Without Rachel?"

"I need you to take responsibility for her," he says. "I know it's not going to be easy, but out there, on the road, you need to look after her. And you also need to recognize that there's a chance she might not..." He pauses again, as if he's reluctant to say what's really on his mind. "It's a miracle that you've kept her alive this long, and I don't want you to think for a moment that I don't realize what a good job you've been doing. I just want you to remember that the circumstances are difficult, and if for any reason Rachel doesn't make it, you shouldn't go blaming yourself too much. Keeping a baby alive, raising her, in this kind of situation... It'd be difficult for someone with experience. For someone new to it all, it's a miracle."

"I didn't have you down as someone who believes in miracles," I tell him.

"What if she was dying?" he asks, changing the subject abruptly.

"Why would she be dying?"

"For any one of a million reasons. Would you be able to make the difficult decisions that would be in everyone's best interest?"

"Like what?" I ask. "Leave her behind?"

"That would be cruel. But it you had to kill her -"

"Yes," I say, even though it's a lie. "Totally."

He stares at me, clearly not convinced.

"I would," I tell him, hoping to make sure he realizes I'm tough enough to make the call. He still thinks I'm some kind of fragile kid, and there's no way I'm going to feed into that impression. Besides, I know deep down that he's right, even if I doubt I could actually abandon Rachel.

"If it would end her suffering," he continues, "and give us a better chance of survival... Could you do it? If, all things considered, it would be the kindest and most effective thing to do..."

"Are you asking me to do that now?"

He pauses, and for a moment I start to worry that I might be right. Is Toad really so hard-hearted that he'd be willing to sacrifice a child's life in order to give us a slightly better chance of survival?

"Not now," he says eventually. "I just want to know that you'll be able to make a difficult decision further down the track, if that's what has to be done."

"I'm not a child," I tell him, even though I want to tell him to go screw himself. "I know I might have had a sheltered life before all of this happened, but I think I'm adapting pretty well. I've been through stuff that you can't even imagine, so you don't have to lecture me on how to deal with things, okay? I'm not that much younger than you, and I've already made tough choices."

"What about your brother?" he asks.

I open my mouth to reply, but suddenly it feels as if a heavy stone has hit my chest.

"When you think back to what happened with your brother in New York," he continues, "are there any moments that you think you could have handled better? Are there any times when you took an easy choice, when a tougher decision might have had a different outcome?"

"Henry's death wasn't my fault," I say firmly, with tears in my eyes. "You don't know anything about what happened back there. There were other people. Bad people. We were waiting for our parents to come home, but they didn't, and we just tried to do the best thing. I guess we trusted the wrong people, and Henry let himself get manipulated."

He stares at me for a moment, as if he's trying to understand me better.

"I'm sure you did everything you could," he says eventually. "It's just that I'm heading out on the road with you, and I need to know I can trust you. Your life is in my hands, and mine is in yours, and then there's Rachel... I just needed to make sure that you've got what it takes. For what it's worth, I think you do, otherwise I'd leave you behind."

"Thanks."

"You know what I mean."

"Well, I'm the same," I reply, sniffing back

tears. "If I didn't trust you, I wouldn't go with you. Simple."

A faint smile crosses his lips.

"I'm not joking," I continue, trying not to let his amusement get to me. "I'm ready for this. I know there's a good chance that we might not survive, but it's better than sitting around here."

Over in the corner, Rachel lets out a faint gurgle. I glance at her, and to be honest I feel a hint of relief. It's the first time all day that she's done anything that seems even vaguely normal, and I can't help but hope that it's a sign of better things to come.

"Is she okay?" Toad asks.

"Of course," I reply, hurrying over and picking her up. "Why wouldn't she be?"

"She just seemed a bit..." He pauses for a moment, as if he's started to notice that something's not right with her. "She was staring at me earlier. Like, really just staring straight at me. It was kinda freaky."

"That's what babies do."

"Is it?" He shrugs, before turning and starting to close his rucksack. "I don't know the first damn thing about them, so I'll have to take your word on it. I don't want to sound like some old-fashioned asshole, but I wouldn't even know how to change her diaper. At least she doesn't cry too much. Hell, she hardly cries at all these days. It's like she suddenly stopped." Tying the top of the rucksack, he pauses for a moment, as if he's not quite sure what to do next. "I think we're ready," he says eventually, before turning to me. "I think we might as well get going."

I nod, but the truth is, I'm terrified. We've talked about the journey a lot, but now we're on the verge of setting out on a long, arduous trek toward an uncertain destination. There's a part of me that wants to stay here at the farm, no matter how foolish that would be.

"You ready?" Toad asks.

I nod.

"And Rachel?"

I look down at her and see that she's staring at me again.

"She's ready," I say cautiously, trying not to sound worried.

"Then you'd better get your shoes on," Toad continues, heading toward the door. "I know a good place for us to camp for the night, and it shouldn't be too hard to get there. I want to get past the main part of the forest before the next band of rain moves in, and I think that only gives us about twenty-four hours. We'll have to move fast, but we can do it."

I wait for him to continue.

"Well?" he says, opening the door and stepping outside before turning to me. "What are we waiting for?"

THOMAS

"STINK'S GETTING WORSE," George says as I drive the truck slowly along the deserted street. He turns to me. "You smell it, boy? You smell that stink?"

"I smell it," I mutter, keeping my eyes on the road. We're getting closer to the heart of the city now, and although the plume of black smoke is still visible up ahead, there's no other sign of life. All around, cars seem to have just been abandoned by the side of the road, while all the buildings seem to be completely empty. I always figured there'd have been looting in the cities, but right now it looks as if no-one had *time* to loot. It's pretty messed-up, but I think I'd feel better if the shops had been trashed. In some weird kind of way, that would be more normal.

"Rats," George says suddenly.

I look over at a nearby intersection just in time to spot something scurrying down into the subway. I've seen rats before, back at home, but never anything so huge, and I can't help but shudder at the thought of encountering something like that. At some point, a rat might become big enough that it feels ready to take on a human.

"Did you see it?" he continues, turning to me. "That was one big-ass rat. Goddammit, I reckon he was the size of a small dog. I wouldn't like to have to deal with one of those things."

"So animals weren't affected by this thing," I reply. "Just humans."

"Humans *are* animals," he points out. "It's almost like whatever happened, it was designed to hit us and only us. Can't say I'm surprised. We acted like we were the dominant species, but now the *real* dominant species has taken a right old swing at us."

"What are you talking about?" I ask, starting to get a little tired of George's roundabout way with words.

"Bugs. Bacteria. Do you know how many bacteria you've got living in the average human body? Millions, and all different types. They're the ones who are really in charge of this planet." He pauses. "Them and dolphins."

I open my mouth to ask about the dolphins, but at the last moment I decide not to bother.

"This is the revenge of bacteria," he mutters. "That's what it is. It's all our chickens coming home to roost at once."

"I don't like this," I reply, glancing over my shoulder to make sure that the road behind us is clear. Turning to look out the front, I watch the smoke for a moment. "It's probably just a random fire. It's probably rats or something, chewing through wires."

"There's no electricity. They can chew all they want, but they won't set fire to nothing."

"But it's probably not people!"

"It almost certainly *is* people!" He pauses, clearly exasperated. "I told you already, if you wanna turn back, that's fine. No-one's forcing you to come with me. I'll walk from here if you're scared."

I keep my foot on the pedal, and even though I'm desperate to get the hell out of here, I figure that we might as well keep going. After all, I've got nowhere else to be, and there's always a chance - no matter how faint - that we'll come across signs of a recovery. When this mess first started, more than a month ago, I kept trying to come up with some kind of plan. These days, it's more like I'm living from moment to moment, never knowing what the hell is going to come at me next.

"Stop!" George says suddenly, reaching over and grabbing the wheel.

I slam my foot on the brake pedal, and the

truck comes to a lurching halt.

"Did you see it?" he asks, his voice suddenly lowered to a conspiratorial hush.

"What?" I ask, starting to feel as if I'd rather be exploring the city alone... or not at all. "Another rat?"

"Only if rats can walk upright," he replies. "Did you really not see her? She was right up by that next corner, on the right."

We sit in silence for a moment. I don't see anything, but George seems convinced, and in some strange way I feel as if the silence is getting louder all around us, until finally I can't take it any longer.

"We're getting out of here," I say, pushing him away and hitting the gas pedal as I try to turn the truck around. I've tried not to panic, but suddenly I figure that panicking might actually be a damn good idea.

"It was a normal person!" he shouts, trying to wrestle control of the wheel from me.

"Those things aren't normal!"

"I saw its face! It was a girl!"

"Then you can get out and go say hi!" I shout back at him, trying to push him away as the truck mounts the sidewalk and knocks on old trashcan out of the way. "I'm not going any further, not if there are things walking about!"

"It was a girl!" he says again. "As soon as she saw us, she turned and ran, but she was normal!

I saw the whites of her goddamn eyes!"

"It was probably one of those -" I start to shout, but at the last moment George grabs the wheel and the truck lurches to the right. I've still got my foot on the gas pedal, and I don't have time to react before the front of the truck crashes into the window of a shop. As glass shatters, the truck finally comes to a stop, with the front section partway inside the building. We've crashed into the front of a clothes shop, and although the interior is dark and unlit, I can make out rows and rows of expensive-looking dresses. It's a surreal moment, and for a few seconds I can barely even process what I'm seeing.

"What did you do that for?" George asks finally.

"Me?" I try to reverse, but we're stuck and all that happens is that the wheels spin. Somehow, the front of the truck seems to have become caught on part of the window, but I'm damn well not going to get out and try to push, not if there's a chance of those creatures being around. I can feel them already, watching and waiting, probably hoping that we'll make it easy for them. They're probably slipping closer with every passing second.

"I told you to stop," George continues. "I said, just stop and we'll take a look, but you're the one who's in the driver's seat. There was no need to go and crash into the front of a building. You're the one who -"

"Shut up!" I shout, flooring the pedal in an attempt to get the truck free. The whole frame of the vehicle is shuddering, but whatever's caught on the underside, it's stubbornly refusing to come loose. The engine's revving so loud, I'm worried it might get flooded, but at the same time I can't find a way to calm down. We have to get out of here before those creatures arrive.

"Thomas -"

"Shut up!" I shout again.

"If you're gonna be like that," he replies, "I think I should just get out and walk! You're acting like a fool."

"Fine," I mutter, changing gear in an increasingly desperate attempt to get the truck to reverse out of the broken shop window. "I don't care about smoke or people in cities or anything like that! I just want to -" Suddenly I spot something in the rearview mirror, and I turn to see several people wandering toward us. They look lost, almost as if they're mindlessly drawn to come closer. One of them, who has almost reached the truck, looks to be a young girl around my age, and she's staring at me with a haunted expression.

"Hang on," George says, reaching out to open the door. "We can ask them if -"

"Don't open that!" I shout. "I've seen these things before! They'll kill us!" At that moment, the truck finally comes loose from whatever was holding it in place, and we reverse across the sidewalk. One of the creatures, apparently unable to react in time, is hit by the back of the truck and falls under the wheels, and the entire vehicle shudders and jolts as first the rear and then the front wheels drive straight over the corpse. As I try to turn the truck, I see a thick red trail on the sidewalk with pieces of bone and skin mashed into the mess, but I don't have time to take it in yet. Instead, I turn the wheel, still functioning on pure adrenalin. There's no goddamn way I'm going to let these things get me.

"Thomas -" George starts to say.

"Shut up!"

"Thomas -"

I turn to shout at him, but suddenly the door next to me is pulled open and someone reaches into the truck, grabbing me by the shoulders and hauling me out until I fall onto the sidewalk. Before I can get to my feet, I feel several more sets of hands grab hold of me and start dragging me away, and although I struggle to get free, I'm quickly pinned down against the ground. Figures are leaning over me, partially blocking the sunlight as they stare down, and I'm convinced that at any moment I'll feel them start to rip me apart. Even though I'm trying to fight back, there's a part of me that knows I'm outnumbered. This is it.

"What's your name?" a male voice asks suddenly, as one of the figures leans closer to me.

"Go to hell!" I shout. "Get -"

Suddenly something strikes me on the side of the face, with enough force to almost knock me out.

"What's your name?" the voice asks again, leaning closer this time. "And give me one good reason why I shouldn't kill you right here and now!"

ELIZABETH

"LOOKS KINDA SMALL FROM up here, doesn't it?" Toad says, glancing over his shoulder as we make our way along the dirt path that winds up through the forest.

Turning, I look back at the farmhouse, and he's right: it looks tiny and completely insignificant, and vulnerable too. It's hard to believe that we spent so long there, and I can't help thinking that if any more of those creatures had shown up, we'd have never been able to defend ourselves. We thought we were sitting tight and staying safe, when in fact we were just waiting to die.

In my arms, Rachel lets out another faint gurgle.

That's good.

That's normal.

She's a normal, healthy baby who just happens to have been through some bad experiences.

Everything's going to be okay.

"It'll be another couple of hours before we reach the site," Toad continues. "It's a good spot, though. We'll be on high ground, away from the risk of flooding, and we'll have a good view of the area. I know the land, and I should be able to tell if it's been disturbed. Those creatures aren't exactly subtle. We'll take it in turns to keep watch, though, just in case. Two hours on and then two hours off"

"Keep watch for what?" I ask.

"The creatures."

"Do you really think they're still out here?"

"Probably not, but it'd be an expensive mistake if I was wrong. There's no way I'm willing to just go to sleep and hope for the best. There are other predators to consider, too. Wolves could be a problem. If you see or hear anything unusual, let me know immediately. I know how to deal with these things."

Glancing at the forest, I can't help but wonder if he's right. Sure, the creatures haven't been around for weeks now, but that doesn't mean they're not still out there somewhere. I guess I've allowed myself to become complacent, when the truth is, there could be millions of the damn things still on the loose. There are so many uncertainties in the world right now, it's impossible to think about every eventuality. No-one can make plans when the world is in such a mess, and when there could be any kind of horror around the next curve in the road.

"Do you see that?" Toad asks after a moment.

Staring at the horizon for a moment, I realize that I can see a very faint black smudge. If Toad hadn't pointed it out, I probably wouldn't even have noticed it, but now I can tell that it's something large and artificial.

"It's a military base," he continues. "They used to fly training programs, mainly, although there were always a few crackpot conspiracy theorists who insisted there was other stuff going on there. You know the kind of thing. Strange flights at night, loud booms... There was a guy who used to camp out near the main gate and try to get photos. He was completely crazy, but for a while he'd come to my home and try to talk to me about it all. Eventually he drifted away. I tried to ignore it for the most part, but if there was any chance of an organized response to what's happened, I'm pretty sure it'd start in a place like that. Not that anything like that is going to happen, though. It'll just be a bunch of abandoned buildings by now."

"Why didn't you mention it before?" I ask.

"I've been keeping an eye on it. Watching for signs of life. So far, there's nothing. I didn't want to tell you about it, in case it seemed like a false hope. Anyway, I figured you'd probably come up with some dumb idea about heading that way."

"We should go and see if anything's happening there."

He shakes his head.

"It might be our best chance! If the government's organizing things, they'll have to start with the military!"

"There'll be no-one there. Anyway, even if there is, they're the last people we want to get involved with. I wouldn't trust them, not even for a second."

"So what are we gonna do?" I ask. "Go around it and make sure they don't see us?"

"Sounds like a plan to me."

"Are you serious?"

"I've had dealings with the military before," he replies. "It was a long time ago, but I doubt much has changed. If there's anyone there, they'd just assess our usefulness and then put us to work in whatever capacity suited them."

We walk on a little further, but I can't help wondering what's really going on in Toad's head. Even though I've been living alone with him for a month, I still don't know him very well, and every so often he displays a hint of stubbornness that makes me wonder about his earlier life. He's never really talked about himself very much, and although

I used to assume that he was just the kind of guy who keeps himself to himself, now I'm starting to wonder if maybe there's something he wants to keep hidden.

"You don't like authority figures, do you?" I ask eventually, hoping to learn at least a little more about him.

"Does anyone?"

"No, but you seem a little more worried than most people."

"What tipped you off? The house in the middle of nowhere? The attempt to prepare for a world-ending catastrophe?"

"So what did you do before you came out here?"

He doesn't reply.

"You must have done something," I continue. "You must have had a life."

"It doesn't matter."

"Can't you tell me anyway?"

"The past is the past," he says firmly, glancing at me. "Old lives don't mean anything, not now. Any of us could have been anything, but it's not going to help. Everything's been washed away and we have to focus on the future. If we spend too much time thinking about the old days, we might as well just sit down and wait to die."

"But -"

"If you want to go to that base," he

continues, interrupting me, "then no-one's going to stop you. You can take Rachel, and you can even take a share of the food and water we brought, but you'll be on your own. There's no way I'm going near that place."

"Because you're scared?"

"Because it'd be a waste of time. Because there's probably no-one there, and if there is, then I sure as hell don't want anything to do with them, not anymore. There's no power, there's no way for anyone to put things right. We need to get over the idea that someone's gonna come riding to the rescue."

"But -"

"Talking wastes energy," he adds. "Let's just focus on the journey."

Although I want to ask him more questions, I figure I should stay quiet for now. After all, he's clearly not in the mood for a conversation, and my attempts to dig into his past seem to be riling him up. Still, I can't help but notice that he seems to have some kind of history with authority figures, maybe even with the military. He's a loner at heart, and although he opens up to me a little from time to time, he slams back shut as soon as I mention the past. As we continue on our journey along the path, I glance over at the smudge on the horizon. Toad's probably right. There's probably nothing over there that can help us. I just wish there was some way to know for sure, though. If there's even a slight chance that we're bypassing someplace that might be useful, I don't see why we couldn't at least give it a try.

I can't strike out on my own, though. For better or for worse, I need to stay with Toad, at least until we meet some other people. When that happens, however, I think I need to consider other options.

DAY 48

THOMAS

"THERE'S NO POINT TRYING to get free," the man says, watching me from the other side of the room. "We're not in the habit of letting murderers walk away."

Ignoring him, I continue to tug on the chain that's been used to secure me to the wall. Having spent all night trying to find a way to get loose, I'm already feeling exhausted, but as the first light of morning shows through the window, I'm starting to panic even more. I knew it was a bad idea to come into the city; I thought we were in danger from those creatures, but now it turns out that *uninfected* humans might be even more of a threat.

"Give it a rest," George says, sitting nearby on the floor. Like me, he's been chained up; unlike me, however, he seems to have accepted his fate with weary resignation. "You're not gonna get out of those damn things, so you might as well conserve your energy. Wait for a more important fight."

"The old man's right," the guard adds. "You should listen to him."

Frustrated, I try yet again to slip my wrists free. All I manage, however, is to cut a little more flesh away. I've been working on this all night, trying hundreds of different ideas, and my wrists are now bloodied and sore. Still, I sure as hell don't like the feeling of being chained up, and all I know for certain is that I have to find a way out of here.

"You haven't even asked her name," the guard says.

I turn to him.

"The girl you murdered. You haven't even bothered to ask her name, or anything about her."

"I didn't murder anyone!" I spit at him.

"Alice."

I shake my head.

"I was there," he continues. "You drove right over her. You turned and looked back, so you must have seen her, and then you put that truck in reverse and went straight for her. Crushed her. You won't even going very fast, so I doubt it was quick. She probably suffered."

"She was attacking us!" I shout.

"She was curious. We were coming to help you. That's what people do when they see other people in need. They go to help them."

"She was infected!"

"No-one's infected round here. That's all over now."

I turn to George, and I can see the concerned look in his eyes. He knows we're in trouble here.

"I didn't murder anyone!" I say again, hoping against hope that he'll back me up. "Come on, you were there! Tell him!"

"I warned you not to go crazy," he replies quietly. "You were panicking. I told you to stay calm, but you wouldn't listen."

"But you saw them!" I continue. "They were coming at us! They were like... They looked like those things!"

"No," George says, "they didn't, and I told you as much. They looked... normal. I saw that girl's eyes right before she was killed, and she didn't look like she was infected, not at all. She looked scared, and tired, and hungry, but not dangerous. She was -"

"Alice," the guard says.

George sighs. "She was -"

"Alice," the guard says again, before walking over to George and kicking him hard in the ribs. "You should have the decency to at least use the name of the girl you killed. Her name was Alice, she was eighteen years old, and as far as I know she never did anything wrong to anyone. She was quiet, kinda reserved and shy, like she preferred keeping herself to herself. She survived all the crap that happened over the past month, and then you two turned up and smeared her across the sidewalk."

"I wasn't driving!" George gasps as he edges away from the man. Turning to me, he seems desperate. "Tell him! Tell him you were the one who was driving! It wasn't anything to do with me!"

I stare at him, disgusted by his attempt to push all the blame onto me. The truth, though, is that he's right. I can't stop reliving the moment when I put the truck in reverse and went straight over that girl. At the time, I was disgusted when I saw her battered body on the sidewalk, but I told myself it was just another of those infected creatures. Now that I know she just a normal person, I can feel a huge, crushing weight of guilt on my shoulders, even if I'm not quite ready to accept what really happened. I *did* kill that girl, but it was an accident and it sure as hell wasn't murder. I'd do anything to go back and change what happened, but I can't. Someone has to understand.

"The tribunal's gonna get together soon," the guard says. "It's for them to decide what happens to you. Shouldn't be much longer now, just a few hours. Fortunately for you, justice moves pretty quickly around here. It's not like the old days."

"Tribunal?" I ask, turning to him. "Like a court?"

"We're not savages," he continues, staring at me with a look of utter contempt in his eyes. "You should be grateful. If we *were*, we'd probably have just finished you off there and then. Instead, we're going to let you have your say." He turns to George. "You too. None of us here has any idea about either of you, and we've got a rule about not letting strangers just wander into our midst. If we don't have certain standards, we're not much better than dogs. Even murderers get to have their say."

"I didn't murder anyone," I say firmly.

"Whatever. She's dead. Someone still had to gather up her body. Someone who knew her, too."

"But I didn't *murder* her," I tell him. "It was an accident."

"So what happens if we're found guilty?" George asks, with a hint of cynicism in his voice. "I mean, I have no doubt that this tribunal system is extremely fair and balanced, and driven by respect for the law rather than some kind of blood-lust. But if common sense doesn't prevail, and if we're deemed to be cold-blooded murderers, what's our fate going to be?" He pauses. "Let me guess. You'll put us to death somehow."

"I have no idea," the guard replies calmly. "We've never actually had to hold a tribunal before, so it's new territory. But what would you do with a pair of murderers? Just let them stay? Let them walk off into the sunset like nothing happened? A life was lost yesterday and someone has to pay. There were rules before and there are rules now. She'll make the right choice."

"She?" George asks.

"We're lucky. We have a very wise leader in charge around here, someone who's very keen to ensure that justice has a place, even as the world crumbles around us. We always knew that one day someone would arrive and threaten us, but we have a system to deal with these things. There have been doubters, of course, but now the system can be put to the test. You should be proud. You're pioneers, and you're going to get a fair hearing before your fates are decided."

"Great," George says, turning to me. "Did you hear that, Thomas? We're gonna be guinea pigs for a brand new tyrant -"

Before he can finish, he's kicked in the gut again, this time with such force that he lets out a gasp of pain. Clutching his side, he seems to be having trouble breathing for a moment. When he finally looks over at me, I can see the fear in his eyes.

"Save your words for later," the guard says with a smile. "You'll be given a chance to explain yourselves, so you should take a little time to work out what you're going to say. It might be the most important little speech either of you ever give in your miserable lives. If I was the one in charge, I'd already have decided what to do with you before the sun came up this morning."

As he makes his way back over to the other side of the room, I turn to George and see that he's clearly still in pain.

"I think he cracked a few ribs," he grunts.

"I didn't murder that girl," I reply, my mind almost frozen blank with terror. "You were there, you saw what happened! I swear -"

"I know you didn't," he replies, "but you killed her, and that might be enough for these bastards. I don't know what kind of set-up they've got going here, but whatever it is, we're gonna be used to make a point, and I doubt they're aiming to show how lenient they can be. This is why I always preferred living well away from other people. The human herd instinct is strong, and it's so easy for them to fall in line behind anyone with an ounce of personality. Whatever the hell's going on around here, we're on the wrong side of the law. They're gonna want to show force, and then they're -"

"They'll have to listen to me," I say firmly, interrupting him. "There were people there, witnesses... No-one's seriously going to think that I killed that girl on purpose!"

"They're gonna think what they want to think," he replies, "and whatever makes them feel safer. No, scratch that... They're gonna think whatever they're told to think." He pauses, wincing at the pain in his side. "If that means executing us, then I think we might need to come up with an escape plan." As he lifts the side of his shirt, I see that there's a dark patch under his skin, right in the spot where he was kicked. "Got any ideas?" he asks finally.

ELIZABETH

"DAY FORTY-EIGHT," I tell Rachel as I finish changing her diaper. "Or forty-nine..." I pause for a moment as I try to work it out. "No, forty-eight. Definitely forty-eight. I should have kept some kind of diary."

Staring back at me, Rachel doesn't respond at all. She's still doing that staring thing, which freaks me out even more now that I realize it reminds me of the girl I met on the road a few weeks ago, the one whose name seemed to be Dawn until I found a chunk of metal wedged in the back of my head. Putting aside my worries about infection for a moment, I've checked every inch of Rachel, looking for some sign of an injury, but she seems to be completely undamaged. Whatever's wrong with her, and I'm convinced that there *is* something, it must be in her head. If that's the case, I have no idea how to help her.

"Hey," I say, forcing a smile. "How are you doing? Are you gonna maybe laugh for me some time? You used to laugh, remember? It was a long time ago, but..."

I wait.

Nothing.

"I'm trying," I say quietly, before looking up at the dull, gray morning sky. "Can you just give me a break? I'll believe in you, I swear, if you just give me one little thing that makes all of this easier. I want to believe, but you need to give me something. Make her act more like a normal baby, or give me more strength, or help me to understand. Anything."

Again, I wait.

Again, the answer is nothing but silence.

Suddenly Rachel lets out a faint gurgle. I look back down at her, but she's already resumed her usual stare. That gurgle was so brief and so faint, it's hard to think it could be a positive sign, but right now I'm willing to latch onto anything. Ignoring the pain in my right ankle, I decide that I just have to hope for the best.

"Please don't be sick," I whisper, holding Rachel up. "Please, please, please -"

Hearing movement nearby, I glance over my shoulder just in time to see that Toad has returned from his scouting trip. He's seemed tense all morning, as if somehow things aren't going according to plan, but I don't quite have the nerve to ask him if anything's wrong. I figure he'll tell me if it's necessary, and right now I've got enough to worry about. Working out a route is *his* job.

"Are you talking to that baby again?" he asks with a faint smile.

"She's a person," I reply.

"It's not like she can talk back, though."

"It's good for her. People talk to babies all the time. It helps her get used to language." I pause as I try to work out if any of that made sense. "I'm bonding with her," I add, although I immediately regret my choice of words. After all, Rachel isn't my child, and even though I'm the one who's looking after her, I'm not sure I should be assuming responsibility for her entire life. Still, right now she's a symbol of hope, and of the future, and she's helping me to keep sane. Well, relatively sane. I can feel myself starting to unravel, but I'm convinced I can hold myself more or less together, at least for now.

I guess I've got no choice.

"There's been flooding," Toad replies, opening the back of his rucksack and pulling out a small plastic bag. "The terrain's shifting, and I don't think now is the time to go taking any risks. You saw what happened last time we were out in bad weather, and we're too vulnerable to go through anything like that again. We're going to have to try a slightly longer route, around the edge of the forest and then across Dan Hodge's old farm. It'll add about a day and a half to our journey -"

"A day and a half?" I reply, shocked by the suggestion. "I don't even think -"

"We can manage," he says firmly. "If there were creatures around, don't you think we'd have run into them by now? They've all rotted away. It's natural, if you think about it. Whatever was controlling them, it couldn't halt the natural decomposition of dead bodies. We just have to focus on surviving the journey, and we have to hope that we can find somewhere that offers a chance for a future."

"Are you sure we shouldn't turn back?" I ask. "At least at the farmhouse, we had food and shelter."

"The food was running low. We might have felt safer in the short-term, but in the long-run we'd have just been sitting around, waiting to die. If I thought someone might eventually show up to put the world straight, then maybe it'd be an option, but that's not going to happen. We're on our own, and this isn't the kind of situation that favors caution, not when it comes to the big picture." He pauses, and for a moment he seems to be searching my face for something. "Are you okay? If there was anything wrong, you'd tell me, wouldn't you?"

"Like what?"

"Like an injury." He stares at me for a moment, as if he's trying to spot any hint of weakness.

"I'm not injured," I tell him. "I'm fine. I just wish I had a better idea of where we're going, or why we're walking such a long way. I want a plan, or at least some kind of destination, 'cause right now it feels as if we're just drifting through the landscape."

"The plan is to find out what's happening," he replies. "Would you really rather stay at the farmhouse and play happy families like we're the last two people on Earth, while we wait for the darkness to close in? I didn't want to scare you back there, but the way things were going, we only had about two weeks left."

"Things were that bad?"

"My food reserves were shot, and the land was dying. Every day, I went out and tried to find some kind of solution, but there was nothing. There was no choice, we had to leave."

Sighing, I look back down at Rachel. I know Toad is right, but I can't help feeling that we're completely exposed out here, as if danger could be coming toward us from every direction. At least when we were at the farmhouse, we had some kind of base, but at the moment I have no idea what we're going to do next. There's a part of me that feels we're going to end up dying out here, whereas at the farmhouse we could have focused on trying to make what's left of our lives a little more comfortable. Even if that was only a few weeks.

"You didn't sleep last night, did you?" he asks eventually.

"I'm fine."

"You don't look fine. Your eyes are dark and you look pale, like you're about to collapse." He pauses, as if he's waiting for me to say something. "We won't be getting many opportunities to rest, Elizabeth. You need to take them when they come."

"I said I'm fine."

"Take half an hour," he continues. "I'll take care of Rachel -"

"No!" I snap, horrified by the idea of Toad looking after her. After all, the more time he spends with her, the more likely he is to realize that something's seriously wrong. I need to keep them apart as much as possible and just hope that somehow she's going to be okay. If that means I have to stay awake for a week straight, then that's just what I'm going to have to do. "This isn't your thing," I stammer. "It's mine. I'm in charge of it."

"Your thing?" he asks, sounding confused.

"I mean my job," I continue, my mind racing as I try not to sound too suspicious. "You've got your job, which is keeping us on the road, and I've gone mine. I'll look after Rachel, okay? You don't need to worry about her." I turn to him, and I can see that he's realized something isn't right. "Don't keep bothering me," I add. "I've got enough to do, looking after her. You said it yourself. We each have to stick to our roles here, and I'm sticking to mine. She's fine. Maybe you should spend less time worrying about her, and more time finding a safe route for us."

He stares at me, and for a moment it seems as if he might be about to call my bluff. I'm pretty sure I'm not fooling him, and that he knows I'm cracking up.

"We should get going," he says eventually. "The sun's up, so we need to make the most of it. Just... Next time we stop for a rest, you need to *actually* rest. At this rate, you're going to end up collapsing -"

"Then you can just leave me behind, can't you?" I reply, interrupting him before realizing that I'm being far too defensive. "I'm okay. Really. I'm just trying to deal with a lot, and it'd be easier if you weren't second-guessing me all the time. I'm fine, and Rachel's fine, and if you're fine then everyone's fine and..." My voice trails off as I realize that I'm rambling. Damn it, I swear to God, I think I'm losing my mind. I never thought that the world could seem so chaotic and confusing.

"Five minutes," he says, clearly concerned. "Then we'll get going. I've got a new route worked out, but it's not going to be easy. I can carry her for a while, if that'd help. She must be heavy."

I keep my focus on Rachel, refusing to answer.

"Okay," he continues. "Let's just get ready to move on."

As he closes the rucksack, I look down at Rachel and try to pull myself together. I thought I'd be able to manage this journey, and it never occurred to me that I could end up turning into such a mess, but right now I'm terrified that Toad is going to realize there's something wrong with Rachel. There's no way he'll be willing to keep her around if there's even a chance of her being infected, but at the same time I'm convinced that I can keep her safe.

"It's going to be okay," I whisper, leaning down and kissing her forehead, while struggling to keep from crying. "Everything's going to be fine. You can trust me. I won't ever let anything happen to you. For as long as I'm alive, no-one's ever going to hurt you."

THOMAS

"HOW MANY ARE LEFT?" George asks as we're led through the empty streets. "A hundred? A thousand?"

"There are sixty of us," the guard says, walking a little way behind us. "Well, there *were* sixty of us until you showed up. Now there are fifty-nine. Although I guess you two count for now, so there are sixty-one. I guess it'll be back down to fifty-nine again soon."

I glance over my shoulder at him. He's got a makeshift weapon pointed at me, and even though I have no doubt that he knows how to use it, I'm already starting to wonder if I could overpower him. The weapon itself looks to be no more than an old rifle with a pair of large hunting knives strapped to the front. The problem is, he hasn't said anything about the rifle itself, so I have no idea whether it's in working order. Then again, I'm almost beyond the point of caring. I'm too weak to do much more than stumble along and do whatever I'm told. Even if I was able to get away, I don't have the truck anymore, so I don't know where I'd go.

Joe would be disgusted.

"Sixty people in the whole of Chicago?" George asks. "My God, there must have been close to three million here a couple of months ago. Three million living, breathing people with hopes and dreams."

"Most of them died overnight," the guard replies. "Some ended up with that... *thing* in them. They were walking about, talking... After a few weeks they started to rot. Their bodies were falling apart, and it only took a couple more days before they were pretty much gone. It was like a miracle."

"Convenient," George mutters.

"It's over," the guard continues. "At first we thought the creatures were going to overwhelm us. For two weeks, we hid and scavenged. It was like some kind of zombie apocalypse. I saw people being cut down by those things and ripped apart. Whatever the hell was going on, it didn't last long, and now we can start to rebuild. It's not about putting everything back to how it used to be. It's about making things better than ever and avoiding the mistakes of the past. We've got a whole city here to work with -"

"Where are the bodies?" George asks, turning to him.

"Keep walking," the guard says firmly, raising the weapon. "If you try anything, I'll cut you down."

"There should be three million corpses littering the streets," George continues as we make our way past an old restaurant, its windows darkened now. In the window, there's a large poster advertising a two-for-one pizza discount, but the door looks to have been forced open at some point, probably by looters.

"We started tidying," the guard continues. "We were worried about disease, so we didn't have any choice. Plus, the rats were becoming a problem, so we cleared a small section of the city. If you want to see real horror, all you have to do is go about four blocks in any direction, and you'll soon find more than enough. There are bodies all over the place, with rats picking at them. We started by quarantining a certain section of the city and then focusing our work here for now. It was hard, but we organized ourselves in groups and we worked day and night. Every street was scrubbed, every trashcan was emptied, every shop was stripped of anything that might be useful. It might sound like looting, but it wasn't; it was more organized and more effective. Everything's in hand and Quinn has it all under control."

"Quinn?" George asks.

"Quinn took charge. It's what we needed. People panic so easily, but Quinn came up with the answers we needed. There's order here now, and a system of rules. We're working together to make sure we have food and water, and to keep the sick and elderly from starving. In some ways, things are even better than before. As Quinn reminded us during a recent meeting, there were too many people in the old days. Life might be better when things have been pared back a little."

"Sounds like a typical dictator," George mutters.

"You should be careful, giving opinions when you don't know a damn thing about what's been going on around here."

"And what does Quinn get out of this?" George asks.

"The satisfaction of helping us all."

"I'd be interested to meet this Quinn individual," George continues. "I'm sure plenty of people set out with good intentions, but they always become bitter and twisted. That's just what happens when people reach a position of power. If I'm going to be killed for the pleasure of a new ruler, I'd at least like to see the color of that person's eyes before I'm cut down."

"You'll find out soon enough."

"Finally we have a name for the man in charge," George continues, turning to me. "It's always good to know the name of the despotic little tyrant who's planning to take over the world. It's human nature, really. Nature hates a vacuum, and where there's a lack of power, there's always gonna be some asshole ready to run into the gap and start issuing orders. Fortunately, I don't suppose there's much this Quinn individual can do from the ruins of Chicago. It'll be a pretty small kingdom."

"You need to shut up," the guard says firmly.

"Why? You're going to kill us anyway, aren't you?" George pauses, and it seems as if he might have finally given up all hope. "There's probably a little tin-foil ruler in every city, puffed up on delusions of grandeur as he tries to convince the idiots around him that he's the one true king. It's pathetic how humanity constantly reverts to type, but you can't deny it. The vast majority of people are so disgustingly credulous, and I include myself in that category. I've made my fair share of mistakes, listened to my fair share of bad advice."

"You should try saying these things when you're at the tribunal," the guard replies. "I'm sure it'll go down very well. You'll be given an opportunity to explain your actions and apologize for your sins, but if you prefer to use that opportunity to gloat and make foolish statements instead, then that's entirely up to you."

"Oh, I plan to," George replies. "Believe me, I have no intention of hiding my true feelings as I prepare to meet my maker. Might as well go out with a bang, huh?" He turns to me. "Don't you think so, Thomas? Who wants to be pleading and begging as the sword slices through their throat? No-one remembers a coward. At least piss people off and -"

Suddenly he trips and falls, landing hard against the sidewalk, and it's clear that the guard tripped him on purpose. Barely able to even think, all I can do is watch as George rolls onto his side and lets out a gasp of pain. It's almost as if he's got a death wish, since everything he says right now seems designed to provoke the guard. I guess he must have given up all hope of finding his family alive, but as he struggles back to his feet, I can't help wondering why he's so keen to invite pain.

"You're an old man," the guard says calmly. "How old exactly? Sixties?"

"Fifty-nine," George says darkly, turning to him, "and all the better for it. I'm sure as hell not going to be fooled by this Quinn person, whoever he is."

"It doesn't matter whether or not you're fooled by anything," the guard replies. "Your personal beliefs and opinions are completely irrelevant. The tribunal exists for one purpose and one purpose only, and that's to determine your guilt or innocence in the matter of Alice's murder. It's really not so different to how things used to be. In the old days, you couldn't run a girl down and get away with it, so why do you think you should have that right today?"

George stares at him for a moment, before finally turning to me.

"I didn't murder that girl," I say, my voice sounding dry and hoarse. "You were there..."

"Come on," he says with a sigh. "Someone gave the dumb little man a big knife, and now he's in charge, so there's not much point fighting, is there? We might as well get this over with. Let's see what kind of twisted attempt at justice these people have managed to come up with. I've got a feeling it'll be rather sick, but at least it'll be entertaining."

I know I should answer him, but the truth is, I feel completely dazed. It's as if I've finally accepted that there's no way out of this situation, and now I'm just trying to empty my mind as much as possible, so that whatever happens next is a little less painful. That's all I really want now; I want to minimize the pain and just try to die without too much misery.

And then I want to see my family again, in a place that's better than this.

ELIZABETH

"Elizabeth."

Ignoring the voice, I focus on moving forward. All I can think about is the fact that my bones are aching. I desperately want to sleep, but at the same time I know I can't stop. The weight in my arms - Rachel, sleeping or maybe just staring - is dragging me down, and as I stumble over a stray branch and almost fall, I feel as if the whole world is spinning around me.

This isn't right.

I feel... off...

"Elizabeth!"

Suddenly someone puts a hand on my shoulder. Startled, I turn to find a man staring at me. It takes a moment before I realize that I've seen him before. I don't remember his name, but I have a strong image of him in a bed, with some kind of bandage. I know I should recognize him, but right now my mind seems to be filled with fog, and all I can do is stare and hope against hope that I'll come up with an answer soon.

"Toad?" I say eventually, the name sounding strange and alien.

Leaning closer, he peers into my eyes, as if he's looking for something specific. I don't like the way he's acting as if he's in charge.

"I'm fine," I mutter, turning to walk away.

"You're delirious," he replies, grabbing my arm and pulling me back toward him. "You can't go on like this. We need to stop again."

"We don't have time," I reply, although suddenly I realize that this entire situation is absolutely hilarious. Toad is so serious all the time, when really there's no point worrying. We are what we are, and we're going to end up somewhere, and if we die then it doesn't really matter. Although I try to keep these thoughts to myself, eventually I start grinning. I can't help it. Everything has seemed so relentlessly serious lately, and I just feel as if I need a break.

"What are you laughing at?" he asks.

"I'm not laughing," I reply, before forcing a brief, awkward laugh as a kind of demonstration. "There, that was a laugh. I'm smiling, though, but that's just because you're being so serious." I take a step back, but the ground seems to dip and swirl all around me and it takes me a moment to steady myself.

He puts the palm of his hand against my forehead for a moment.

"You're running a fever," he continues, before checking my pulse. "We need to rest. At this rate, you're going to collapse, and that'll slow us down even more. We'll just stop here for an hour. I'll look after Rachel and you can -"

"No," I say, turning away from him in an attempt to make sure he can't see Rachel's face. "She's mine."

Looking down at Rachel, I realize that she's still just staring at me. I want more than anything for her to act normally, to show some kind of sign that she's not sick, but as tears roll down my cheeks I can't help but realize that I'm just fooling myself. I've been trying so hard over the past couple of days to hide the truth from Toad, and during that time I've been building up a wall of resilience and determination; right now, however, that wall is starting to crack, and I can tell that it's going to come crashing down at any moment.

"Talk to me," Toad says. "Tell me what's -"

"I'm fine," I whisper, holding Rachel tighter. He's going to try to take her away from me, and then he'll probably murder her for being some kind of monster, and if that happens, there's no more hope. Everything seems so clear and obvious right now, as if all the lies have been lifted away.

I just want to go to sleep, but I can't.

"Tell me what's wrong with the baby," Toad continues. "You've been acting strange since we left the farm, Elizabeth, and I need you to tell me the truth. Whatever it is, we can work it out, but only if you're honest with me." He pauses, waiting for some kind of grand confession that I'm never going to offer. "Can I see her?" he asks eventually. "You can hold her, but I want to look at her. Is that okay?"

I don't reply, but as he steps around me to get a better view of Rachel, I realize that I might as well let him.

"You can't hurt her," I tell him, my voice trembling as I hold back the tears. "Please, she's okay, she's just upset."

"This is all she does all day, isn't it?" he replies. "She just stares."

"She's been through so much."

"But it's not normal, is it? A baby should be more active and alert."

"What do you know about babies?" I ask him.

"What do *you* know?" he replies.

"She's going to be okay," I tell him, taking a deep breath as I try to stay calm. "She's a little off-color right now, but she's not a threat to anyone. If she can just have some time to recover, she'll be fine in a day or two. She's not getting the right food. It's not like I can breast-feed her. I tried, just in case somehow it might work, but obviously it was useless. There were no books at the house, so I had to guess about the food..." Pausing, I realize that I might have been poisoning the poor little thing. "I just want her to be okay. That's all that matters. If a baby can't survive in this world, then nothing can and we're all doomed." I turn to him. "You can't kill her. I won't let you!"

"I'm not going to kill her," he replies. "Has she done anything that makes you think she might be infected by the same thing that was in those creatures?"

I shake my head.

"Then you're probably right," he continues. "She's just had a bad diet. I know you've done the best you can, but it's a huge job keeping a baby alive. But even if she's sick, she's still here, and if we're lucky we'll find someone who knows what to do, and then we can turn her over to them." He pauses, before suddenly leaning closer and planting a gentle kiss on my forehead. "It's not the end of the world, Elizabeth. Not yet. Things look bad, but we're out here fighting and we're not going to give up."

I nod, even though I'm worried he's just saying these things because he wants to trick me.

The moment I go to sleep, he might take Rachel and hurt her.

"I need to take a look at your right foot," he adds. "You've been limping more and more, and I need to see it."

"My what?" I ask, momentarily confused before I remember the cut from a few days ago. "It's nothing, I just -"

"Let me see it."

"Why?"

"Because you're limping, Elizabeth."

"It's just a scratch from some barbed wire," I tell him, worried that he's trying to trick me into putting Rachel down. "If you -"

Before I can finish, he kneels next to me and reaches down. Although I want to push him away, I figure I might as well just let him take a look, but as he pulls the side of my sock away, I feel a jolt of intense pain shoot through the bone and it's all I can do to keep from dropping Rachel. Instinctively, I pull away, shocked by the pain. I knew my foot wasn't quite right, and I was planning to take a look some time soon, but I figured it was nothing too serious. Or maybe I was just hoping I could ignore it and it'd get better.

"It's infected," Toad says getting to his feet.

"It's not infected," I reply, even though I'm starting to worry. "All that happened is I scratched myself on some old barbed wire on your property. It was days ago."

"And did you clean the wound?"

"Yes!" I reply, trying not to sound too exasperated, before I realize that maybe I didn't clean it after all. I was going to, but in all the fuss and confusion with Rachel, I guess I might have forgotten. "Maybe," I add. "I'll do it soon. Look, it's not as if I'm infected by whatever was in those creatures. It's just a cut, and if it's got a slight swelling, that's totally normal. It'll be fine!"

"You're an idiot," he says after a moment.

"Excuse me?"

"You're a goddamn idiot," he says again, as he checks the temperature of my forehead. "The wound on your ankle is infected, and you've got a fever. If there was barbed wire anywhere near my property, it must have been old, which means it was probably rusty, which means..." He pauses, and he seems genuinely worried. "I need you to sit down so I can look at it properly," he says eventually.

"What kind of infection?" I ask. "Do you mean -"

"Not the kind that created those creatures. This is a much more regular infection, but it's just as dangerous. Stay still while I -"

"No way," I say firmly. "I'll wait 'til we find a doctor -"

"What doctor?" he replies, interrupting me. "There are no doctors around here! Now sit down and take your goddamn shoes off, okay?"

I want to argue with him, but I figure I should probably go along with whatever he wants, at least for now. It takes a moment for me to arrange Rachel on a nearby patch of grass, but finally I sit on an old tree stump and start unlacing my right shoe. The pain is much worse than I'd expected, and by the time I peel the shoe off to reveal a yellow-and-red-stained sock, I'm starting to realize that something really bad might be happening here. I glance at Toad, and it's clear that he's worried, but I force myself to focus on the positive. Reaching down, I start to peel my sock down, but it's partially stuck to the wound and I find to my horror that one entire side of my ankle is swollen and bloody. For a moment, all I can do is stare at it and try to pretend that it's not as bad as it looks.

"Your shoes were too tight and too airless," Toad says. "The cut must have been deep enough to let the bacteria thrive, and then the shoes provided the perfect incubation site."

"Do you have anything for it?" I ask, trying not to panic.

"In the old days, you'd have had to go to hospital."

"Okay, so what do we do now?"

He pauses, staring at the wound as if he's not sure how to fix it. Maybe I've allowed myself to become too accustomed lately to the idea that Toad has an answer for everything, but the look of helplessness in his eyes is extremely worrying. I'm waiting for him to come up with an idea, to tell me that everything's going to be okay, but it's as if I've finally presented him with a problem that he can't fix. The problem is, if Toad can't fix it, then I sure as hell can't either.

"What do we do?" I ask again.

"The infection could spread a lot further," he replies, clearly lost in thought. After a moment, he reaches down and tilts the wound toward him. "This is going to hurt," he continues, "but I have to see how deep it's gone." With that, he presses a finger against my skin and starts pulling the wound open.

As a jolt of pain hits me, I instinctively pull my foot away.

"Just stay still," he hisses, grabbing my ankle again and taking another look. "It's deep," he says eventually. "I think it's reached the bone, and there's slight swelling a little higher up."

"What kind of infection is it?" I ask, wiping sweat from my brow. "Give me some good news here."

"I don't know. I'm not an expert. I knew a guy in the army once who had something like this, and..."

I wait for him to finish, but he remains stubbornly silent.

"And what?" I ask.

Again I wait, but again he seems lost in thought. I want to be patient, to pretend that I'm not panicking, but right now I'm terrified. I hold back for as long as possible.

"And *what*?"

"You're not going to be able to walk on this soon," he replies, dodging the question. "It's going to be too painful. Look how tight the skin is around the back of the ankle and down to the heel."

"It's just a scratch," I point out, trying to keep him from over-reacting. "People scratch themselves all the time!"

"It's a deep scratch on rusty barbed wire. I guess you don't often have that kind of thing in the city, but when you're out here, you need to be more careful. In the old days, you'd have gone to hospital and been treated, and you'd have almost certainly been okay. Right now, out here, I can't even begin to help you! Do you have any idea how serious this might be?"

"Fine," I reply, "then you might as well leave me behind if I'm just gonna slow you down by hobbling! I mean, I don't want to put you out! I know how you feel about people who are weak!"

He stares at me, and suddenly I realize that he might actually be considering doing just that. I open my mouth to tell him he's crazy, but finally it hits me that this is serious. The pain in my ankle is getting worse, and I'm starting to feel the fever that he said I had a little earlier. Looking deep into his eyes, I can see a hint of indecision, and that's when it hits me: my foot *is* going to get worse, and I *am* going to slow him down, in which case the only logical thing for him to do would be to leave me here. After all, it's not like we really mean anything to each other. To him, I'm just this girl who showed up a month ago.

I wait for him to say something, but it's as if he can't speak.

"Are you going to go?" I ask eventually, with tears in my voice.

He doesn't reply.

"Are you?"

I wait for an answer.

"I'll die," I tell him, trying not to panic. "I'd die anyway, without help, but if I can't walk."

Nearby, Rachel finally lets out another faint gurgle.

"You're gonna leave her too, aren't you?" I continue. "You're gonna just walk off and forget about us, and we'll die here."

"Elizabeth -"

"You *are*!" I shout. "I can see it in your eyes! It's gonna be so easy for you!"

"I'm not going to leave you anywhere," he replies, but I can tell he's not sure whether he really means it. He's clearly weighing up the options and trying to decide if he can do something so horrific.

"I don't blame you," I continue. "This is all my fault anyway. If you want to go -"

"I'm not going to leave you!"

"You should!"

He shakes his head.

"But if you -"

Before I can finish, he suddenly leans forward and hugs me. It's a shocking moment, unlike anything I've experienced with him since the days immediately after his injury last month. I have no idea how to respond, so I just wait as he holds me tight, and that's when I realize that this is the first proper human contact I've had since Henry died. All I can do is close my eyes and hope that this moment lasts forever, because I'm terrified that this is his way of saying goodbye.

THOMAS

PEOPLE.

Actual people.

As we reach a small area of parkland, flanked on all four sides by large buildings, I'm shocked by the sight of forty or fifty people standing around, as if they're waiting for us. They all look disheveled and gaunt, which I guess is only to be expected after spending more than a month living here in the ruins of what used to be Chicago, but as they turn to look at us, I can't help feeling as if I'm very exposed. If I was going to make a run for it, that chance has definitely passed.

"Don't let them see that you're scared," George hisses. "That's what they want. People like this, they feed off the suffering of others."

"What does it matter?" I whisper. "If they're

going to kill us anyway -"

"Shut up," the guard mutters, poking me in the back with the butt of his weapon. "Just keep moving. You'll have a chance to speak soon enough."

As the crowd parts, a small platform is revealed up ahead. It's not much more than some old wooden crates arranged in a pile, with a section of flat-board over the top, but as the guard leads George and me up onto the raised section, I suddenly feel as if we've been brought here to be displayed to the gathered survivors. Turning, I realize that they're all staring at us, and it's hard not to wonder what they're waiting for. At least there's no noose, but I'm sure they could think of plenty of other ways to finish us off.

I should be screaming with fear, but I'm too numb to do anything other than stare back at them.

"Sheep," George mutters.

"They think I'm a murderer," I say out loud, even though the words aren't really directed at anyone. "They think I murdered one of them."

"They've been told to think that," George replies. "This isn't justice. It's politics, and theater. Whoever's in charge here, they must be thanking God for delivering such a great opportunity right into their hands. Putting us up here and pretending to dispense justice is going to provide excellent cover for whatever cowardice and evil lurks at the heart of this bullshit. All the best tyrants are able to dress themselves up as warriors of virtue."

Before I can reply, I spot movement to one side, and I watch as another guard brings a girl up onto the platform. She looks to be about my age, maybe a little older, and she has bright blonde hair that has begun to betray dark roots. With a weathered, teary look in her eyes, she barely even glances at me before taking her place next to George. It's as if she's accepted her fate, whatever that might be, and can't even muster the energy to struggle. After a moment, however, I realize that she's shivering slightly.

"At least we're not the only ones," George whispers. "Oh God, did I really say that? What's wrong with me?"

"Ask her what she did," I reply.

"What's the point?" he sighs. "They'll let her off, I guarantee it. She's one of their own, so they'll show leniency, just so they can claim to be fair and just. It's a typical tactic to make sure that they don't develop a reputation for being barbaric. Then, when they -"

"Silence!" the guard shouts, shoving George so hard in the back that he takes a step forward before recovering his composure.

Taking a deep breath, I stare out at the crowd and watch as the dead-eyed survivors stare straight back at me. They're waiting for something, but I have no idea what; it's as if they've simply been told to come here and observe whatever fate is handed out to us, and I can't help wondering if they're even capable of independent thought. They're not talking or showing any sign of interest in proceedings. They're just standing and waiting, almost like zombies. I guess this is a kind of entertainment for them.

"So these are the prisoners," says a female voice suddenly, from behind.

Turning, I see a woman approaching the back of the platform. Unlike everyone else around here, she seems a lot more alert, and she smiles as she steps up to join us. I want to ask her who the hell she is, but I get the feeling that I'd only end up with the butt of a rifle in the back of the head. Besides, it's not as if there's much I can do to get out of this mess. George is undoubtedly right; this is less about justice and more about bolstering support for whoever happens to be in power around here. As she makes her way around to the front of the platform and stops in front of the blonde-haired girl, the woman pauses for a moment, and finally a smile crosses her lips.

"You stole food," she says eventually, staring at the girl. "Look at me."

The girl continues to stare straight ahead.

"Look at me, darling," the woman continues, putting a hand under the girl's chin and tilting her head up until they make eye contact. "That's better. You stole food, didn't you? You're a thief."

The girl doesn't respond.

"You considered your own hunger to be more important than the health of one of your fellow survivors," the woman adds. "You're young, though, so there's still time to change you, to make you see the world more clearly. For that reason, I'm going to allow you to stay with us. After all, it would be unnecessarily cruel to throw away such a young life."

Silence.

"Don't you have anything to say?" the woman continues.

The girl opens her mouth, but no words come out.

"What's that?" the woman asks. "I didn't quite hear..."

"Thank you," the girl replies, her voice sounding bare and devoid of almost all emotion. "If you -"

"I considered banishing you," the woman continues, interrupting her. "I could have ordered that you were sent away from this place, to roam the rat-infested streets or to strike out on your own beyond the city. In fact, before I saw your face, I was seriously considering such an option. Would you have liked that?"

"No," the girl says, finally sounding scared.

"You'd have died," the woman replies, clearly taking great pleasure in this demonstration of her power. "It wouldn't have been pleasant, either. You'd have starved, and most likely rats would have started chewing on your body before you were quite dead. I saw that happen to a man a few weeks ago. My God, you should have heard his screams as the rats' teeth scraped against his bones. I should have finished him off, but I needed to expose myself to that kind of suffering. Instead of helping him, or running, I stepped closer and forced myself to watch. He was twitching for hours, even as the rats chewed to the bone. Once you've witnessed something like that, it no longer holds quite so much power over you." She pauses. "If you steal again, I will have no hesitation. You'll be sent out to meet that exact same fate. Do you understand?"

"Of course, but -"

"Use this opportunity. Learn from it. Become a better person and try to teach others how to live decently. There'll be no stain on your character, and no-one will hold this incident over your head, so long as you repent and reform. You're free to go. For now."

"Thank you," the girl mutters, before hurrying down from the platform and joining the crowd. She quickly takes a position near the front, and it's shocking to realize how quickly she's gone from being part of the show to being part of the audience. I guess she's just grateful to have been released, but it's as if all the people here are in awe this ceremony. I still don't quite understand what the hell's happening or how this woman ended up in charge, but there's something very creepy about the way she seems to be in charge.

As the woman wanders along the platform and stops in front of George and me, I can't help but look down at my feet. There's something about this woman's strong gaze that makes me feel uncomfortable, as if she can see directly into my soul. I wait for her to say something, but so far she seems content to just get a closer look at us, and her eyes - so brown, they almost seem to be dark red - have been fixed on me with unblinking precision for what feels like an eternity. After a few minutes, I start to wonder if she's waiting for one of us to say something, but I don't dare break the silence. Finally, however, I force myself to look at her, and I find that she's staring straight at me. An older woman, in her forties at least, she has shoulder-length black hair, and she seems to find me amusing.

"Murderers," she says eventually.

I stare at her.

"Murderers," she says again. "No-one likes a murderer, do they? Well, no-one's *supposed* to like a murderer, but then sometimes social conventions are supposed to be broken. You kill one man, it's murder. You kill another, it's a strike for freedom. Everything's subjective, don't you think?" She leans closer. "I murdered a pigeon the other day and ate it for dinner."

Unable to answer, I wait for her to get to the point. If she's going to have us killed, I wish she'd just get on with it.

"It was a good meal," she adds. "Plump and juicy, although I suppose that was largely due to the way I cooked it. Still, I'm sure all the other pigeons would call me a murderer. The question is, do I care? And the answer would have to be no, because they're just pigeons. But we... We're human beings, just like you. That makes things different, doesn't it?"

Standing next to me, George lets out a snort of derision.

"You find something funny?" the woman asks.

"Oh, I'm sorry," George replies. "Is this *not* supposed to be a stand-up comedy act?"

"The world's ending," the woman continues. "The pack has been shuffled, so to speak." She turns to me. "You were the one driving, weren't you?"

I stare at her, but it's clear she won't believe me. She's probably already made her mind up.

"I can only assume that it was an accident," she continues. "No-one would come to us and immediately kill an innocent young woman. Such a move would be insane. Unless you're monsters, which I don't think is the case. There was some concern that you might be creatures, infected by whatever caused this disaster in the first place, but I can see now that you're no such thing. You're scared, frightened men who came crashing into our little world without a plan. It's so inept and foolish, it must have been the result of blind panic. Am I correct?"

"The boy thought she was infected," George replies. "He was trying to get us out of here. I was with him, I can vouch for his actions."

"Infected?" She pauses. "There's been no infection for weeks. The creatures are gone, and they won't be coming back."

"You can't be sure of that," George tells her.

"Have you seen one recently?"

"I didn't say I disagree with you," he continues. "I just said that you can't be sure."

"I watched them rot. I was the first to come out of hiding on these streets, and I walked among the monsters as they fell apart. It was a foolish thing to do, perhaps, but it inspired others and it made them look at me as if I'm brave and wise. Obviously that's a little off-target, but I can only accept their praise. The creatures were dying, and I knew it, and by that stage I was willing to take the risk. They were still talking, some of them, and goading me.

Gradually, as other people saw that I was safe, they too came out to witness the final moments of those... *things*. Eventually, there was only one left, and I stood before him as his body fell apart. Do you want to know what his last words were?"

"Not particularly," George mutters.

"Do *you*?" she asks, keeping her gaze fixed on me. "Come on, you must at least be curious. This is important stuff here, and I can see from your expression that you're not a dumb kid. You've made it this far, so you must have your wits about you."

I stare at her, trying to work out what kind of game she's playing.

"He said he'd be back," she continues. "He said he'd mis-calculated, but that his virus would mutate and evolve, and that eventually he'd see us again. And in return, I told him that whoever and whatever he really was, he suffered from delusions. I told him that there was no way back for him, no possibility of survival. And then I watched as he tried to speak, and then I laughed as his body gave way completely, and I kicked his bones once he was gone." She pauses, as if she's trying to gauge my reaction. "I imagine the same scene was playing out all over the world," she adds after a moment. "The creatures weren't viable, but they *did* perform a useful service. They wiped away billions of worthless people who were only taking up space and consuming resources."

"My family died," I tell her, trying to hide my anger.

"Everyone's family died," she replies. "Don't see this as a disaster. See it as an opportunity. Humanity was struggling under the weight of its own success, there were too many of us. What we needed was this mass extinction event, to bring us to our knees. Now, those of us who are left can rebuild the species without having to worry about over-population. All it took was one virus."

"See?" George mutters. "I told you the person in charge would turn out to be insane. Only a very special type of lunatic is drawn to take control like this and start spouting so much bullshit."

"My name is Amanda Quinn," the woman replies, turning to him, "and I have something very important to show the pair of you. Something that I've been keeping to myself. Most of the people here aren't ready to see it, they're too dazed or too stupid, but I think I should give you a nice reward. After all, you murdered a girl who was only draining our resources. That makes you very..." She pauses, as if she's trying to find the right word. "Interesting. This tribunal isn't here to punish you for what you did. Oh no, it's here to reward you. Now, it's a great responsibility, but I would very much like an outsider's perspective, so I absolutely insist that you back to my home so I can show you what I've found. It's very important and very rare, and I think it could change everything. Are you ready to see it?"

"I'm good, thanks," George says. "No special favors for me."

"Fool," she says with a smile.

"I know plenty of very smart people who died young," he replies. "If being a fool keeps me alive, then that's fine by me. I only came here to look for two people, and I don't see them in your little group -"

"Then they're dead," she says calmly. "Believe me, this is the only safe part of the city."

George stares at her, but I can see that he believes her.

The woman turns to me.

"Well?" she asks. "Are you stubborn, like your friend, or are you interested in seeing what I've found? I could use a second opinion, and unfortunately the other people around here aren't really much use. There's no reason to be scared. If I wanted you dead, you'd be dead by now."

I stare at her, convinced that at any moment she's going to change her mind and order our execution.

"It's a computer," she continues, keeping her voice low. "It works, too. I've got it linked up to an old wood-burning generator. Not exactly efficient, but still... Anyway, that's not even the most exciting part. Here's the kicker." She leans toward me, with a look of wonder in her eyes. "I've picked up a very interesting signal from somewhere not too far away."

ELIZABETH

"THIS IS GOING TO HURT," Toad says as he squeezes some clear gel from a tube. "It's only a mild disinfectant, and it won't be enough to clean your wound properly, but it'll buy us time."

"Time until what?" I ask, sitting on the forest floor with my bare leg out-stretched.

"Time to think of something else," he replies, before he starts to rub the gel over my wound. He was right: it hurts. In fact, it's agony, and although I try to keep from crying out, eventually I let out a gasp of pain. I can feel the gel slowly being worked deeper into the cut, and although I'm just about managing to stay still, the pain is getting worse and worse. Leaning my head back, I close my eyes and desperately try to keep myself from screaming.

"Done," Toad says suddenly.

Turning to look at him, I see that he's finished. My bare ankle glistens in the midday sunlight, and I can tell that pus has already begun to leak from the wound. I keep telling myself that somehow everything is going to be okay, but the truth is, I can tell that my ankle is only going to get worse. Already, it's almost too painful to walk, and in another few hours' time I'm going to start slowing us down.

I can't ignore the truth.

Maybe Toad *should* leave me. If I'm going to die, he and Rachel should still try to find safety. These thoughts have been in my mind for a few hours now, and slowly I'm edging toward thinking the unthinkable. Having spent my whole life worrying only about myself, I can finally feel a different kind of strength welling up in my soul. I just haven't had the guts to put them into words yet, although I'm running out of time and I need to get this over with before the fever brings more delirium. If my fate is sealed, I can't let anyone else suffer.

"I've been thinking," Toad says after a moment, "and I've come up with a solution -"

"Leave me," I say suddenly, interrupting him.

He stares at me.

I pause, wondering whether I really said

those words.

"What/" he asks eventually.

"We both know it's the best thing," I continue, taking a deep breath in an attempt to keep from crying. "My ankle's not going to get better, is it? You can keep putting gel on it, but the infection'll just spread. Even if I keep going today, I'll end up collapsing tomorrow, or the day after that. It's inevitable."

He opens his mouth to reply, but it's clear that he knows I'm right.

"And I can't carry on any other way," I point out. "It's clear. The pain's too bad, I can't walk, you sure as hell can't carry me, and then there's Rachel..." Looking over at her, I watch as she stares back at me. After a moment, I turn to Toad. "I've always been a selfish person," I tell him, "and I've always done whatever I wanted, whatever suited me. And this injury to my leg is something *I* caused. It was my fault I cut myself, and it was my fault I didn't pay attention to it. I'm not cut out to live in the world when it's like this, and..."

I sniff back tears, but deep down I suddenly feel as if I'm finally doing the right thing. It's terrifying, but also strangely fulfilling.

"Take Rachel and get going," I continue. "Right at the end of my life, let me do the right thing. She's got more of a chance than me, and so have you. If leaving me here helps you two, then I want you to do it. I've never, ever done anything selfless, but I can see now that this is the right thing to do, and if Rachel survives, then that's all that matters."

"There's another way," he replies.

I shake my head, but the tears are running freely down my cheeks now.

"We can keep going," he continues. "You can use me for support, and I'll carry Rachel, and we'll try to find another route, one that's more direct. Or we can find shelter for a while and wait while I try to fix your ankle. There are a million ways we can beat this, Elizabeth, and none of them involve you sacrificing yourself."

"But all of your answers involve compromise," I point out, my lower lip trembling as I try to persuade him to see the truth. "We're not friends. Not really. We were thrown together by events, and I appreciate everything you've done for me, but I know that you'll just put yourself and Rachel in danger if you try to save me." I pause, stunned by the words that are coming from my lips right now. I never thought I'd do something so selfless, but the crazy part is that I don't even feel scared. As long as I know that Toad and Rachel will be okay, I know I can face this. "Please," I whisper, hoping and praying that he'll understand.

He shakes his head, but there are tears in his eyes too and I can tell that he knows I'm right.

"Please," I whisper again.

He pauses, and then finally he leans closer and kisses my forehead. After a moment, he looks deep into my eyes, and just when I think he's going to pull away, he leans even closer and our lips touch. It's not much, barely a kiss at all, but it lasts for a few seconds. I keep expecting him to turn and leave, but something seems to be holding him close to me, as if he doesn't want the moment to end.

Finally, he pulls back.

"I'm not leaving you," he says quietly.

"Yeah," I reply, sniffing back tears. "You are, and you're taking Rachel with you. And you're going to find somewhere safe, and she's going to get a chance to grow up. You can tell her about me, and you can make out that I'm some great hero who did a really brave thing, but all that matters is that you two are okay. There's a future out there somewhere, a place for survivors, and I wish I could go with you, but I can't. You've always treated me like I'm some kind of kid, but I'm not. I'm an adult, and I can make my own decisions. This is the best option for all of us."

"We'll talk about it in the morning," he says. "You're tired and delirious -"

"I've never been more sure about anything in my life," I continue. "Let me do this. I'm going to die anyway, so at least let me know that you two are going to be okay."

179

I wait for him to reply, but I can tell that I've won the argument. He's going to leave, and he's going to take Rachel, and I'm going to die with the comfort of knowing that they have a chance. The truth is, I'm convinced that they can get to safety so long as they're able to keep moving, but with me slowing them down, they've got no chance.

"You should sleep," he says calmly.

"I want you to be gone when I wake up," I tell him.

"Elizabeth -"

"Both of you. If you're still here, I'll refuse to come with you. I probably won't even make it until morning anyway. I can tell I'm burning up, and the pain is getting worse. Just promise me you'll be gone when I wake up."

He pauses.

"Get some sleep," he says finally. "Rest. You're in pain."

"But you'll -"

"Sleep."

"But promise -"

"Sleep. Don't make me tell you again." He reaches down and squeezes my hand. "Everything's going to be okay. I promise. You're right. You can't go on like this. Some decisions just can't be avoided."

I want to make him swear that he'll be gone when I wake up, but somehow I can tell from the look in his eyes that he's accepted the inevitability of this moment. I guess he just doesn't want to say the words, but this is goodbye, and the craziest thing is that I can't help smiling as I think of them carrying on and reaching safety. Maybe I'm delirious from the pain and the infection, but I feel as if all that matters is these two other people. Hell, I didn't even know them until about a month ago, but now they mean everything to me. I wasn't able to save Henry, but I can save Toad and Rachel.

"Thank you," I say eventually.

"Here," he says, grabbing a blanket from the rucksack and putting it over my shoulders. His hands are shaking, and although I want him to just walk away right now, I figure he has to do this his own way.

"Thanks," I reply as I settle down to rest.

"I'll -" he starts to say, but his voice trails off.

I stay awake for a while, listening to the sound of him fiddling with the rucksack. I feel strangely calm, and when I finally close my eyes, I find myself imagining what it'll be like when Toad and Rachel reach safety. I hope that one day he'll be able to tell her about me, and although there's not a chance in hell that she'll remember anything about this part of her life, she might at least realize that after her mother died, there was someone else who took care of her. I know there's a chance that she's sick, or maybe even infected, but right now I feel that she at least has hope. I helped her get this far, and now Toad's going to help her to keep going. She'll be fine.

Eventually, finally, I slip into sleep. I just hope that Henry and the rest of my family are waiting for me.

THOMAS

"MOST OF THEM DON'T know about this," Quinn says as she leads us through the door, into the wrecked remains of an old sandwich bar. "I prefer to keep a tight rein on information."

I don't reply, because I don't really know what to say. This woman seems... *off* somehow. For one thing, back on the platform she actually seemed to be pleased with me for running someone over with the truck; for another, she clearly has the loyalty of the people who were gathered in the crowd, but I can't see why that might be. So far, Quinn is coming across as a kind of scatty woman whose thought processes don't entirely make sense. I don't trust her at all.

"We're heading down the rabbit-hole," George whispers, keeping pace with me.

"Should we try to run?" I ask.

"I can hear you!" Quinn says, stopping up ahead and opening a cabinet to reveal a laptop, which she removes and places on a table in front of us. "Please don't whisper to each other. If you want to discuss me, or to talk about the situation in any way, you might as well just do it in the open. I don't bite, I promise."

"We were just trying to figure out how crazy you are," George says, with a hint of derision in his tone. "My vote is that you're about a six on the scale, but you're playing to the crowd and trying desperately to seem more like a ten. People like you aren't exactly rare." He turns to me. "What about you, Thomas? Do you think she's faking it?"

I stare at Quinn, who's too busy plugging the laptop into some kind of large black box.

"Thanks to a very complicated system that I set up," she explains, "I've been able to generate small quantities of electrical power and store them in some redundant batteries. I know, I'm a genius, but this is a time for geniuses, so what else can I do other than step up to the plate? Most people, they're not very smart, but I *am*, and that's why I get to do all the fun things, like this -"

She presses a button on the laptop, and it whirs into action.

"Impressed?" she says, turning to us.

"Mildly," George mutters.

I watch as the laptop boots up. To be honest, I never thought I'd see anything like this again. It's only been about a month and a half since the world went to hell, but the laptop already feels like something from another age, almost as if it's out of place in the new order. Nevertheless, even though I keep expecting it to break down, it eventually completes the boot process.

"There's no internet," Quinn says with a smile. "I'm not *that* smart. Hell, I only really started the damn thing out of nostalgia, the first time at least. But I know a thing or two about computers, so I started rooting around and managed to link a low-frequency transmitter to the system, and that's when I came across something very interesting." Turning to the machine, she opens some kind of dialog box and types in a series of commands.

As she continues to work, I walk over to join her. I don't know a lot about computers either, but I can tell that she's working in a DOS dialog box, and once I'm close enough to see the screen properly, I realize she's using the transmitter to ping a server. I stare at the command lines, and at first I tell myself that I must be misunderstanding what I'm seeing, because it looks a hell of a lot like she's getting some kind of signal back from a remote location.

"Someone's out there," she says, turning to me. "You understand what you're looking at, right? Someone's running a server."

"Who?" I ask.

"I don't know *that*," she replies. "Jesus, if I knew that, I wouldn't have to keep digging, would I? I'm not a mind reader. I've been trying to narrow down the physical location, but so far I haven't had any luck. There are programs I could use, but I don't have them, and I'm not gonna try writing them myself. Still, there's no doubt about it. Someone out there is running a server, and as far as I can tell it's up all the time, which indicates a stable and continuous power source, which indicates..."

I wait for her to continue.

"Well?" she says, raising an eyebrow. "You seem reasonably smart. What does it indicate?"

"Someone's out there," I reply, staring at the screen.

"Someone's out there *and* they've got a system running," she continues. "A proper system, with a proper power source. Much better than this pile of junk I managed to rig together. Given current conditions, that's hardly the work of a moment. It's clear that we're talking about someone who knows what they're doing, someone with resources and intelligence. And then there were the booms."

"The booms?"

"You must have heard the booms. Everyone heard the booms. It was like the whole planet shook. The last one was a few weeks ago, and they've been completely irregular, but they *have* happened."

"I remember," I tell her. "I just figured something was exploding somewhere."

"Oh, you're such an optimist," she replies, patting me on the shoulder. "No, something's going on out there, something big and something... Something that someone's controlling. In all this chaos and dust, someone has managed to either retain or regain control of at least some of the old techniques. The world isn't collapsing into disorder after all. If we can find whoever's running this server, we can make contact with other groups like our own, and then we can think about rebuilding properly. This is the beginning of... something!"

"What if it's just automated?" I ask.

"The power supply can't be automated, not after all this time. It would have cut off. Someone's keeping it running."

I turn to George.

"Don't ask me," he says with a shrug. "You two might as well be talking in goddamn Mandarin for all I understand."

"It's a computer system," I tell him. "Someone's got a server going and it's broadcasting a signal."

"It must be powerful, too," Quinn adds. "It's quite faint, but it's distant too. I don't think it's coming from within the city. It could be fifty, maybe sixty miles away, but that's really just an educated guess. I need to find a way to calculate the direction, 'cause right now it could be based anywhere in that radius, maybe even further."

"Great," he replies, "but why? What's the point?"

"Good question," Quinn continues. "I doubt it's just there for the benefit of people like us. Someone's planning something, maybe they were even planning it before all of this crap started to happen. But don't you see? There's order in the chaos. This one, lone signal is proof that the whole world hasn't fallen apart. Someone's out there. It's like a test. They want to make contact, but only with people who have the ability to find them."

"That's something of a stretch," George points out.

"It's a new world order," she continues, ignoring him. Whatever else I might think about her, I can't deny that she's filled with enthusiasm. "It's the start of something huge and wonderful. The human race could never have continued along its old course. Over-population, diminishing resources... We were headed for a crash, so really this whole thing has been a huge blessing. It almost makes me want to believe in God."

Staring at her, I realize that she might have lost her mind. It's almost as if she's enjoying this, as if she thinks it's some kind of huge game.

"So..." I pause as I try to work out what I'm

supposed to say next. "What do we do?" I ask eventually. "There's a signal, but now what?"

"I'm glad you asked," she replies, with a mischievous grin. "I've got a plan. We have to go and find the source of this signal. It's almost like a test, a way for us to prove that we're smart enough. Only the best can survive in this strange new world, and those who are too dumb or too weak are just going to have to..." She pauses, and it's almost as if she's enjoying the situation. "You did such a good thing when you ran that girl over," she continues. "She was worthless, just another piece of human flotsam drifting through life. So we're going to have to continue your good work and thin out the ranks by leaving the detritus behind, and then we're going to march forward and embrace the future of the human species. It makes sense, doesn't it? The whole thing makes perfect, crystal clear sense!"

I look at George.

George looks at me.

"Come on," Quinn continues. "Face the future!"

Staring at her, I realize that she's actually serious. She isn't horrified or shocked by the fact that I ran that girl over; she thinks it's a good thing, and she thinks it means that I'm like her. I want to tell her she's insane, but at the same time I'm worried about making her angry.

"So what do you say?" she continues,

189

holding a hand out toward me as the smile finally leaves her face, replaced by a darker expression that hints at danger. "Are you with me, or are you against me?"

ELIZABETH

"TOAD?"

Sitting up suddenly, I realize I must have been asleep for several hours. Sweat is pouring down my face and I feel as if I'm burning up, and as I look around the clearing, I'm shocked to find that the light is starting to fade. A kind of hazy gray dusk is descending, making the whole place seem almost unreal.

"Toad?" I say again, wiping my eyes.

No answer.

"Toad?"

I look around, but there's no-one here. For a moment, I can barely remember anything that has happened over the past few days. Memories of the farm are mixed with older memories, of Henry and my family, of that psychopath Bob and... The fever seems to be keeping me from thinking clearly, but eventually I remember my ankle, and then I remember the conversation I had with Toad a few hours earlier.

"Rachel?" I call out, pulling the blanket close as I feel a cold breeze blow past.

Silence.

"Rachel?"

When I try to get to my feet, I immediately find that my balance is a little off, and it doesn't help that my ankle is throbbing. Crawling on all fours, I make my way over to where Toad placed the rucksack earlier, but it's gone. Taking a deep breath and trying to stay calm, I finally realize that he did what I asked: he took Rachel and he left. I guess he wanted to wait until I was asleep, so he wouldn't have to endure some long, drawn-out goodbye. Still, it's good that he left. If he'd stayed, we all would have died. He did the right thing.

And now I'm alone.

I look across the clearing.

This is it.

This is where I'm going to die.

Elizabeth Marter, born in a New York hospital, raised in Manhattan, and died in a forest shortly after the collapse of civilization...

Reaching down, I touch my ankle and find that it's swollen even more. The pain is intense, but in a strange way it's also bearable. I feel as if my whole body's on fire, which I guess means that the infection is spreading. Rolling onto my back, I stare up at the early evening sky. This is probably the last time I'll ever see the world, but my mind is too muddled to take it all in. All I can think about is the fact that somewhere out there, Toad and Rachel are continuing the journey, making their way toward a possible future. I know it's still a long-shot, but at least they have a chance, which is more than they would have had if they'd stayed here with me.

"Dear God," I say out loud, "please look after them. Keep them safe. Forget about me, but make sure Rachel gets a chance to grow up. Please, whatever has to happen to me, just keep her safe. Just... please..."

I wait, hoping that there might be some kind of reply, but instead the pain in my ankle seems to be building. I hold my breath, trying to push the pain back, but it's no use. Digging my fingers into the ground, I hold on tight, desperately forcing myself to stay strong; as the pain gets worse, I dig my fingers deeper, but it's not working and finally I let out an agonized scream that seems to last forever.

DAY 49

THOMAS

SITTING BY THE WINDOW, I watch as the first rays of sunlight start to spread across the remains of the city. Shorn of human attention, the skyscrapers look old and abandoned now, and it's hard to believe that this was once a bustling home to millions of people. Every building has become a kind of tomb, filled with the bodies of those who fell and died when this catastrophe hit. Somehow, I feel as if we should abandon the cities now and leave them undisturbed, as a mark of respect to the people whose lives were lost.

"Are you thinking anything specific," George asks suddenly, "or just staring vacantly out the window?"

I pause, not really knowing what to say.

"I'll tell you what *I'm* thinking," he

continues. "I'm thinking about the past. I'm thinking about the people I took for granted, and all the things I never got a chance to say. I'm thinking about the world that was suddenly pulled away, like part of some magician's trick. I'm thinking about how complicated everything was, and how quickly it was destroyed."

"I'm thinking about the future," I reply, not turning to him. Instead, I keep my eyes focused on one particular building, which towers a little higher than its neighbors. There's no point to its existence now. It might as well fall down. If I could, I'd destroy the city completely. I hate the idea of Chicago, like every other city, still standing now that most of the people are gone.

"What *about* the future?" he asks.

"Whether there'll be one."

"I'm sure Lady Macbeth'll be along shortly," he continues. I hear him shuffling over to join me, and eventually he sits a few feet away. "She doesn't seem like the kind of person who has much downtime, if you know what I mean. I'd rather avoid her, if possible. What are *your* plans?"

"Plans?" I turn to him.

"There was talk yesterday about some people who left town," he replies. "Just a handful, but apparently they headed north. I've been thinking, maybe Melissa and Katie were with them. I know it's a long-shot, but right now it's the *only* shot." He pauses, and it's clear from the look in his eyes that he knows there's no chance. "If I stop looking for them," he adds, "I'll die. I'll just sit down and waste away, or God help me I'll find a gun from somewhere and I'll blow my goddamn brains out. I know this is going to sound pathetic, but they're all I've got left. Even if I only catch up to them briefly, or I just hear from someone that they got away, I need to know they're okay. Once I've done that, there's nothing else I want in the whole world. I can..."

His voice trails off, but I figure I know what he was going to say.

"Are you gonna head north?" I ask.

"Got no choice. If that's where they went, then it's where I'm going too. I don't believe in miracles, but this once... What about you?"

I open my mouth to reply, but the truth is, I have nowhere to go. Sure, there's Martha out in California, but even if she survived all of this, there's no way I could ever hope to find her. She might have gone back to the farm, in which case she'll have found nothing but a set of burned ruins, and then what? If Joe and I had been smarter when we left, we'd have put some kind of message up for her, but then again it's not as if we even knew where we were going when we set off. Whatever we'd said, it would have been useless by now. I guess we could just have written goodbye, but at the time we were focused on hitting the road. Still, I figure I shouldn't spend too much time thinking about Martha. She's probably dead, anyway.

"I don't suppose you fancy making the trip north, do you?" George continues. "I sure could use that truck of yours. I've got a bad knee, did you know that? I'm a brave soldier and I hide it, but my left knee feels like there's razor blades tucked between the bones. Imagine me trying to make such a long journey on foot. I doubt I'll last more than a couple of days."

"I don't know," I reply. "I think..." Taking a deep breath, I try to imagine another long journey, but I'm too tired to even *think* about traveling anywhere. "I think I wanna stay here for a bit," I tell him, "and then head off somewhere else once I'm rested. I don't know how long."

"I can't stick around. Every second I'm here is another second that they're getting away. I figure I'll try to find out some more information about whatever direction they took, and then I'll strike out this afternoon. I'd like to say I'll keep in touch with you, boy, but we both know that's not gonna be possible. With the world as it is, I reckon there are gonna have to be an awful lot of goodbyes."

"It's okay," I tell him. "I understand."

"That little girl..." He pauses, and there are tears in his eyes now. "Katie's the most wonderful child you could ever meet. She's fearless and smart and kind. I know the world's in a terrible state right now, but I refuse to believe that anything bad could have happened to her. Maybe I'm naive, maybe I'm stubborn, but my granddaughter is too precious to fall victim to whatever the hell's going on. It doesn't make sense that someone as good as her would be cut down by this random misery. No god would allow it. It's not natural."

I want to argue with him, to point out that his granddaughter is almost certainly dead, but at the same time I don't want to take his hope. He's going to head off toward the horizon, looking for his family, and even though I'll never see him again I know that this is something he has to do. He's basically heading off to his death, but there's nowhere else for him to go. In a way, I admire him; he knows what he's going to do with the rest of his life, whereas I'm just stuck here with no reason to go and no reason to stay.

"Do you think it's all going to go back to normal one day?" I ask.

He smiles. "No chance."

"But at least a little bit?"

"You're not one of those idiots who thinks the government'll ride to the rescue, are you? There's no-one out there in a position to do anything. The whole goddamn system fell apart, and the most we can do is pick up the pieces. I'm sure some people are gonna do okay out of it.

Probably the lunatics, like Ms. Quinn, while the rest of us fade away. I guess the building blocks of a decent world are still scattered all over the place, something for the children to play with, but the human race had its chance. It's over now."

"But that signal -"

"It's just a blip, or a malfunction, or some other kind of fuck-up."

"There has to be someone somewhere," I continue. "Someone's doing something, and maybe it'll help us all."

"We're cooked," he replies. "Maybe a few of us'll keep going, but we'll never get back to where we were. I have no idea how many people are left on the planet, but it could be as low as a few hundred thousand. Things'll probably get worse before there's a chance for them to get better, and that's without taking into account things like disease and infections. It's only been about six weeks, so there's still food left over from the old days, but when that starts to run out, I don't see many people surviving. There's gonna be mass starvation, including the people here." He pauses. "If you want my advice, you'll get out of the city, find yourself some land out of the way, and try to get by with subsistence farming. Maybe someone'll come along and help you out, maybe even a woman and you can think about bringing some children into this world. But that's really the absolute best you can hope for."

"When are you leaving?" I ask.

"As soon as I've done some asking around," he replies, getting to his feet and gasping as his knee cracks. "There's no time to sit around chatting. Just take my advice, boy, and don't hang around here for too long. The city's a bad place to be, and I don't trust that Quinn woman. There's something dangerous in her eyes. She might seem friendly, but she's crazy, and not the good kind of crazy either. If I were you, I'd get the hell out of here before sundown." He reaches out a hand. "I know we met in awkward circumstances, and I'm truly sorry for trying to blow your head off that time. It was nice getting to know you, even if it was only for a few days, and I wish you all the best."

"You too," I reply as I shake his hand. "I hope you find your daughter and granddaughter. They really might be out there somewhere."

He nods, but he clearly knows that there's no chance.

Once he's gone, I stay by the window for a moment. There's a part of me that's tempted to go with him, since we could cover so much ground if we used the truck, but I don't feel like going on a doomed quest. I need to come up with something, anything, that gives my life purpose, and then I need to make a proper decision. The craziest thing is, I'm starting to wonder if Joe and I should have just stayed at the farm. At least we knew the land,

and if we'd worked together, we might have been able to grow enough food for us to survive. One thing's for sure: I definitely can't stay in the city. The people who cling to this place are deluded. The only chance for survival is to hit the road and, as George said, to find a new home.

Or, if not a home, then at least somewhere that offers some kind of hope.

THE BUNKER

"SHIT," I MUTTER, holding the main cable in one hand while I reach around the back of the machine and try to blindly operate the secondary valve. It's a balletic operation that would reward someone a little more delicate, but gradually I'm able to turn the handle, releasing pressure on the pipe and reducing the intake load. Straining to look back at the meter, I watch with relief as the needle quivers a little and then finally moves back down out of the red zone.

Danger averted.

For now.

"Fuck!" I shout, as my hand suddenly brushes against the pipe itself, instantly burning the flesh around my wrist.

I instinctively pull back and stumble over

some cables on the floor, which cause me to tumble against the desk. Just about managing to maintain my balance, I look down at my wrist and see that the flesh on one side is seared pink. It hurts, but I know it's going to hurt *more* soon.

"Fuck!" I mutter again, annoyed by my own stupidity. I'm always so careful. What if this mistake is a sign of mental erosion? I might be losing my mind, which in turn might lead to clumsiness and then problems with coordination, and finally I'll just make mistake after mistake until I end up killing myself through sheer stupidity. Still, I'm on top of the situation. I'm not crazy yet.

Glancing at my reflection in the mirror, I stare at myself for a moment.

"No," I say finally. "You don't look crazy at all."

Making my way to the supply cupboard, I search for some anti-bacterial wipes and finally I find an open packet on the top shelf. Even the slightest injury could become infected and then blow out of control, so I'm careful to cover the burn in three layers of gel. It stings, and I'm going to have a hell of a blister in the morning, but this approach is definitely preferable to dying of some goddamn stupid little scratch. That would be an absolutely pathetic way to leave this world.

"Just keep on truckin'," I mutter as I examine the wound. It's pretty bad, and it's clear that I've burned the flesh deep. I guess it'll hurt like a bitch for a week, maybe two, but all I can do now is make sure I never do something so dumb again.

After a few minutes, I wander back over to the computer and watch the screen as the signal continues to cycle through its three stages. Keeping this damn thing running is a constant struggle, but fortunately I don't really have anything else to do. Grabbing the tin of cold beans I was eating earlier, I use a spoon to scoop some into my mouth before giving up and just pouring the contents straight down my throat. Some of the sauce spills over my chin, but I don't care. It's not as if anyone can see me, anyway. I haven't been anywhere near another human being for forty-eight days straight now, and I don't expect to see one any time soon either.

Unless...

Leaning closer to the screen, I watch as the inbound IP tracer cycles through another scan. It's been twelve and a half hours since the last ping, but someone out there has sure as hell located the server. So far, all they're doing is pinging it a few times a day, almost as if they can't be sure that it's really here. I guess they're surprised to find that someone has managed to keep such a sophisticated rig up and running for so long, and I have to admit that I've done a damn good job. The problem is, pinging my server is only the first stage. Whoever this asshole is, I need him (or her, I guess, if I'm being politically correct and all that other bullshit) to actually come and find me. After all, how hard is it to triangulate a signal?

"Come on, motherfucker," I whisper, watching the screen intently. "Use your head. If you've got the intelligence to get a basic system running, you should be able to come up with my position and grab a few shovels. It's not rocket science."

Glancing over at the window, I realize that it's daylight again. Damn it, the nights and days just seem to sneak up on me. Sometimes I worry that I'm going just *slightly* crazy, which wouldn't be too much of a shock. Still, I've got my anti-crazy set-up arranged on the desk: a copy of *Ulysses*, a set of headphones for the computer, a notebook, and a pen. When things seem to be getting too much, I can just take some time out and try to calm my mind. Damn it, I wish I had some opera recordings, but that would just be too perfect. A man must suffer.

"It'd be so easy to go nuts down here," I whisper, staring at the desk. "So easy to just... flip out and become a total psychopath. Good job I'm -"

Suddenly, I pause.

"Was that out loud?" I ask, genuinely puzzled.

I wait.

"Huh."

Taking a deep breath, I realize there's a faint smell of rotten meat in the air. Looking over at one of the other desks, I realize I forgot to finish off the ham from yesterday. Damn it, at this rate, I might actually have to start worrying about my food supply before the year is out. I should probably tidy up, but I figure the bunker's probably about as neat as it's ever going to get. Besides, I'm the only one down here, and I got used to the stench a long time ago. I've got far more important work to be doing, so the plates of half-eaten food can just stay in place. Feeling a ticking sensation in my throat, I break into a coughing fit that eventually causes me to double over. I'm still not doing so good, but I don't have time to rest. Once I've brought myself under control, I resume my relentless gaze at the monitor.

I'll do some sudoku later. Just a few from one of the books I stashed down here, to make sure that I don't get lazy. And then I'll play a game of chess against myself. I need to keep my mind alert and sharp, because eventually I'm going to need to put phase two of my plan into operation. God damn it, I need to be sharp as a pin when someone finally finds this bunker.

I need to be ready.

"Come on," I mutter, desperately willing the system to show another ping. "What are you waiting for? I'm right here. Come and get me!"

THOMAS

"IT'S BEEN THE CASE throughout human history that most people are expendable. You know that, don't you? You must have noticed? Most people are just... worthless."

Sitting in the room that Quinn describes as her 'office', I keep my eyes fixed on the laptop. It's hard to believe that she's got it up and running, and even harder to believe that someone somewhere out there has managed to maintain a server. I can't help trying to work out who could be on the other end of the signal. The government? The military? Some lone hacker? Someone like Quinn?

"I've always had a very realistic view of the world," she continues, apparently not too bothered by the fact that I'm not responding to her. In fact, this whole encounter is more like a soliloquy than a conversation. "Most people try to maintain the fiction that human beings, in general, are useful, but the truth is rather different. There were seven billion people on this planet before last month, and now how many do you think there are? A hundred thousand, maybe? That's one sweet-ass cull. It's almost enough to make me believe in God. I mean, I never had much of an opinion one way or the other in the old days, but now..." She pauses for a moment. "God just became interesting, so I'm finally paying attention."

"Can't you work out where it is?" I ask, still staring at the laptop.

"The signal?" She wanders over and looks at the screen for a moment. "I'm working on it. I've got a few ideas. I always considered myself to be not very good with computers, but I had the benefit of being able to look stuff up online. I never bothered with hard copies of system information, and now I'm struggling a little. I'll work it out eventually, though. Nothing ever beats me, not in the long-run." She pauses again. "Where's your friend?"

"What friend?" I'm genuinely puzzled for a moment, until I realize she means George. "I don't know. He... I think he left. He's looking for his family."

"Family?"

"His daughter and granddaughter."

"Oh," she replies, sounding distinctly

211

unimpressed. "So he still clings to traditional patriarchal definitions of societal structures, does he? How gauche."

I turn to her. "He wants to find his -"

"I know, I know," she says dismissively, "but it's all just pissing in the wind, isn't it?"

"Aren't you looking for anyone?" I ask.

"Only smart people. Bright people. People who can help me." She stares at me for a moment. "What about you?"

"I've got a sister, but she was out in California when all of this started so -"

"Forget her."

"I just -"

"Forget her. She's old news." Putting a hand on my shoulder, Quinn seems to be trying to make friends with me, although there's something stiff and off-putting about her, as if she's pre-determined her every move. "California's a hell of a long way from here, Thomas. The odds of you finding your sister are huge, and why does it matter, anyway? Just because someone is biologically related to you, it doesn't mean that either you or she will benefit from working together. You have to get past these old ideas about family and recognize that the world has moved on. What do you really think is going to happen to your friend George?"

I pause. The truth is, I don't want to say what I really think.

"He's going to die," she continues. "He's going to fill his head with dreams of looking for his family, he's going to go out there, and he's going to fail, and then he's going to die. He'll probably collapse and starve. It'll be a horrible, lingering and painful death. He'll feel his stomach starting to digest itself as he dies. If he's lucky, rats will finish him off a little quicker. And why will his life end like that? Because he was fixated on family. Families are absolutely fatal. Am I right?"

I stare at her.

"Thomas, I need you to show me that you understand. Am I right?"

I nod.

"Say the words."

"You're right," I whisper, even though I feel as if I'm making a mistake.

"Louder."

"You're right."

"That's better." She smiles. "The way I see it, you've got two choices. The first is that you can sit around here, or sit around some other place, and scrabble in the dirt until you die. Do you realize how bad your life could get before the end? There's no dignity left in the world, no promise of love or tenderness. It's every man for himself from this point forward, and screw the weak."

"This is some serious shit," I hear Joe's voice say suddenly. "You're changing. You're letting this psycho freak make you see things differently. Be careful, kid. She doesn't strike me as someone you can trust."

"Worms," I reply, ignoring Joe's imagined voice and turning instead to face Quinn. "I was eating worms the other day. They were the only thing I could find."

"Exactly. And who wants to end up like that?" She pauses again, as if this whole performance has been calculated from the start. "Or you could take the other choice, which is to make something of yourself and adapt your skills to the new world. There's a reason I took you into my confidence, Thomas. I'm a good judge of character and I could tell immediately that you're someone who can see the world from my perspective. You're not like all those assholes out there, wandering the streets, waiting for me to tell them what to do. There are lots of different types of zombie. At least those infected creatures were interesting, but a lost, mindless human is dull and boring."

I open my mouth to argue with her, but I can't. I know deep down that if I stay here, or if I strike out on my own, I'll die. When George left earlier today, I knew that it would be the last time I'd ever see him, and I also knew that his chances of success were zero. Worse still, I could see that same realization in his eyes.

"We're going on a journey," she continues

with a grin. "You and me, Thomas. We're going to find the source of this signal and we're going to go and find it. I've been waiting for someone to show up, someone I could take with me, someone smart and resourceful. Fate has brought you here, or maybe it was God, but either way, we're going to find that source and we're going to take bold steps into the new world. Are you with me?"

"I don't know," I reply. The truth is, she seems to be completely insane, but at the same time I feel as if she's at least offering something positive. I don't want to hang around here in Chicago, and I'm not sure I could really make it as a farmer.

"Be better than the others," she whispers, leaning closer until her face is almost touching mine. "You arrived here because this is where you were needed."

"What about all the other people?" I ask.

"What other people?"

"The ones here. The ones who follow you."

"They're not people. They're sheep. They'll die once I'm gone, and it doesn't even matter. Let them starve. The world won't benefit if smart people waste their lives worrying about the weak. You and I, Thomas, carry the burden of being better than the rest. We owe it to the future of the human race to maximize our potential." Reaching out to take my hand in hers, she pauses, and again I get the feeling that she's working through some kind of script that she prepared in advance. "Let's do our part to rebuild the human race. Let's go and find the source of this signal. It's a beacon for people like us, and it's our duty to respond."

"I..."

She waits for me to continue.

"I have a truck," I say eventually.

"I know," she replies, her eyes bright with excitement. "That truck of yours is going to make our journey so much easier! It's another gift from God!"

"We don't know which way to go."

"I'm working on that. By sundown, I should have worked out the direction of the signal. I've got a few different systems set up, and once I've triangulated the signal's strength, I can mark out an area that should be no more than five or six square miles. Then all we have to do is go and search. I'm pretty sure it should be easy enough to find whoever's running the server. After all, they seem to *want* to be found."

"But then -"

"No more hurdles," she says, silencing me by placing a finger against my lips. "It's decided. As soon as I've got the information we need, we'll leave. If the people here are worthy of life, let them save themselves. It's every -"

Before she can finish, there's a knock at the door, and a man wearing rags steps into sight.

"What is it?" Quinn snaps, clearly annoyed that we're being interrupted.

"There's..." He pauses. "There's been another... It's that girl again."

"What girl?" Quinn asks, before a faint smile crosses her lips. "Oh. *That* girl." She pauses, before turning to me. "If these people are going to survive once I'm gone," she continues, "they'll need discipline. I might as well try to help them one last time." She squeezes my hand tight. "Come on, Thomas. Let me show you the power of tough love."

THE BUNKER

NOTHING.

Day forty-eight, and still no sign of the creatures. That makes it three full weeks since the last one, which in turn means that I have to at least be hopeful that the first phase of this nightmare is over.

After scribbling a few items in my notebook, I take one more look out the window and stare at the scrubland on the other side of the hatch. When I came down into this bunker, I wasn't entirely sure what would happen, but I was worried that I'd end up being besieged by those creatures. I imagined them banging on the glass, desperately trying to get inside. I knew they'd never be able to get to me, but still, it would have been unsettling. I had nightmares about the whole thing; some nights I'd wake up, covered in sweat and convinced that somehow they'd be able to prize the seal open.

As usual, my fears were completely unfounded. I'd done too good a job, and prepared too well.

In the end, a few of them showed up, but basically they died off pretty quickly. I watched as a handful of my children made the pilgrimage here to find me, and then I watched their impotent anger, and then I watched them die. Some of them tried to talk to me, begging me to let them in and calling me a god, but I just stood and watched as they fell apart. It was a beautiful thing to experience.

Well, beautiful and sad. Two sides of the same coin.

Sometimes I wonder if I should open the hatch and step outside, but I know I need to be patient. The server is up and running and I'm convinced that sooner or later, someone is going to get the goddamn message and find me. I mean, is it really too much to hope that there are still people out there who can rise to the challenge? The creatures might be gone, and they might have been something of a mistake, but the world should still have a few stragglers left behind. Besides, I know for a fact that someone has been pinging my server, which means that I've been noticed.

All I ever wanted, really, was to be noticed.

I just hope they get here soon. I only have

enough food, water and air for another 351 days, and I've got a feeling my sanity might get down to the bone a lot sooner.

THOMAS

"DON'T YOU REMEMBER WHAT I told you?" Quinn asks, stepping behind Kaylee. "Didn't you listen to a word I said yesterday?"

A small crowd has gathered in front of the platform. Dead-eyed and weak, the survivors seem to be almost hypnotized by the sight of the girl being judged. I've got to admit, Quinn has a sense for the theatrical, and she seems to know how to keep people interested. As she walks all the way around Kaylee and finally stops in front of her, she has a curious look in her eyes, as if she's already decided what to do.

"I told you not to steal again," Quinn says eventually. "I told you to become a better person. And how did you respond? You tried to become a better thief instead. You were more sneaky, more cunning. You'd have succeeded, too, if it wasn't for the fact that I made sure someone was watching you the whole time. Unfortunately, Kaylee, I already suspected that you might disappoint me."

Kaylee doesn't respond. She just stares straight ahead, with a look of fear in her eyes. It's almost as if she knows what's coming next, and she's ready for her fate.

Quinn pauses, before turning to me.

"See?" she says after a moment. "This is a perfect example of what I was talking about before. This girl had a chance to better herself, but instead she just ran off and stole from the communal food supply. She put her own needs above the needs of everyone else here, and she thought she was smarter than all of us when, in fact, she's just another fool." She turns to Kaylee. "Isn't that right?"

Again, the girl doesn't reply. There are tears in her eyes, but she seems to be forcing herself to remain stony-faced.

"And now she arrogantly remains silent," Quinn adds. "What do you think, Thomas? Should I teach her a lesson? How should I punish this young lady, since my efforts yesterday seem to have failed so spectacularly? I mean, I've tried reason and logic, I've tried kindness, and she just knocks it back in my face. It's tempting to believe that some people are utterly beyond salvation, which leads me to..." She pauses again. "What would you do, Thomas? If you had the power, how would you punish her?"

"I don't know," I say, worried that I'm being tested. "I just..."

"Should I just let her go?"

I shake my head.

"Of course not. She's a thief, and she's been caught twice now. Something has to be done to ensure that she doesn't do this again. She needs to be removed from the rest of the community, not only to protect the dwindling food stocks but also so that she can have another chance to learn her lesson." She pauses, before reaching under her shirt and pulling out a hunting knife with a large, serrated blade. "Or I could kill her."

"No!" I shout, stepping forward.

"Why not? She's worthless."

"But you can't -" Turning to look at the crowd, I realize that they're all staring at the platform with varying degrees of disinterest. It's as if they don't care that a girl might be murdered right in front of them, and I can't help feeling that whatever Quinn decides to do, her actions will be met by more or less the same blank reaction.

"I can't what?" Quinn asks with a frown. "Kill her? Of course I can. I can do anything I want. Who else is going to administer justice around here? These sheep would probably just let the little bitch carry on stealing from them, which..." She pauses. "Which," she continues after a moment, "might actually be something that sets Kaylee apart from the others." Still holding the knife, she seems lost in thought. "Maybe a thief is someone who refuses to sink into the crowd. Maybe this young lady has a little more sense than I'd anticipated."

"Kill me," Kaylee says suddenly.

"Did you hear that?" Quinn asks, turning to me with a broad smile.

"Please," Kaylee continues, with tears streaming down her face. "I don't want to live like this. I'm hungry all the time..."

"Then why haven't you ended your own life?" Quinn asks.

Kaylee's lips move, but no words come out. A moment later, she buries her head in her hands and starts to sob.

"Are you too scared?" Quinn continues. "Do you worry about how much it's going to hurt? That's a very human way of looking at things." After a moment, she takes Kaylee's right hand and gently forces her to hold the knife. "Here. I'm sure you can be inventive. If you truly want to die, then end your life right here. Don't be shy. Everyone dies eventually, and I'm sure some of these people might even envy you. After all, who hasn't craved death since the world ended? Go on. If you can't be good, be brave."

Kaylee stares at the knife, her hand trembling as if she's genuinely considering her options. I watch with horror as she slowly moves the blade toward her chest, and although I want to shout out and tell her not to do it, I feel as if I'm frozen in place.

"Go on," Quinn says softly. "After all the cowardly things you've done, be brave right at the very end of your life. It's more than most people manage. I mean, how many truly brave people have you ever met in your life? Two? One? None?" She leans closer to Kaylee's face. "Do it!"

I wait.

The crowd waits.

Silence.

Suddenly Kaylee jerks the knife toward her chest, only for Quinn to reach out and grab it at the last minute, pulling it away again. Twisting the girl's wrist until she lets out a cry of pain, Quinn forces her to drop the knife before shoving her roughly down to the ground. When Kaylee reaches out to grab the knife again, Quinn kicks the weapon away before crunching her heel down hard against her hand.

No-one in the crowd really reacts. A few coughs and grunts here and there, but nothing more.

"You surprise me," Quinn says, finally freeing Kaylee's hand before stepping across the platform and picking the knife up. "It's so very rare for someone to truly surprise me, but you've managed it. I don't mind admitting that I really didn't think you had it in you. I thought you were a coward who'd always choose life. It's a good job I learned the truth, though. This way, you're going to be extremely useful to me. That's all that really matters anymore... Whether or not people are useful in the grand scheme of things."

"Please," Kaylee sobs, "I don't want to -"

"Get up," Quinn says firmly.

"But -"

"Get up!"

Slowly, and with obvious pain, Kaylee gets to her feet and starts wiping her eyes.

"Please," she whimpers, "let me die. I just want to be allowed to die. There's nothing wrong with -"

"Shut up!" Quinn shouts.

Kaylee takes a step back, clearly shocked by the outburst.

"You're going to come with us," Quinn tells her, "and you're going to listen to what I have to say. You've managed to redeem yourself, and I think you'll be very surprised when I tell you what's going to happen next. The world is moving at a faster pace, and there are jobs to be done." She turns to me. "Don't you think so, Thomas? We could have managed the journey alone, just the two of us, but a girl with Kaylee's strength of character might be a real asset. I'm sure we'll make a wonderful little team as we set out to find the source of that signal."

Although I'm being dragged way too fast into this situation, I feel as if I'm in no position to argue. Quinn is a force of nature, and as she turns and heads back toward her building, Kaylee follows almost without question. Glancing at the small crowd, I realize that everyone here just seems to accept whatever Quinn says and does, and I don't know whether to be horrified or impressed. Finally, feeling that I don't belong up here on this platform, I turn and head into the building. For now, at least, I figure my best bet is to see what Quinn has to offer. If she's right about this signal, it means there are other people out there in the world. I have no idea if there's a real chance for the human race to recover, but I have to at least find out.

For the first time in weeks, I feel as if there might actually be a future.

THE BUNKER

"BANG," I MUTTER as I hold the rifle up, admiring its long, smooth barrel for a moment. I never used to be the kind of guy who liked guns. Hell, I was in favor of strict gun control. Now, however, with my life riding on my ability to protect myself, I find myself appreciating these fine weapons so much more.

Aiming at the hatch, I close one eye and peer down the scope with the other. For a moment, I try to imagine what it would be like to have some poor bastard right in the crosshairs. With a faint smile, I pull the trigger, although the gun only makes a satisfying clicking sound.

"Boom," I say calmly as I lower the rifle. "One more goddamn asshole out of my way."

Before I came down to the bunker, I stocked

up with plenty of rifles, handguns and grenades. I've got enough weapons here to hold back a full army, and even though I doubt I'll have to face off against anyone with too much firepower, it feels good to be prepared. Placing the rifle on a table, next to the rest of my weapons, I take a moment to admire them all. Damn it, I feel like a kid in a candy store, and there's a part of me that actually wants some bastard to come and cause me trouble, so I can take a pop at him.

Once I'm certain that all my weapons are in good working order, I head over to the desk and pick up my copy of *Ulysses*. Just because I've become a man who likes firepower doesn't mean I'm not cultured. I've already read this particular book twice over the past month and a half, and now I intend to start again from page one. Joyce was always such a master of prose, and when I read his greatest achievement, I find myself idly wondering if perhaps I could write something just as powerful. The problem is, since there's no-one around to read anything I come up with, I find it hard to get motivated. I'll just have to be happy with the knowledge that in another life, I was almost certainly a literary genius.

Opening a bottle of whiskey - one of several that I saved for my long sojourn down here in the bunker - I pour myself a glass and then settle in a chair. After glancing at the laptop and checking that everything is more or less under control, I raise my glass in a mock toast to whichever poor souls eventually come and find me here.

"Cheers," I say with a grin. "Same procedure as every year!"

After taking a sip, I open the book and stare at the inscription on the first page. It's been so long since I received this beautiful gift, and it's hard to believe that the hand that wrote this inscription is now cold and dead. Still, love outlasts the soul, and I know that she'd be proud of me. In fact, these words of hers feel to me like the real start of the book, and I read them several times over:

To Jacob,
with all my love,
Annalise

If only she could see me now. Glancing at the hatch, I remind myself that someone out there is probably headed this way. When they finally arrive, I can put phase two of my plan into action. Until then, however, I've got nothing to do apart from eat, drink and read.

Sometimes, life is good.

THOMAS

"ARE YOU REALLY GOING to come with us?" I ask, keeping my voice low as I sit with Kaylee.

She turns to me, but she seems a little dazed, as if she's not sure what to say. When she glances over at Quinn, who's still working frantically on the laptop at the other end of the room, I realize that Kaylee's problem is that she's not certain she's *allowed* to talk to me. I don't know exactly what's happened to her, but something's definitely wrong.

"She thinks she's found a signal," I explain, hoping to at least get some dialogue started. "She's trying to triangulate the source and then I guess we're gonna go and check it out. I guess I understand it, at least a bit. I think she knows what she's doing, but..."

My voice trails off as I realize I'm not

getting anywhere.

After staring at me for a moment, Kaylee finally allows herself the faintest of smiles, although she still seems scared and uncertain.

"I've got a truck," I continue. "We're gonna use it, so we won't be too tired. There's enough gas to keep us going for about a week, and I figure that should be enough time." I pause as I realize that I'm not sure how I got dragged so deep into this situation. There's a part of me that thinks I should have stuck with George; no matter how stubborn or deluded he might have been, at least he wasn't crazy.

"I don't mind," she says suddenly.

"You don't mind what?"

"Whatever." She pauses. "Living or dying. There's no point to either."

"We might as well at least check it out," I reply. "If there's something out there... What if the world's not ending? What if someone's got a plan?"

"Maybe," she mutters, although she really doesn't seem to care either way. It's almost as if she's high on some kind of drug, although I think the more likely cause is some kind of post-traumatic stress problem. "It kinda... hurts to think about it," she adds. "I'm sure it's all gonna be okay."

"I can hear you two chatting away," Quinn says after a moment, not looking up from the laptop. "I don't mind you talking, but just be aware that I can hear every word." Finally turning to us, she stares for a moment, as if she finds something amusing. "I wasn't going to reveal this yet," she says, getting to her feet and heading over to a cupboard at the far end of the room. Opening the door, she rifles through a box before pulling out a sheet of paper and looking at it for a few seconds. "I don't want to freak either of you out," she continues, "but sometimes I have these very powerful dreams, and I like to keep a record of them."

As she comes over to join us, I can't help feeling that Quinn's madness is becoming more and more evident.

"Do you believe that dreams can tell us things about the future?" she asks. "I know this probably sounds a little cuckoo, but just hear me out. Do you believe that dreams are the mechanism by which our subconscious mind picks up on echoes from the future?"

I look over at Kaylee, but it's clear she's not going to answer. In fact, as she frowns, I realize she probably doesn't even understand what Quinn's talking about. She seems somehow disconnected from the world.

"Thomas," Quinn continues. "Did you hear the question?"

"Dreams are dreams," I reply, turning to her. "I mean, they're just stuff that comes up from deep in our heads. It goes in when we're awake, and then it comes out when we're asleep. All, like, jumbled."

"How quaint," she says, before turning the piece of paper around so we can see a crude sketch of three figures. "But if that's true, how do you explain this?"

As soon as I see them, I realize that the figures are Quinn, Kaylee and me. The likenesses aren't great, but there are enough similarities and, besides, the clothes are a perfect match. She's even written T, Q and K under each of us, as if she had some idea of our names. I'm not sure whether to be amused by the fact that Quinn drew this, or genuinely freaked out. Still, there has to be some kind of logical explanation. I'm sure as hell not about to believe that this crazy woman had an accurate dream about the future.

"This was from a dream I had on the very first night," she continues. "It was so powerful and vivid, I had to get an image down immediately. In the dream, I was setting out on a journey, and I had two people with me. When I woke up the following morning, most of the dream had already faded from my memory, but I had a strong image of the three of us. It's like it was some kind of vision, and even though I don't usually believe in such things, I kept the drawing in case..." She pauses, as if she's stunned by this development. "It must mean something," she adds eventually. "After everything that's happened, with all this chaos surrounding us, somehow a message has been sent to me."

I glance at Kaylee, but she's just staring absently at the piece of paper.

"Thomas," Quinn continues. "You can see that this is the three of us, can't you? There's no doubt about it."

I want to disagree with her, but I can't. Unless she whipped the picture up some time in the past few hours, it's undeniable that something seems to have caused her to draw us, and if the dream came so long ago... I've never been the kind of person who believes in this kind of thing, but I have no doubt that Quinn is telling the truth. It's either the biggest coincidence I've ever encountered, or it's a sign that something strange is happening here.

"It's our destiny," she adds with a smile. "It might even be the destiny of the whole human race. Maybe this all happened for a reason, and some kind of force is pushing us to the heart of that reason, and now we're on the cusp of uncovering something huge. What if it's -"

Before she can finish, the laptop lets out a brief buzz. Dropping the piece of paper, Quinn turns and races back over to it. Staring at the screen for a moment, she seems completely enthralled by whatever she's reading. She taps a few buttons on the keyboard, bringing up different windows, and although I'm still skeptical of pretty much everything she says, I'm starting to wonder if there might be at least a small amount of sanity at the heart of what she's doing.

"I've done it," she continues eventually, sound as if she can barely believe what she's saying. "I've found the source of the signal. To within a few square miles, anyway." After a few more seconds, she turns to me. "It's not even that far away. Someone's transmitting from somewhere along the shore of Lake Erie. Do you realize what this means?"

"We have to go there?" I ask.

"Not only that. We can be there in a day or two! We can find these people, whoever they are, and we can make contact." Grabbing a piece of paper and a pen, she starts making notes from the laptop screen. "Everything's coming together perfectly," she continues. "The dream, the signal... It's as if some divine force is guiding us to an endpoint. There has to be a reason, though. After all the chaos, order is finally being restored and..." She pauses, and then she turns to me again. "Order is being restored, and we're right at the heart of it all. The world is being reorganized in a new manner, and while the vast majority of people have been left to die, the three of us are destined to play some part in whatever comes next."

Hurrying back to the laptop, she closes the lid and unplugs it from the various wires that have been connecting it to the wall.

"There's no time to waste," she says, grabbing a bag from the desk and turning to us. "Thomas, fire up that truck of yours and let's get moving. I've got the directions, I already have some supplies packed, and if I'm right, there's some kind of force guiding us on our way. The future of humanity is waiting for us!"

***

A few hours later, with dusk starting to fall, we hit the road. Although I keep telling Quinn that we should wait until morning, she insists that we start the journey as soon as possible, and eventually I'm too tired to argue with her. With the truck packed, the three of us leave behind the sixty survivors, who have started to huddle around burning trashcans for heat. I want to ask Quinn what'll happen to them, but I figure I know the answer. They're going to die slow and painful deaths, probably starving or becoming dehydrated, or maybe the rats will get them. Quinn seems to excited to even care, but I can see that Kaylee understands the situation. Again, though, I'm too exhausted to argue, so we leave.

Quinn tells me that I have to drive.

As we reach the outskirts of the city, I glance toward the horizon and watch as the sun casts a beautiful red and orange glow across the desolate landscape. In the distance, a lone silhouette is walking slowly toward the north, and I realize that it's George, setting out on his lonely, doomed quest to find his daughter and granddaughter. For a moment, I consider telling Quinn to go to hell, and maybe joining George instead. Finally, however, I steer the truck onto a road that leads toward the east, figuring that we should stick to our plan and head to Lake Erie. Still, I keep glancing over my shoulder until finally George can no longer be seen.

The road ahead is dark.

DAY 50

ELIZABETH

WHEN I OPEN MY EYES, I immediately realize that something's wrong. My skin is cold and wet, and finally it hits me: I'm covered in a fine layer of dew.

Sitting up, I wipe beads of water from my face. I'm shivering, but I'm not sure if that's because of the high fever or the fact that I seem to have been passed out for more than a day. I'm simultaneously hot and cold, and I can barely even squeeze a coherent thought out of my head, but as I sit in the silent clearing I finally realize that something *else* is also wrong. I take a deep breath, but there's a sharp pain in my chest. Whatever's wrong with me, it's spreading.

Suddenly, there's a sound nearby.

Whatever it is, it's repetitive, and getting

closer. Like a kind of rustling, or footsteps...

Turning, I see something moving in the distance, a dark shape making its way between the trees. I can barely even remember who I am, let alone how I ended up here, but finally the shape gets close enough and I'm able to make out a tall, well-built man with a small bundle of fabric cradled in his arms and some kind of cloth sack slung over his shoulder. He's making straight for me, and although I have no idea if it's safe for me to be here, all I can do is wait for him. Something about the guy feels safe and reassuring, but I'm still not certain...

I open my mouth to ask him what's happening, but no words come out. I try again, but it's as if my body is no longer fully under my control.

Feeling a faint pain, I look down and see that the skin around my right ankle looks to be swollen. I can vaguely remember something about this, as if deep in my memory there's a range of facts that make sense, but my mind is far too jumbled. Again, I try to ask a question, but again my mouth barely even moves.

"You're alive," the man says as he sets the bundle of fabric down nearby. To my surprise, the bundle moves slightly, and a moment later I see a small hand reach out. It's a child.

There's a name in the back of my mind.

Rachel.

I want to ask the man who *he* is, but I feel as if my head is burning.

"I wasn't sure you'd still be here when I got back," he continues as he places the sack next to me and starts pulling out various items. "Last night was much colder than I'd expected. There was a real risk of exposure, even with the blanket I left. I traveled as fast as I could, but it wasn't easy with Rachel in my arms the whole way. I never realized quite how tiring it could be, carrying a baby for such a long time. I've got no idea how you managed it."

Me? Did I carry her once? She's not my child, I'm sure of that.

Squinting a little, I stare at his tools. There are a couple of saws, along with some bandages and various other items I don't even recognize. I feel as if I know this man, as if I should be pleased that he's come back, but my mind is still a little foggy. Focusing on trying to remember his name, I hold my breath for a moment, but it's useless. I feel as if there's a fire burning in my body.

Nearby, the child lets out a gurgle. For some reason, this seems to reassure me.

"Are you okay?" the man asks.

I turn to him, but's it's difficult to focus on his features. Everything seems slightly blurry.

"Let's take a look," he continues, leaning closer and using his fingers to pull my eyelids back.

There's a flash of light, as if I'm not used to having my eyes fully open, and I can tell from the look on his face that the guy is concerned. "Your pupils are dilated," he says after a moment, "one of them more than the other, and you're having trouble focusing, aren't you? The fever's getting worse. Can you even remember your name?"

"Eliz..." I whisper.

"What's that?"

"Eliz..." I pause, trying to get it right. "Elizabeth." I pause again. "Marter. Elizabeth Marter. I'm from Manhattan. My brother's... Henry..."

"That's good. And do you remember *my* name?"

I stare at him, but the answer won't came.

"What about her?" he asks, indicating the child nearby.

"Baby," I whisper, before I feel my mind start to clear a little. "Rachel... Is she okay?"

"Given the circumstances, she's great. She's been a little more responsive over the past day." Turning to my right foot, the guy reaches down and examines the skin. "I wish I could say the same for you. This is as bad as I feared, Elizabeth, maybe even worse. You're developing a serious infection, and even if we had access to the best medical science the old world could provide, I don't think there's much they could do at this point. You're going to have serious necrosis of the flesh around the wound soon. If I had to guess, I'd say this is a case of tetanus complicated by a tight shoe and maybe some other environmental factors."

It takes a moment, but I'm finally able to focus on my own foot, and that's when I realize that it's swollen to double its usual size, while the flesh has become a kind of black and green color. Taking a deep breath, I can feel pain throbbing through my body, but somehow I'm almost like an outside observer, *noticing* the pain but not really feeling it.

"I couldn't find everything I was looking for," the guy continues. "I went back to the farmhouse to pick up some things. It was the only solution."

"I thought you'd left me," I reply, even though the words barely even make sense. "I thought you'd..." I pause for a moment, trying to breathe steadily. "I thought you'd gone off without me."

"I'd never do that," he says, turning to his tools and arranging them on a small piece of cloth. "However, what I'm going to do next is going to hurt, Elizabeth, and I'm afraid there's absolutely nothing I can do about that. Believe me, I've tried to come up with an easier approach, but there's nothing. All I can promise is that the pain shouldn't last too long, and at least you'll have a good chance once it's over."

"Toad?" I say suddenly. "That's your name, isn't it?"

He turns to me. "That's right."

"What's happening?" I ask.

"You're sick."

"I know, but..." I stare at the tools. One of them is a large saw, while another is the same but smaller. "What are you going to do?" I ask eventually, starting to feel a knot of panic in my gut. "What are you doing to me?"

"The only thing that might save your life."

"What?" Instinctively, I try to inch away from him, although I'm not very mobile. "Tell me..."

"Your foot isn't going to get better," he explains. "It's only going to get worse, and once it passes a certain point you're going to end up with blood poisoning, and then you're going to suffer a slow, painful death. I've tried to come up with another approach, but there's no point delaying the inevitable. If you're going to stand any chance of survival, I'm going to have to take the foot off."

"What do you mean?" I ask, dragging myself a few inches away.

"I'm going to amputate," he continues. "That's why I told you that this is going to hurt."

I shake my head.

"It's the only way."

"No."

"The actual procedure won't take too long. I did something similar to a cow once. I know that probably won't make you feel much better, but if I work quickly it can all be over in a couple of minutes."

"You're not cutting my foot off," I tell him, starting to really panic as I realize that I'm not strong enough to stop him. I try to get up, but as soon as I put any pressure at all on my right foot, the pain is intense and I collapse in a fit of agony. "Please," I whisper as I try to get up again, "don't touch me!"

"I know what I'm doing. More or less, anyway. Once the foot has been removed, I'm going to fold the skin over and then bandage it properly. I can't lie to you, though. It's going to hurt, and then you'll have to endure more pain while it heals, but I think we can keep it clean. Dan Hodge's farm isn't that far away, maybe five hours. I was going to try to get you there first, but I don't think we can afford to wait a moment longer. As soon as the amputation is complete and I've bandaged you up, I'll take you there for recovery. It'll just be a few days -"

"No!" I shout. "No, I don't give you permission for this! You can't do it!"

"Do you want to die instead?"

"I thought you'd left me!"

"I almost did," he continues, "but eventually I realized... If Rachel and I had gone on without you, we might have had a marginally better chance of survival, but I'd never be able to live with myself. So here we are, and I hate to say this, but your opinion on the matter doesn't really count. You can't stop me, and I'm prepared to use force here. It's for your own good."

Reaching out to one side, I try to find a rock or a stone, anything that I might be able to use to defend myself. Rolling over, I feel a jolt of agony in my foot but all I can think about is somehow getting away from this maniac. As I try to crawl, however, I can already feel myself getting weaker and weaker, and after several minutes have passed I've still only managed to get a few feet away. Turning, I see that Toad seems to have finished preparing his tools, and finally he looks at me.

"It's time," he says calmly.

"No!" I shout. "No! You're not doing this!"

"I'm going to have to tie you down," he continues, pulling a length of rope from the cloth sack. "It's only to make sure you can't struggle once I start cutting. Please try to understand."

"No!"

"It's the only way, Elizabeth. You'll thank me later."

"No!" I shout again, as he comes around behind me and grabs my shoulders. Although I try to fight him off, I'm too dazed and weak to have my effect, and soon he's got my arms tied firmly behind my back, at which point he drags me across the clearing and uses a second piece of rope to tie me to the side of a tree. Even though I know I can't make him stop, I keep trying to get free, but finally I feel the last of the ropes being pulled tight around my chest and I realize that I can barely even move.

"This is going to save your life," he says eventually, holding a small piece of wood toward my face. "Here, bite down on this. It'll help with the -"

"Go fuck yourself!" I shout, still struggling to get free. He tries to put the piece of wood in my mouth, but I immediately spit it out.

"Elizabeth -"

"Help!" I scream, hoping against hope that there might be someone nearby who can hear me. "Somebody help me!"

"I'll make it as quick as possible," Toad says, turning and heading back toward his tools.

I keep screaming, even as he picks up the large saw. He pauses for a moment, examining the blade, and then he turns and starts walking toward me.

THOMAS

"THIS IS THE MOST amazing thing ever!" Quinn shrieks from the passenger seat. "It's like we're roving investigators on some kind of amazing road trip, and look! I can even ping the server remotely. We're technological road warriors in a post-apocalyptic landscape. It's almost as if we're living in a movie!"

As I keep my eyes on the road, I can barely even summon the energy to respond. We've been driving through the night, and while Quinn has spent the whole time enthusing about our plans, I can barely keep my eyes open. With the sun having finally risen in a cloudy gray sky, I'm starting to get to the point where I have to sleep if I'm going to keep from driving straight into a ditch. As Quinn taps excitedly at her keyboard, I bring the truck to a halt at the side of the road.

"What's wrong?" she asks, sounding worried. "Thomas, is there a problem with the truck? Do you know how to fix it?"

"No," I reply wearily, barely even able to find the strength to get any words out, "there's not a problem with the truck, there's a problem with me. I need to sleep."

"There'll be time to sleep later," she says dismissively. "Let's keep going for now."

I shake my head.

"Do you want something to eat? Would that help?"

"I need to *sleep*," I tell her again, starting to feel frustrated. Why the hell doesn't she understand?

"Oh, whatever," she replies, playfully punching my shoulder. "Come on, find some more energy from within. Did you know that we have enormous untapped reserves of strength that we never use? Our bodies naturally try to slow us down when we get to the halfway point, but with a little mental strength you can free up those reserves and use them for an extended period. It's a wonderful skill to have. How do you think I manage to remain so perky all the time? Just try to feel the enthusiasm rise up from your soul, Thomas. We'll be in the target zone in another nine or ten hours, you can -"

"I need to sleep," I say again, still staring at the road ahead. "It doesn't matter what you say, okay? You're going to have to drive."

"How?"

I turn to her.

"I can't drive," she continues, with a frustratingly blank look in her eyes, as if I've just asked her to operate a rocket ship or perform brain surgery. "I never learned."

I stare at her.

"What are you looking at me like that for?" she asks. "It never came up! I wouldn't know how to drive this thing if my life depended on it. Everyone has a blank spot in their skill-set, and I'm afraid this is mine. I can do so many useful things, but drive a vehicle? Sorry, no way."

"What about Kaylee?"

"She can't drive either," she replies. "She can't really do much at all at the moment. That's why I made her ride in the back of the truck." She leans closer and lowers her voice to a conspiratorial whisper. "She's really just here to bulk up the numbers, you know. She's a bit of a red shirt, if you get my meaning. Still, she was in my dream, and who am I to argue with the forces of the universe?"

"So I'm the only one out of the three of us who can drive?" I ask, genuinely shocked.

She nods.

"Then we're gonna have to take a break, 'cause I need to rest for a few hours."

"You can't, Thomas," she exclaims, setting

the laptop aside for a moment and turning to me. "Please, we need you. *Humanity* needs you. We're so close to getting some answers, and I know it's hard, really I do, but we're all having to extend ourselves a little further than we might want, and sometimes you just have to push yourself and summon up the strength from deep within." She pauses, as if she's searching my face for a sign that I agree with her. "Come on," she adds, forcing a smile. "I wouldn't have brought you on this trip if I didn't think you could do it. We're all operating outside our comfort zone here. Don't let the side down."

"You wouldn't have brought me if you didn't need my truck," I point out, "and I wouldn't have come if I thought I'd have to drive for a whole day without stopping. It's physically impossible."

"Your truck?" She lets out a faint laugh. "I could've just stolen your goddamn truck, Thomas. I mean, really, that's hardly a big stumbling block, is it? You've got to think about how the world has changed. People aren't always going to ask your permission when they want to use something. Often, they'll just take it. Hell, property rights have gone right out the window, haven't they? It's survival of the fittest, and the smartest, and the toughest. This truck, like everything else in the world these days, belongs to whoever can take it."

"I'm going to make this very clear for you," I

continue, starting to lose my patience. "I can't drive without taking a few breaks every so often. If I try, we'll crash."

She stares at me, and there's a look in her eyes that makes it seems as if she's heart-breakingly disappointed in me. Frankly, her constant enthusiasm is starting to piss me off.

"Fine," I mutter, opening the door and climbing down onto the side of the road. Making my way around to the back of the truck, I find that Kaylee is wide awake, sitting in one corner with her knees drawn up toward her face. She looks terrified, which seems to be her default facial expression, but right now I really don't have the energy to be diplomatic. "You need to drive," I tell her. "It's the only way."

She stares at me.

"Drive!" I shout.

"I don't know how," she says quietly.

"It's really not that hard. There are no other vehicles on the road, so you just have to focus on following the signs and keeping the truck on the road. I'll show you the basics."

"I don't think I can do it..."

"You have to. I need to sleep, and apparently we can't even afford to stop for a couple of hours."

She stares at me, and it's clear that she's stunned by my request. The truth is, I'm too tired to really care about her feelings, and I'm starting to feel annoyed by the fact that both Quinn and Kaylee seem to have been relying on me to do everything. As I wait for Kaylee to show some sign that she's going to help, however, I realize that we probably wouldn't even be safe with her behind the wheel. At the same time, I really don't think that Quinn's going to be much use.

"I don't think I can do it," Kaylee says again.

"What's going on back here?" Quinn asks as she climbs out of the passenger seat and comes around to join us. "Are we having some kind of meeting? We really don't have time for long, meandering discussions, you know. The future of humanity is waiting for us, and even a half hour could make quite a difference."

"Either someone else drives for a few hours," I say, turning to her, "or we stay here while I sleep. There's no way I can keep driving. At this rate, I'm going to fall asleep at the wheel and then we're going to end up crashing. I'm not being lazy or weak, I'm just stating the obvious."

"But -"

"We'll die," I say firmly. "Either that, or we'll get injured, or at the very least the truck'll be wrecked. Can't you at least *try* to drive? It's just steering and choosing the right roads. You can even go a little slower than usual if that helps. Most of it's just about pointing in the right direction."

Quinn opens her mouth to argue with me, but finally a look of irritation reaches her face.

"Fine," she says. "I'll drive. Like you said, it can't be that difficult. I mean, billions of people used to do it. Even though I've got absolutely no experience with vehicles whatsoever, I'll just use my natural skills to work it out as I go along. Hell, a trained monkey could probably drive one of these things."

"It's a manual," I point out.

"A manual what?"

"Gearbox."

"I'm sure I'll work that out just fine," she replies, making her way around to the driver's side. "I pick things up fast, you know. Give me a few miles under my belt, and I'm sure I'll be driving like a professional."

A few minutes later, I'm sitting in the back of the truck as Quinn gets us underway. To my surprise, she doesn't seem to be having any problems at all, and I can't shake the feeling that she was lying when she said she couldn't drive. In fact, I'm convinced that she was just making that claim so she could get out of taking her turn, and now that she's got no choice, she's going to pretend that she's some kind of genius who picked it up in an instant. Settling into the corner, I close my eyes and try to get some sleep as the truck speeds along the road. After a moment, however, I open my eyes and see that Kaylee is staring blankly at me.

"You okay?" I ask.

She nods.

"You want anything?"

She pauses, and then she shakes her head.

Closing my eyes again, I figure I just need to ignore her. It's not as if I'm going to get a decent conversation out of her, no matter how hard I might try. Finally, as I sink into sleep, I find myself thinking again about George making his lonely trek to the north. Sure, he's never going to find what he wants, but at least he believes in something. Right now, I feel as if I'm on some kind of crazy journey with a mad woman and a girl who's borderline catatonic, and I can't shake the feeling that Quinn's not exactly the best person to leave in charge.

ELIZABETH

"NO!" I SCREAM, still struggling as Toad gets in position next to my ankle. "Someone help me! Please!"

"It'll be over in a couple of minutes," he explains calmly.

Seconds later, I feel the edge of the saw being placed gently against my swollen throbbing ankle. As I try to get free, the blade moves a little and ends up closer to my knee. It's as if he's trying to determine the best place to start.

"You can't do this!" I shout. "I don't give you permission! You can't do this to me without my permission!"

"I'm going to cut here," he continues. "I need to be sure that I'm getting the entire damaged area, so I might end up taking an inch or two more than is necessary. Still, it's the best approach. I know you probably can't understand this, but -"

"If you even touch me," I shout, "I'll kill you!"

"Try to understand -"

"I'll kill you!" I scream, pulling on the rope so tight that it starts digging into my wrists. "I swear to God, I will kill you if you don't let me go! If you do this, and if I get better, I will wait until you're not looking and then I will kill you! I swear to God, I won't let you get away with this!"

I feel him adjusting the blade, getting ready to cut.

"I'll kill you!" I shout again, before breaking into a series of sobs. Tears are running down my face and although I'm still trying to get free, I feel completely helpless. "Please God, don't let him do this," I shout through the tears. "Somebody help me! Anyone! Please!"

Nearby, Rachel has finally started to cry.

"I'm sorry," Toad says calmly.

"Stop!!" I shout. "If you touch me, I swear to God I'll -"

And that's when he starts.

I let out a cry of pain as I feel the blade slice through my flesh and scratch against the bone, a little way below my right knee. To my shock, he immediately starts sawing, and I can feel my entire leg vibrating and throbbing with pain as he grinds the blade through the bone. The pain is beyond anything I've ever experienced in my life, and even though I scream as loud as I can manage, the agony quickly rises through my body until it becomes a kind of white hot flash in my mind, pushing all other thoughts away. For a few seconds, it's as if my personality has been pushed to the edges and the pain has become all of me.

The worst thing is the sound. I can hear the saw squealing as it grinds through my bone, like fingernails being dragged down a blackboard.

After a few seconds, the pain changes, becoming deeper and more intense. I can feel the blade going through the marrow in the center of the bone, and suddenly there's a jarring moment of agony as the saw seems to get stuck. I continue to scream as Toad adjusts his angle and resumes the job, but the pain is now so overwhelming that I can't even think. My eyes are squeezed tight shut and I try to scream even louder in an attempt to drown out the sound of the saw, and finally I feel as if I've reached a point at which it's no longer possible to feel any more pain.

And then I feel something snap in my leg. Something's different, not only about the weight but also the way Toad is holding me. It's as if my body has fundamentally changed. At first, I assume it must be the blade, but as Toad moves away from my leg for a moment, a more horrifying thought hits me.

That was my leg.

It's gone.

"Stop!" I scream, suddenly overwhelmed by a powerful sense of grief. I can't stop thinking about my leg - *my* leg - being take away from me. I want it back.

"It's okay," Toad says, his voice somehow getting through to me.

"Stop!" I scream again, unable to stop sobbing. "Please, stop..."

After a moment, I start to feel something warm and wet flowing from my body, and it takes me a moment to realize that it must be blood. Toad immediately raises my leg and applies a thick bundle of bandages. Opening my eyes, I find that I can barely see; my vision has become blurry, but I can just about make out a bloody red stump, with Toad holding some kind of instrument in his hand as he continues to work on me. The pain is still overwhelming and after a few seconds I tilt my head back and scream at the sky. I feel as if someone has to come and save me, but after a moment I realize that I might have briefly passed out.

"Where are you?" I whisper.

No reply.

"Toad, where are you?"

Again, no reply.

Suddenly I realize that I don't think I said those words out loud. They were just in my head. I try to move my lips, but somehow I seem to have forgotten how to communicate.

"Where are you?" I try to ask again, but it's useless. "Please. Talk to me..."

Looking back down toward the lower half of my body, I see through my blurred eyes that Toad is still working, although he seems to be a lot further along. I blink, trying to improve my vision, and finally I'm able to make out my raised right leg with a thick collection of bandages wrapped around the knee. Toad is frantically working, and eventually I realize that he seems to be trying to sew the edges of my skin together. I stare at him, and for a few seconds the pain seems to dissipate and I feel almost as if I'm watching him work on someone else.

Time seems to slow down.

Rachel is crying, but she sounds as if she's so far away. I can only hope that she doesn't understand what's happening, and that she can't see anything. Even though she's so young, something like this could scar her for life.

"It's okay," Toad says, his voice echoing in my head. "It's all going according to plan. You just have to sit tight."

I try to ask him what he's doing next, but I still can't quite manage to speak.

"You're doing great," he adds.

I open my mouth, trying to speak, but I can feel something moving through my soul. After a few seconds, I realize that it must be the pain. My mind has somehow found a way to block it out, but I know it's going to come back soon, like a huge wave waiting to break and wash over the shore of my consciousness. Holding my breath, I try to push it back, but I can feel my soul starting to strain under the pressure. Finally, it happens: the pain bursts through me and I let out an involuntary scream. I know it's crazy, but I just want someone to come and help me. I don't care who they are, just so long as they get me away from Toad and put my leg back on.

All I can think about is the fact that he should have left me to die. Anything would have been better than this. As another burst of pain rushes through my body, I scream again, and this time I can't stop.

THOMAS

AT FIRST, IT'S JUST a vague sensation that something's wrong. As I emerge from sleep, I can feel... *something* nearby. Finally, opening my eyes, I find myself face to face with Kaylee.

Literally face to face.

In fact, almost touching.

She's kneeling in front of me, staring straight into my eyes as if she has no idea that she's being weird. As the truck continues to speed along the road, all I can do for a moment is stare back at her until, finally, I slip to one side, managing to get a little space between us at last. To be honest, I'm kind of stunned by the way she's gone from blatant disinterest to rampant fascination in the space of just a few hours.

I wait for her to say something.

She just stares at me, still looking sad.

"You okay?" I ask, feeling a little dazed. I'm not sure how long I was sleeping, but it sure as hell wasn't long enough. I'm pretty sure I was having bad dreams too, although they've already faded from my memory.

"You were talking in your sleep," she says eventually, keeping her eyes fixed on me.

"What about?"

"You kept mentioning someone named Joe."

"Huh." I pause for a moment. "He was my brother. He died."

"Oh." She seems lost in thought. "There was something about an old man too."

"That'd take too long to explain."

"And someone named Robert... Helms or Harms or -"

"Haims. Robert Haims." I pause again. "He was a cop. He died too. A lot of people have died lately."

I wait for her to say something else, but she seems so completely blank, it's as if nothing really gets through to her. Turning, I look through the front of the truck and see that Quinn is doing a fine job of keeping us on the road; in fact, she's going way faster than I'd prefer, and it's clear that I was right when I suspected she was bluffing about her driving skills. I guess she just wanted to pretend that she'd picked it up fast.

"My parents died," Kaylee says suddenly.

I turn to her. "How?"

"Those creatures."

"What happened?" I ask.

"They were just..." She pauses. "The creatures got them. We were in the street. I managed to hide behind a car, but they couldn't get away. I heard..." Another pause, as if she's reliving everything in her head, over and over. "I didn't see what happened to them, but I heard the sound of them being torn apart. It was like a kind of sticky, slurpy noise. I know that sounds silly, but it's really how it was. They were screaming at first, but after a while it was like their mouths were full of blood, but they were still calling out for help, and then that stopped and I think it was kinda worse. I could hear their bones cracking as they were just being..."

Her voice trails off.

"I couldn't run," she adds. "I just had to wait."

Staring at her, I finally realize what's wrong with her. She's in shock. I guess it must have been a month or so since her parents were killed, and she's still trying to deal with it. That faraway, vacant look in her eyes is obviously due to the fact that she's reliving those final moments over and over again, never quite managing to get past them. For the first time, I feel as if I can actually understand a little of what she's going through. All those people back in

Chicago were probably in shock as well; they'd all lost loved ones, and they'd all seen their lives being torn apart. It's impossible to know how different people will react when something like that happens, but all those people staring at the platform... They were all in shock.

"Sorry," Kaylee says quietly. "I didn't mean to say too much. It's just something I think about a lot. Like, all the time. I wish things were different."

We sit in silence for a moment as the truck speeds along the road. The wind is whipping Kaylee's hair a little, but she doesn't seem to mind. In fact, right now, she doesn't seem to mind anything. It's as if she doesn't really care about the world around her.

"My parents died too," I tell her. "My father went into town, and later we found his body. Then my mother got sick. We burned the house in the end, but then my brother died, and he came back as one of those things, but he still kinda had his own mind." Pausing, I realize that maybe I'm still in shock too, albeit in a different way. "I killed a girl too," I add. "The other day, when we arrived in Chicago, I thought she was one of those creatures, and I panicked..."

"Her name was Alice," she replies.

"Did you know her?"

She nods.

"What was she like?"

"Shy." She pauses, as if she's finding it hard to remember. "She didn't say much, but we used to go searching for food together sometimes. I usually had to be in charge, 'cause she'd just follow me around without saying much, but I didn't mind. I managed to get her to talk sometimes, but she wasn't the most interesting person in the world."

"I'm sorry," I reply. "I didn't mean to kill her, I swear, I just -"

"I understand," she says, interrupting me. "Things happen. You shouldn't blame yourself. Everyone's dying anyway. No-one knows what's going to happen next, but you could tell, back there in Chicago... They were all just waiting for the end. Quinn kept telling us that we had a chance to survive, that we were the lucky ones, but I don't think anyone believed her. The city is the worst place to be right now, 'cause that's where all the diseases are spreading, but people still want to be there. It's like some kind of nostalgia thing. Habit, maybe. I guess everyone deals with things differently. Like Quinn."

"She's crazy," I mutter.

"Her son died."

I stare at her for a moment.

"Didn't she tell you?" she continues. "It wasn't long after everything went wrong. I didn't know her at all back then, but I heard a lot of stories. She had a son, he was about nine or ten. I think she was raising him alone. I didn't see what happened, but I think it was similar to when my parents died. She left him alone or something while they were out looking for food, and then she heard him screaming. That's when she changed, apparently. She started to be... weirder. Like she couldn't stand to deal with the world in the same way. I met someone who knew her before all this stuff happened, and apparently she was, like, a junior accountant at some firm. Pretty normal stuff."

Looking through to the front of the truck, I stare at the back of Quinn's head for a moment as she continues to keep us speeding along the road. I was always sure that something wasn't quite right with her, but it never occurred to me that she might have suffered some kind of trauma. I guess her enthusiasm for this journey is understandable; she wanted to get the hell away from Chicago, but at the same time she wanted some kind of destination. It also explains her disdain for George's mission to find his family; if her son died, she probably sees no need for that kind of thing anymore. For the first time, I actually feel sorry for her.

"Are we really going to find anything?" Kaylee asks after a moment. "She keeps going on about this signal, but do you think it's real? I'm worried it's all just in her head, or she's making it up. It's just so hard to believe that this could actually be happening."

"I think there's something out there," I reply. "I don't know what it is, and I'm not sure it's a person, but there's something. Either way, it's good to get away from the city. Like you said, that's not the best place to be right now. I don't think the people we left behind are going to last much longer. At least out here, we've still got a chance."

"I just don't want it to hurt," she continues. "When I die, I mean. It's inevitable that it's gonna happen. No matter how I try to stay alive, I'm not equipped for a world like this, so there's a part of me that's okay with getting it done as soon as possible, just so long as it doesn't hurt. Whenever I see a dead body, I kinda envy them, like they've already been through it all and now they're at peace. I want it to be painless."

"I don't think there are many painless ways to die," I tell her.

"But there have to be *some*, right? Like, maybe something that's so quick, your body doesn't even have time to send pain signals to your brain. Vaporization, or just getting blown to pieces in a fraction of a second. That can't hurt, can it? Or getting killed while you're asleep. You wouldn't even know! That'd be, like, heaven!"

"Maybe," I reply, "but I think I want to live. At least long enough to see if there's anyone else out there."

Although I've had a few moments when I've

considered giving up, the truth is that there's some part of me, deep down, that keeps pushing onward. I guess I've got this feeling that somewhere there's still hope, and that there's still a chance that life could somehow become a little more normal. I'm also very aware that if Martha's dead, I'm the only member of my family left alive. If there's any chance for the human race at all, I want my family's bloodline to stay alive. Turning and looking toward the horizon, I realize that I'm never going to give up.

I'd rather die.

ELIZABETH

"ELIZABETH, CAN YOU HEAR ME?"

Of course I can hear him, why does he keep asking? All I want is to sleep, and to wait for the pain to go away.

"Elizabeth, if you can hear me, open your eyes."

I don't know why he keeps bothering me. Now that the pain has stopped, or at least shuffled to one side of my mind, I just want to stay perfectly still. Even breathing feels like an unnecessary risk, and I'm far too tired to respond to whatever the hell he wants me to do.

Suddenly I feel something against my face, and he uses his fingers to pull my eyelids open. I try to move my head away, but as light floods my vision, all I can do is stare as Toad's face peers down at me. It's as if he's looking for something, as if he's trying to see directly into my soul. It's annoying, but there's nothing I can do to stop him. I just wish he'd stop bothering me.

"Elizabeth, I need you to give me some kind of sign that you can hear me. Anything. Just something that lets me know you're okay in there."

He waits.

"Elizabeth?"

Finally, I let out a faint groan. It's not much, but it's all I can manage right now. I just hope it's enough for him.

"It's over," he continues. "The operation went as well as it could have done. I managed to remove the infected part and then seal up the wound, so now it's just a matter of waiting for everything to heal. The biggest danger is that the stitches could come loose, and then I'd have to try to put them back together. I don't have much spare material left over, so it's vital that we get it right the first time. There's still a danger of infection. Do you understand? You *can't* put pressure on your leg at all."

I try to blink, but he's still holding my eyelids open.

"Elizabeth, do you -"

I groan again, hoping that he'll take the hint and leave me alone. Something feels very wrong with my body, but I can't quite work out the problem. My leg hurts, but I feel as if the pain is far weaker than it was just a short time ago. I'm also very warm, but I'm too weak to wipe the sweat off my face.

"You need to sleep," he adds. "Don't worry, I've got everything under control. Rachel's fine, and we're just going to wait here until you wake up. There's not much further to go until we reach the Hodge place, but the most important thing is that you get some rest." He pauses, and then he lets my eyelids close again. I think maybe he says something else, but the words drift away.

I can hear him moving about, but I don't care what he's doing. All that matters right now is that I ensure I don't wake up fully. If I wake up, I'll have to deal with everything that's happened, and I'd rather just stay like this forever, in a kind of haze. I don't know if it's exhaustion or blood loss that's making me feel so weak, but either way, I don't even care. As I sink into a deep, blank sleep, the last thing I think about is Henry.

If he could see me now...

THOMAS

"FELLOW TRAVELERS," QUINN SAYS, as we stand next to the truck on the side of a seemingly innocuous dirt road that runs between a pair of vast green fields, "we have reached the point of no return. We're on the cusp of the signal field, which means the source could be anywhere in the immediate vicinity. From this moment on, we are entrusted with the solemn task of connecting with whatever form our destiny has chosen to take."

She pauses, before lowering her head as if she's entering prayer.

"To any deities that might be listening," she continues, "we offer our profound thanks. We understand that we have been entrusted with a sacred honor, and we can only assure you that we will not let you down. Before this day is over, we will find the source of this signal, and we will take our rightful place at the heart of whatever plans you see fit to implement. Amen."

Another pause, and then she turns first to Kaylee and then to me.

"I don't believe in any gods," she adds with a smile, "but it's always better to be safe, right? Just in case."

We all stand in silence for a moment. The only sound comes from the wind, which is rustling through some bushes nearby and which seems determined to at least partially interrupt proceedings. After a few seconds, however, it becomes clear that Quinn is actually waiting for either Kaylee or me to respond to her little pronouncement, and with Kaylee having retreated back into her shell, I guess the pressure is on me.

"There's nothing here," I say eventually.

She frowns.

"There's *nothing* here," I say again. "Look around. We're in the middle of nowhere!"

"Maybe to the naked eye," she replies, as if she'd anticipated my comment, "but we must learn to look closer. I'm afraid this isn't something that has been hidden out in the open."

I turn and glance across the rolling fields that run to the horizon in all directions. It looks like we're in the middle of farming country, and as much as I want Quinn to be right about this signal, I can't help feeling that this is a very unpromising location. If someone was really going to set up a system for contacting other people following a huge apocalyptic event, I really don't think this is the spot they'd choose.

"No," I say eventually, turning back to her. "Still nothing."

"Maybe it's buried," Kaylee suggests.

"Exactly," Quinn says, pouncing on the idea. "Whatever we're looking for, it won't have been left out in the open so that just any old person can find it. This is part of a game, designed to ensure that only worthy individuals are able to locate the source. For that reason alone, we must exercise caution. We can't possibly imagine what we're dealing with here. A great intellect is reaching out and looking for others of its ilk, so we must expect the task to be difficult."

"So what's the plan?" I ask, still weary after only getting a few hours of sleep on the back of the truck. "Did anyone think to bring a metal detector? Or should we just shout and hope someone hears us?"

"The laptop can help us move in the right direction," Quinn replies. "The closer we get, the more accurate the signals should become, until finally we'll hopefully be standing right on top of the damn thing. We must all be aware, however, that we might be being observed. It would make sense for someone to keep an eye on us once they've managed to lure us to this area. We must also be aware that there's a small chance we might be joined by others who have detected the signal."

"Or someone got here before us," I point out, "and we're too late."

"I doubt it," Quinn replies calmly.

"Why not?"

"Because it's highly, *highly* unlikely," she continues, and it's clear that she's straining to keep from letting her irritation show. "The vast majority of people are completely incapable of picking up this signal, given the way the world has fallen apart. Whoever set this up, they must have been aware that there was a danger of it never being located. I'm sure we'll be welcomed with open arms just as soon as we find the spot." She fiddles with the laptop for a moment. "I only have another hour's worth of battery left before I need to recharge it," she adds. "We should get moving. Any questions?"

I open my mouth to tell her that I've got nothing *but* questions, but at the last moment I realize that there's no point. She's off on her own little mission, and it's my fault that I allowed myself to be dragged along. I feel as if I've still got a little power, though, since the truck is mine and at the end of the day I can threaten to abandon them both if they don't come with me. To be honest, the idea is really tempting right now.

As we start walking away from the truck, Quinn stays out front and I find myself hanging back a little with Kaylee. Since our conversation on the back of the truck, she seems to have clammed up again, but I figure I can at least try to get her talking. Given that Quinn is clearly insane, I feel as if I want to try to get Kaylee on my side. Besides, I can't deny that she's very pretty, and even at a time like this, I want to get to know her better.

"What do you think?" I ask after a few minutes, keeping my voice low so that Quinn can't hear. "Are we gonna find anything apart from dirt and a bunch of bushes?"

"Maybe, I guess," she replies. "If the signal's real."

"You think it might not be?"

"I don't understand computers. I don't even know how she's got that one working."

"She wouldn't bring us out here for no reason," I reply. "One way or another, she definitely believes that it's real, and I saw the screen. It was picking up something, which means there's a server somewhere. I'm not sure how she's managed to narrow the source of the signal down, though. She was a bit vague when I asked."

"But what if it's, like, a crashed satellite or something?" she asks. "Or maybe a crashed plane, and the black box recorder is sending out a signal? If this turns out to be nothing, I'm not going back to

Chicago. That place is like a giant cemetery."

"So where *would* you go?" I ask.

"There's nowhere. What about you?"

"No idea," I reply with a shrug. "I feel like I'm pretty much at the end of the road. I've never been this far from home in my whole life."

"Will you two cut it out?" Quinn says suddenly, turning to us. "What is this, a party? We're here to do some serious work, guys." She stares at us for a moment, as if she's genuinely annoyed by the fact that we've started to become a little friendly. "I need you to be constantly on the alert," she continues. "We could be within a few hundred meters of this thing, whatever it is, and I'm relying on you to be able to spot anything that's out of the ordinary. You're hardly going to be able to do that if you're joking around all the time."

"We were just talking," I reply.

"Sorry," Kaylee adds plaintively, like a schoolkid who's just been told off for speaking in class.

"Jesus Christ," Quinn mutters, turning and resuming the search. "Sometimes I wonder if I should have just come out here alone."

"With whose truck?" I mutter.

"I heard that!"

"What crawled up her ass and died?" I whisper to Kaylee, but Quinn's little outburst has clearly ended all hopes of a conversation. Looking distinctly embarrassed, Kaylee moves a few steps away from me and then makes sure to keep looking in the opposite direction, almost as if she's scared of pissing Quinn off again. All I can do is sigh and hope that eventually she'll come around, although it's going to be tiring if I have to coax her out every time I want to get more than a few works from her.

For the next hour or so, we keep walking through the undergrowth, while Quinn constantly checks things on the laptop. She seems to have everything under control, although there's a part of me that worries she might only have a tenuous grip on reality. I wouldn't mind taking a look at the screen myself, just to make sure that this isn't some kind of wild chase into nowhere, but I figure Quinn wouldn't react too well if she thought I was checking up on her. As my legs start to ache more and more, however, I can't help wondering how much longer we're going to spend out here.

"Wait a moment!" Quinn says eventually, stopping up ahead.

Kaylee and I come to a halt next to her.

As she adjusts some settings on the laptop, Quinn seems totally absorbed in whatever she's doing. After a moment, she turns toward the west, and the laptop lets out a couple of beeps. I'm not sure if it's genuinely picked something up, or the battery's just dying.

"I've re-calibrated the settings," she says

finally. "According to the latest data, we need to be heading this way."

"Over there," Kaylee says suddenly, pointing in the opposite direction.

"No," Quinn says, "*this* way."

"Look!" Kaylee shouts, pointing the other way. "I see someone!"

Turning, I look toward the horizon. At first I don't see anything, but finally a moving figure catches my attention. A couple of hundred feet away, someone is running low, trying not to be seen and heading toward a small crest. It's hard to make out any details, but the person looks to be wearing ragged clothes.

"Hey!" Quinn shouts. "You!"

Without even glancing in our direction, the figure dips down over the crest of the hill, leaving behind nothing but a faint cloud of dust until this, too, drifts away.

"Who the hell was that?" I ask, stepping forward.

"Wait!" Quinn says, grabbing my arm and holding me back. "That's the wrong way, Thomas. The signal's coming from the east."

"But that was an actual person!" I point out, struggling to get free from her grip. "Didn't you see? Someone was over there!"

"It's probably just another starving loser," she replies, although I can tell she's worried. "We don't have time to worry about every dust devil we spot in the distance, okay? I'm sure there are plenty of scattered individuals in the wilderness, but they're none of our concern. We're on a mission."

"What if they know something?" I ask. "If people are living out here, they might have a better idea of what the hell's going on. Maybe they've picked up the signal too!"

"Or they might get in our way," she replies. "Think about it. If there's anyone living nearby, they're almost certainly no-hopers. They're probably living off the land, degenerating beyond the point of civilized society and..." She pauses. "My God, they could be cannibals for all we know. Think it through, Thomas. We need to hurry up with our work. In fact, we need to get back to the truck and get moving as fast as possible. I simply won't allow any distractions!"

"There's more of them," Kaylee says suddenly.

Turning, I watch for any further sign of movement, but I don't see anything.

"They were there a moment ago," she continues, pointing toward the spot where we saw the other figure a moment ago. "At the top of that hill, there were three of them. They were looking this way. I couldn't see them properly, but they've definitely noticed us. They moved out of sight, but I swear to you, I'm not making this up!"

"Get to the truck," Quinn says firmly, half dragging me back the way we came. "Come on, we might be in danger. We'll drive a little further to the east and then try again."

"You're not in charge!" I shout, pulling my arm free from her grip.

She turns to me with genuine anger in her eyes. "Excuse me?"

"I want to see who they are," I continue, standing my ground. "From the way that person was moving, they sure as hell don't seem like those creatures from back in the city. What if they're actual people who can help us? We can't just ignore everyone we meet along the way!"

"We sure as hell can," Quinn replies. "In fact, it's by far the best approach. You can't seriously want to go and poke every hornet's nest we come across, Thomas. Even if they're just regular people, they could still be dangerous. For all you know, they might steal the truck, take all our provisions, and then kill us where we stand! Human nature isn't always a good thing, especially when people are desperate."

"I'm going to see," I tell her, turning and walking toward the crest.

"Get back here!" Quinn calls after me. "Thomas! What the hell do you think you're doing? We're a team! You have to get back here immediately and stick to the original mission!

That's an order!"

Ignoring her, I keep walking.

"We'll leave without you!" she shouts. "I swear to God, we'll just drive off and leave you here!"

"Good luck with that," I mutter, double-checking that I've got the truck keys in my pocket.

Up ahead, there's no sign of anyone near the crest of the hill, but I have no doubt that Kaylee was telling the truth when she said she saw three more people. Maybe Quinn's right and this is a dangerous move, but I'm sure as hell not about to let her tell me what to do, and I figure it'd be good to widen my circle of acquaintances a little. Anyway, whatever that signal is, I doubt it's going to vanish in the next few minutes. Scrambling up the side of the hill, I glance over my shoulder and see that Quinn and Kaylee are still standing and watching me. There's a part of me that really wants to find something useful, just so I can give Quinn something to chew on.

And that's when I get to the top of the hill and see what's on the other side.

The first thing I notice is the shore of Lake Erie, with the water stretching for miles ahead. It's a beautiful sight, and strangely calming after everything I've been through recently. More importantly, however, there are people, lots of people, maybe a couple of hundred. Tents have been erected here and there, and I watch with amazement as various distinct groups seem to be getting on with work. Some of them are carrying logs, others are working around small campfires, and another group is closer still, tending to what looks like some kind of allotment. As I take it all in, I can't help but notice that it seems like a fully-functioning community, with everyone working together. It's such a beautiful sight, and so hard to believe, that I almost want to drop to my knees and thank God.

"Hey," says a voice nearby.

Turning, I see that a man has begun to approach me. He looks to be in his forties or fifties, and although his clothes are a little torn, he doesn't look nearly as pale or sick as the people back in Chicago. He's also quite hesitant, as if he's not sure whether he can get too close to me. I guess his fear is understandable; after all, as far as he's concerned, I could easily be dangerous.

"Hey," I mutter, taking a step back and holding my hands up so he can see that I'm unarmed.

"It's okay," he replies, stopping a few feet from me. "The children said they saw someone. I'm guessing you weren't expecting to have company up here, were you? It's probably been a long time since you were amongst other people. There are so few of us left."

"Not..." I pause as a group of children come running to join the man, although they stop a little further back, as if they too are nervous of me. "I had no idea there were people here," I tell the man. "We were just up here looking for something else, and we spotted movement over here. We didn't know anyone was going to be here, but then we saw someone from a distance."

"What were you looking for?" he asks.

"A -" I pause as I realize that maybe I shouldn't tell him everything. "It doesn't matter," I add finally. "It was just some crazy idea."

"Then I guess I should be the first to welcome you," the man says, stepping forward and holding out a hand for me to shake. "My name is Mark, and I'm one of the founding members of the community here. There aren't many of us, but we're working together to try to survive and so far we're doing okay. The land around here is good and we've managed to get hold of some animals from a couple of local farms, and now we're trying to get things set up for a good harvest next year. We don't have much, but we're happy to share our resources with anyone who's willing to dig in and help us. Even if you don't have any special skills, I'm sure there's something you can offer. Are you alone?"

I shake my head.

"How many of you are there?"

"Three," I reply. "Well, more like two and a

half, really. One of the others is kind of -"

"Thomas!" Quinn shouts, suddenly sounding much closer. "What the hell are you doing? We don't have time to -"

I turn just in time to see her scrambling up the hill, with her laptop balanced in her hands. As soon as she sees Mark, she stops in her tracks, and I have to admit that I'm quite amused by the look of utter shock in her eyes. For a moment, it looks as if she might turn and run. Seconds later, Kaylee arrives as well, and she looks equally shocked.

"Welcome," Mark says, not missing a beat. "We're glad to have more people here to join our community."

"There are people here," I continue, turning to Kaylee. "Look at them! Real people, and they're actually organizing themselves! They're making things work."

"Huh," Quinn says. For the first time since I met her, she seems genuinely lost for words as she turns to me. All the old certainty and arrogance seems to be been drained from her face, replaced by an expression that almost looks like panic. "This wasn't part of the plan, Thomas," she says finally. "What the hell have you gone and done now?"

ELIZABETH

"HENRY!"

Sitting up in the dark, I stare straight ahead, looking for my brother. Seconds later I hear movement nearby, and I turn to see a figure coming closer. I reach out to him, but something's wrong. He's taller than my brother, and as his face becomes visible in the light of the moon, I realize that it's Toad. For a few frantic seconds, I genuinely can't work out what's happening. It's as if two completely separate parts of my life are colliding.

"Henry?" I continue, turning to look across the clearing.

"It's okay," Toad says. "You've been dreaming."

"Where's Henry?" I ask, turning back to him.

"Your brother..." He pauses. "Your brother's dead, Elizabeth."

"I know he is," I reply, still trying to make sense of the dream I was just having. It felt so real, so vivid, and Henry was there, talking to me and telling me that everything would be okay. The dream is already fading, but I can picture Henry so clearly, and I can feel him holding my hand. My heart's racing as I sit and wait for the sense of panic to subside, and as Toad puts an arm around my shoulders, I realize that I've started to shiver.

"It's okay," he says, kissing the side of my head. "You were talking in your sleep a lot. I almost woke you." He puts a hand on my forehead. "Your fever's already going down. I've got to admit, you're already doing a lot better than I expected."

"I thought he..." I start to say, before my voice trails off. Suddenly I feel so stupid, like a child who's woken screaming in the middle of the night and who now has to be comforted by Mom and Dad. I want to push Toad away, but at the same time his arms are so warm. Finally, I lean in to him a little more.

"I'm here," he continues. "For what that's worth."

Nearby, in the dark, Rachel lets out a brief cry.

"She's here too," Toad adds. "I guess she doesn't want to be forgotten."

"I don't want to dream," I tell him, staring into the darkness. "Not ever again. Not if he's going to be there."

"You don't want to see your brother?"

I shake my head.

"I'd have thought it'd be good to see him from time to time," Toad continues. "A lot of people would like it if their loved ones came back to them every so often."

"Would you want to see people in your dreams?" I ask, before turning to him. "Do you have anyone?"

"Like who?"

"Anyone you miss? Anyone from the old days?"

He pauses, and I can tell that the answer isn't going to be simple.

"No," he says eventually.

"But you must have had -"

"There's no-one," he adds, before gently settling me back down on the blanket. "You still need to rest. We'll assess the situation in the morning and see if it's okay to move you. For now, try to get some sleep. I can't help you with the dreams, but I hope you can learn to take some comfort from them."

As he heads back over to comfort Rachel, I try to catch my breath, but I feel completely awake. Finally, I try to sit up, but it's not an easy job and I feel as if my body is suddenly strange and unfamiliar. Looking down at my legs, I try to make sense of what I'm seeing, and that's when I remember everything that happened earlier. There's just about enough moonlight for me to be able to see my left leg, but my right leg ends at the knee, where a large bandage has been wrapped around the stump.

"Toad..." I whisper.

"Get some sleep," he replies.

"Toad!" I shout, reaching down and trying to pull the bandages away. Toad rushes over, but it's too late and I've already managed to expose the bloody stump with thick wire stitches holding the flaps of skin together. "What have you done to me?" I shout, with tears streaming down my face as he tries to comfort me. "What the hell have you done to my body?"

DAY 51

THOMAS

"FISHING IS EASY," Mark says, as he attaches a brightly-colored lure to the end of the line. "You just have to know what your target likes, and offer it to them."

I watch as he attaches a small piece of meat to the lure. There's something strangely reassuring about the way Mark works, and after the craziness of the past few days I feel as if I can finally relax. It's a little after sunrise and we're out on Lake Erie, just the two of us in a small boat. One of Mark's jobs each day is to come out here and catch fish for his group, and today he's after salmon. He's already spent a few minutes explaining how to pick the perfect spot, and how to move with the currents and anticipate where the fish will be. Now he's showing me the more intricate details of the job, and I can't help but feel that he's training me so I can contribute tomorrow.

"In this case," he continues, still working on the lure, "it pays to be aware of the kind of thing that attracts salmon. A brightly-colored lure is a must, along with something to add a little scent. In this case, I'm using sardines. Salmon are attracted to this kind of thing, and if I've picked a good spot..."

He lowers the rod and smiles as he turns to me.

"We're on the edge of survival out here, Thomas," he explains. "We can't afford to make mistakes, or to just go blindly searching for food. We have to learn, *fast*, what works and what doesn't. If I don't manage to catch anything, I need to find something else for people to eat tonight, and that's gonna be a problem considering I'm supposed to be fetching wood after lunch. There's no margin for error here."

Turning to the shore, I'm stunned to see that everyone seems to already be up and working. It's a strangely tranquil scene, with everybody apparently knowing exactly what they're supposed to be doing, and I can't help but feel impressed by the way things work around here. Chicago was chaos, but here on the shores of the lake, these survivors have adapted remarkably quickly to the new world.

"And here we go," Mark says.

Looking back at him, I watch as he casts the

lure into the water.

"Now what?" I ask.

"Now we wait."

"How long?"

"As long as it takes," he replies, "but hopefully not more than a half hour or so. As I explained earlier, the community here is divided into ten groups, each of them with about twenty people. For each group, there are designated roles, and in this case I'm the fisherman. I need two salmon, ideally, to feed everyone in our group tonight. If I only get one, I need to find something else to bulk up the meal, and that's going to take resources from other areas. We've got a pretty efficient system running here, but only if everyone plays their part." He holds the rod toward me. "Here. Try it."

Wanting to seem keen, I take the rod and stare down into the water, waiting and hoping for something to bite.

"So what skills do you have?" Mark asks.

"I don't know."

"There must be something."

As I watch the surface of the water gently rippling in the morning breeze, I try to think of a skill that might set me apart, but the truth is, there's nothing.

"Don't worry," he continues. "You're young and strong, and I can tell that you're reliable. Those are useful qualities. We'll set you to work. For one thing, I'm getting a little tired of coming out here at the crack of dawn every day. If you learn fast, you could take over the fishing job from me, at least for every other day. Then we'll put you to work chopping wood or maybe fetching water. There are a million things to be done. What's important is that you're able to put aside your ego and work for the common good of the group."

I nod.

"It's harder than it sounds," he adds.

"I want to help," I tell him. "If you just tell me what to do, I'll do it."

"But for how long?"

I turn to him.

"How long are you gonna stick around?" he asks. "There's no point in me teaching you things if you're just gonna drive off in a week or two."

"I've got nowhere to go," I point out.

"Doesn't stop people from getting itchy feet," he replies. "Your friend, for example. Quinn. I'm worried about her. She seems like the kind of person who won't fit in around here. She's noisy and disruptive, and I could already tell yesterday that she might slow things down rather than contribute."

"She's just..." My voice trails off as I realize that I can't really defend her. For the past couple of days, I've become increasingly annoyed by Quinn's behavior, and I genuinely can't see her contributing to the community. I know she's been through a lot, but there's a part of me that already appreciates the set-up here at the lake and I don't like the idea of Quinn causing problems.

"We'll give her a chance," Mark says after a moment, "but if she doesn't pull her own weight, we won't carry her. We'll have to ask her to leave. If it came to that, how would you react? Would you go with her?"

"She's not really my friend," I reply. "I don't even know her. We only met a few days ago."

"Acquaintances can be fleeting."

"If she doesn't work out," I continue, "then I guess you have to do what you have to do. I understand."

"She can always drive off and look for somewhere else."

"It's my truck," I tell him. "She's not taking it anywhere."

"Then she has no choice," he replies. "She *has* to fit in. Either that, or she'll wander off and..."

I watch the line for a moment, trying not to imagine Quinn wandering through the landscape and eventually collapsing. I guess she'd probably go off looking for the source of that goddamn signal, but there's no way I'd go with her, not now. After everything that's happened over the past few weeks, I just want to -

"You've got something!" Mark says

suddenly, as the line goes tight.

Panicking slightly, I start to pull the rod up, but Mark immediately grabs it and holds it in place.

"You don't want to move too soon," he says, staring intently at the water for a moment as the line continues to tremble. "Let him really get caught on the lure first, so there's no way he can slip off, and then..."

He pauses for a moment, before hitching the rod back. Seconds later, he raises the lure and pulls a large salmon out of the water, before depositing it at the other end of the boat. With lightning reflexes, he grabs a knife from nearby and slides the blade into the fish's head, severing it cleanly as dark red blood pours out onto the floor of the boat. The fish twitches a few times, but finally it falls still.

"And we're done," he says eventually, turning to me. "That's one hell of a salmon we've got, Thomas. In record time, too. We just need one more and then we can head back to shore. Why don't you try to set the lure this time. See if you can remember what I told you, huh?"

As I get to work, I'm very aware that Mark is watching my every move. I want to impress him, to show him that I was paying attention and that I can be trusted, but it's a little difficult trying to remember everything he told me. Still, after working slowly for a few minutes, I finally manage to get the lure in place, and although it's not quite as neat as Mark's effort from earlier, I'm pretty pleased with what I've done.

"Not bad," he says as he examines the lure. "That should do nicely. Now cast off."

Once the lure is in the water, I sit with the rod in my hands and finally I feel as if I'm doing something useful. For weeks now, I've been traveling without a real destination, and I even ended up eating worms at one point. Finally, for the first time since this craziness started - hell, maybe even for the first time in my life - I feel as if I've got a purpose, and I feel useful. Filled with a sense of pride, I wait for the line to twitch again. I want to catch the fish this time, and to land it as well. I need to show Mark that he can trust me.

"You're doing a really good job there," he says eventually. "I'm really impressed, Thomas."

I keep my eyes on the water, but I can't help smiling slightly.

"See?" he says, keeping an eye on me. "It's easy to get something on the end of your hook. You just have to offer it what it wants."

ELIZABETH

"IT'S NOT TOO BAD," Toad says as he examines the stitches. "You shouldn't have pulled the bandages off like that, but at least you didn't damage the stitches."

All I can do is stare at the bloody stump just below my right knee. I'm trying not to let Toad see that I'm panicking, but the truth is I'm still not sure I can believe what happened yesterday. The worst part is, I can still feel my right leg, all the way down to the foot. It's like there's a ghost attached to me, and I have to keep staring at the stump in order to make myself realize that the lower half of my leg is really gone. To test myself, I try moving the toes of my right foot, and I swear I can feel them wriggling, but they're not there. It's like I've got a phantom foot.

"How's the pain?" he asks.

"Bearable," I reply, which isn't quite true. The pain is intense, although it's more like several different pains: there's the torn flesh, and then there's the meat, and then there's the bone, and each of them is hurting in its own way. Although Toad has given me some basic over-the-counter tablets to take the edge off, I'm not sure I can handle this for much longer. Still, I almost feel as if I'm too dazed to really process the pain signals that are being sent to my brain. It's as if I'm observing myself and noticing the pain without really letting it get through to me. My biggest worry is that suddenly everything will change and the agony will take over.

Also, I keep reliving the moment when he started sawing through my bone. I can hear the sound of the saw cutting through me, and even though I know it's not helping, I keep thinking back to it. It's like I'm in shock.

"There's still a long way to go," he says after a moment, as he starts to wrap a fresh bandage around the stump, "but you're already doing a lot better than I expected. At this rate, the worst thing you're gonna have to deal with is a butt-ugly scar in a few months' time." He smiles, but I don't smile back at him. "You know I had to do it, right?" he continues as his smile fades. "You'd be dead by now, Elizabeth. I didn't want to hurt you, but I had no choice."

Instead of replying, I continue to just stare at the stump as he finishes wrapping the bandage around it. Already, a small amount of blood is starting to soak through the fabric. This whole situation feels hopeless.

"I'll change it again in a few hours," he explains. "I don't have too much spare material left, though, so we're gonna have to be careful."

"Can I see it?" I ask suddenly, surprising myself. My voice sounds harsh and damaged, and I had no idea I was going to say anything until the words left my mouth.

"I don't have a mirror," he replies.

"Not that." I pause for a moment, trying to work out if this is really what I want. "My leg. I want to see it. What did you do with it?"

He stares at me, and it's clear that he never expected me to make this request.

"I want to see it," I say again, despite the fact that I know I'm being totally macabre. "It's still mine, even if you took it away from me. What did you do with it?"

"I buried it," he replies.

"Why?"

"I was worried about it attracting animals. While you were resting, I buried it nearby. It was the best -"

"Then dig it up," I say firmly, trying not to cry.

"Elizabeth -"

"It's *my* leg," I continue, interrupting him. "I'm not saying I want to carry it around with me or wear it as a goddamn necklace, but I want to see it one more time. I have that right."

"I don't think it would help -"

"Screw you. Get it."

He pauses, and I can see that he's reluctant.

"You cut my leg off," I continue, "and you did it while I was screaming for you to stop. It's not like I can make you put it back on, but it's my leg, my flesh and bone, and I want to see it one more time." I wince as I feel an itch on my right foot. Reaching down to scratch it, I watch as my hand passes through the air where the foot should be. I can still feel the itch, but there's nothing to scratch. "I need to see it," I continue. "I can still feel it, so I know it's gone."

After a moment, he gets to his feet and wanders across the clearing. As I watch him go, I hear Rachel wriggling in her blanket nearby. Glancing over at her, I realize that she's behaving a little more like a normal baby. I guess I should be happy, but right now I can't really think about her properly. She heard my screams last night, and I can only begin to imagine how that must have affected her. She's only a month old, but already she must have been traumatized by everything that has happened to her.

Even if she makes it to adulthood, she's probably damaged already.

It takes several minutes for Toad to return. I sit patiently, trying to hold back the tears that I know are coming. The truth is, part of me is horrified by the idea of seeing my severed leg, but another part of me feels there's no other choice. Every few minutes, I find myself reaching down to scratch my non-existent right foot, and I can feel the sense of its presence getting stronger and stronger. I've heard of phantom limbs before, and I'm worried I might end up going completely crazy if I don't see the leg for myself. I need to shock myself into understanding that it's gone.

"I still don't know if this is a good idea," Toad says as he comes back, carrying my leg in his hands. "There's no -"

"Give it to me," I say, reaching out to take it.

Reluctantly, he passes the leg to me. The first thing I notice is that it's still covered in soil, so I wipe it clean until, finally, I spot the small butterfly tattoo on my right heel. I still remember the day, about six months ago, when Sammy and I went and got our tattoos done. We were both sneaking out without telling our parents where we were going, and of course we both ended up in trouble when they found out, but it was totally worth it at the time. Now, staring at the tattoo on my amputated leg, I feel a shiver pass through my body. Sammy's almost certainly dead, and my tattoo is no longer a part of me, so it's as if that day has been completely removed from my life.

"Elizabeth -" Toad starts to say.

"Be quiet," I hiss, as I turn the leg over in my hands. It's not very heavy, and it feels strange to be holding something that's simultaneously mine but not mine. I remember painting these toenails in the old days, and picking them clean, and stubbing them and biting them, and I remember the feel of my bare feet on the carpet in our Manhattan apartment. As I run a finger against the sole of the foot, I swear I can feel my phantom leg being tickled, and I instinctively reach down to give it a scratch before I realize that there's no point. Finally, I turn the leg around and examine the edge where it was amputated: the skin is torn and I can see dark red meat glistening, with a sawn-off section of bone just about visible. I guess the worst part is the dark marrow I can see running through the bone. This time yesterday, all of this was still a part of me.

"Okay," I say after a moment, passing it back to Toad. "You can bury it again now."

"If you -"

"You can bury it," I say firmly. "There's no need for a big discussion about the damn thing. Just go stick it in the ground. Or if you prefer, leave it out for the wolves. It doesn't matter anymore."

Instead of arguing with me, he turns and

heads back across the clearing. I want to punch him right now, to make him suffer. I know he thinks he was doing what's best for me, but I can't get over the fact that he took a goddamn saw and cut off a part of my body. Feeling another itch in my right foot, I reach down and once again find that my hand has nothing to touch. Letting out a gasp of frustration, I look up at the dull gray sky overhead, and finally I allow the tears to start rolling down my cheeks. It feels as if a huge part of my soul has been taken away, as if I'll never be complete again.

I hate Toad. I hate him for what he's done to me. As soon as we get to somewhere with other people, I never want to see him again. Feeling another itch on my right foot, I reach down to scratch it before letting out a cry of frustration.

THOMAS

"THOMAS!" A FAMILIAR VOICE SHOUTS. "Thomas! Wait! Thomas! It's me!"

Sighing, I realize that Quinn has finally caught up to me. I don't stop or look back; instead, I continue to make my way along the shore, carrying the two large, heavy salmon to the spot where two women have already got a fire burning. I can hear someone running toward me from behind, though, which I guess means I'm going to have to deal with more of Quinn's drama. Maybe I'm being harsh, but I kind of just want her to disappear. I put up with enough of her crap over the past few days, but things have changed now. I've got better options.

"Wow!" she says as she reaches me. "Those are two huge fish! Where did you get them from?"

"Where do you think?"

"Where?"

"Have you noticed the large body of water nearby?"

"Really? Did you catch them?"

"It was either that or go to the local store," I reply. "I kinda figured they'd probably be all out."

"That's very impressive," she continues, keeping pace with me. "I thought I saw you going out on a boat, but I wasn't sure. To be honest, I never had you down as much of a fisherman, but good for you if you've decided to take up a new hobby. It's absolutely amazing to think you were able to just go out there and catch these two huge things. It's so lucky that you were able to -"

"It's not luck," I say, stopping and turning to her. "Mark knows what he's doing. He taught me, too, so I can do it by myself tomorrow and contribute to this place. People around here actually work to keep the community running, unlike..." I pause as I try to work out if I'm being too harsh.

"Unlike what?" she asks a little reticently.

"I just think this is better than what you had going in Chicago," I continue. "People are actually working together here, instead of dancing around on a platform while a bunch of dazed zombies mill around and wait to die. I mean, do you really think that set-up was going anywhere? The whole thing was completely pathetic."

"It's very different here," she replies

defensively. "They have resources, and a lake -"

"I'm busy," I tell her, turning and heading toward the part of the shoreline that has been marked out as a cooking area for our particular group. I'm already starting to get a good idea of the layout here, and although no-one has said anything about it yet, I'm pretty sure that I must be exceeding expectations. The only thing holding me back is Quinn, and if I can just get her to quit pestering me, I'll be just fine.

"I need to talk to you about the signal," she says, hurrying to keep up with me. "I've spent all morning working on the laptop. The spare battery I brought is almost out of power, so we don't have any time to lose. If we're going to locate the source of the signal with any accuracy, we need to work faster to triangulate the exact site. We also need to find some shovels, because I'm worried that maybe whatever we're looking for has been buried. Do you think the people here might be able to lend us some digging equipment? You seem to get on with them quite well, can you -"

"I'm busy," I say again, this time more forcefully.

"I know," she continues, "but I'm sure there are other people who can take care of the fish. Just find someone who likes cooking."

"I have to go and help chop wood later," I tell her. "I'm going to be doing it all afternoon, so that there's enough to keep people warm tonight. A group of us need to head further along the shore and find a good spot, and then once we've got the trees down we'll have to divide them into smaller pieces and bring them back. So if you think about it, I really don't have time to help you with your dumb quest."

"Wood?" she replies, stepping past me and trying to get in my way. "This is more important than wood, Thomas! This is the future of mankind!"

"Take Kaylee," I say as I side-step my way around her. "I don't know if they've put her to work yet, but maybe you can persuade her to drop her responsibilities and run off with you."

"Responsibilities to who?" she asks, trying yet again to block my way. "To these people, Or to our mission? You saw the drawing of my dream, Thomas. We're supposed to go and find the source of this signal, and we can't allow temporary concerns to get in the way. I know it's important to have food and heat here, and I'm sure that there are plenty of people who can get all of that done, but we have a different task. In fact, what we're doing is *more* important, because we're trying to find a future for the entire human race!"

"I'm busy!" I tell her yet again.

"So am I!" she hisses. "And what I'm doing is more useful than any of the bullshit they're dealing with around here! Can't you see that? This is about finding a new path for humanity. These people are trying to recreate the old ways, and I understand why they might want to do that, but it's not a long-term option. We need to embrace change rather than reverting to the way things used to be."

"Can you just -"

"Are you even listening to me?"

This time, when she tries to get in my way, she manages to get her foot caught up with one of mine, and although I try to keep my balance I end up falling forward and landing on top of the fish. I scramble to get back up, but the sides of the salmon are already caked in dirt. I swear to God, right now I just want to tell Quinn to get away from me and never come back.

"Are you okay?" she asks.

Gathering the fish up, I try to brush away as much soil as possible. I figure they can be cleaned, and that they should still be edible, but I'm starting to feel as if Quinn is pushing me way too far.

"Thomas," she continues. "I'm sorry I knocked you over, but you have to see sense. Our mission -"

"Go to hell," I say, turning to her.

She stares back at me, clearly shocked.

"I've told you over and over," I continue, "that I'm busy. I've got things to do, and people here are relying on me. I don't have time to go running around while you wave your laptop in the air, okay?

You don't need me, anyway. You don't even need Kaylee. You can go off by yourself and spend all the time you want just searching for the source of that goddamn signal. It's probably just some old automated thing anyway, but if it's not, you can come back and prove us all wrong, okay?"

"You can't give up," she replies, sounding a little dejected. "Thomas -"

"Leave me alone," I say firmly. "I don't want anything to do with your stupid quest, okay? I hope you find something, and I hope it makes you happy, but there are more important things to worry about, like finding food and keeping this community alive. If that doesn't interest you, you're just going to have to go off and do your own thing. No-one's forcing you to stick around."

She stares at me, and it's clear from the look in her eyes that she's shocked by my response.

"Can I..." She pauses. "Can I at least borrow your truck?"

I shake my head.

"I'll bring it back."

"I might need it," I reply, "and anyway, you said we were already close to the source of the signal, so you can do the rest by foot. Just try not to cause any problems, okay?"

"But we're friends -"

"No, we're not. We're just people who ended up traveling together for a while because it was convenient, but that's all over now. I don't know what Kaylee wants to do, but I'm sticking it out here. This place is the closest thing to a real life that I can imagine right now, and I want to help Mark and the others keep it going."

"You've really been brainwashed, haven't you?" she replies.

"I'm sorry, I'm busy. This conversation is over. Permanently."

With that, I turn and head to the cooking area, where I set the fish down and explain that they might need a little extra cleaning. Once I'm done, I accept a plate of food and eagerly wolf it down. When I glance over my shoulder, I realize that Quinn is nowhere to be seen. I guess she's headed off to resume her search, which is fine by me. In fact, I really wouldn't mind if I never see her again.

ELIZABETH

"OKAY," TOAD SAYS as he reaches under me, "just try to hold on and make sure you don't shift your weight suddenly. This is going to be a little tricky."

Reluctantly, I put my arms around his neck and wait as he lifts me up. It's hard to believe that he's going to carry me, Rachel and the two rucksacks, but I guess he's been working the land for years and he's probably strong enough. I can tell that he's struggling, and as I arrange Rachel against my chest, I can't help worrying that at any moment we might end up tumbling down to the ground. This whole plan is completely ludicrous, but I'm not exactly in a position to refuse.

"You okay?" Toad asks, sounding as if he's really finding this hard.

"I'm fine," I mutter, not really wanting to talk to him too much. "Are you?"

"Don't worry about me," he says, turning and making his way slowly across the clearing, with heavy, lumbering steps. "I've carried heavier things."

"Thanks."

"You know what I mean."

"I guess I'm lighter than I used to be," I say darkly, staring at my bandaged stump. "How much does a human leg weigh, anyway? It's gotta be a few pounds. I'm not a cripple, though. You know that, right?"

"As soon as we get to the next farm, I'm going to make a set of crutches for you." He takes a couple more heavy steps forward. "You'll have to be careful for a few weeks in case you open the wound up, but you'll be up and about in no time. The only problem might be your upper arm strength, which -"

"I'll manage," I reply, hoping to shut him up.

"You're angry at me, aren't you?"

"Of course not," I mutter bitterly. "What makes you think that?"

"I had no choice, Elizabeth," he continues. "Would you really rather be dead?"

"I'd rather not be in pain," I tell him, "and I'd rather not have a huge chunk of my body missing. What the hell am I supposed to do now, anyway? It's not like I can be useful. You've just turned me into this *thing* that's gonna need to be helped all the time." I wait for him to reply, but as he carries me between the trees, I realize that I'm probably being ungrateful. Still, I can't deny what I'm feeling. "I thought you'd left me to die," I continue. "I was okay with that. I'd come to terms with it."

"I wouldn't leave you," he grunts, obviously struggling with all the weight he's carrying. "The only thing that would have kept me from coming back would have been if I'd died."

Pressed against me, Rachel lets out a brief cry.

"Maybe you should just leave me when we get to this other farmhouse," I continue. "I don't want to be a burden for you two."

"That's not going to happen. I've already got a plan -"

"You've always got a plan," I point out. "You've had a plan since the start, and now look at us."

"We're going to stay put for a while -"

"But you said that was a bad idea before," I continue, trying not to let my frustration show. "You're just changing your opinion to support whatever course of action means that we stay together."

"That was when you were able to walk properly. This time, we're going to have to wait while you learn to get about properly on crutches, and then we're going to have to alter our plans. I need to study the land and work out if there's any way we can survive out here. I don't know what was going wrong with the soil back at my farm, but hopefully it's not the same everywhere. I still believe we can live off the land."

"We'll all die," I tell him. "You'll sit around trying to help me until I die, and then you'll die, and then Rachel will die too. Three lives will be lost instead of one."

"Not necessarily."

"You know it's true," I continue. "I don't know why you're trying to be all noble and strong about this, but things are getting worse day by day, and sooner or later you won't be able to fix anything. Right now, you can patch everything together and find a way to make it work, but that's not always going to be the case. Anyway, I used to be able to help, but now I'm just going to be holding you back."

"The other way to look at it," he replies, "is to say that you're going to be less mobile, while means you'll be more likely to stay put when I tell you not to get into trouble."

"Is that supposed to be a joke?" I ask.

"Let's just focus on getting to the Hodge place," he continues. "Once we're there, we can look into our other options, but at least we'll be able to rest. The Hodges ran a good farm, and hopefully there'll be something there we can use. Either way, it'll be better than being out here, and it'll be an improvement on the situation back at my place. We can adapt to whatever we find. I used to think we needed to plan everything out, but now I realize that adaptation is the most important thing. We'll see what we have, and we'll make it work."

I want to argue with him, but I figure there's no point. I don't understand why he's so keen to save me, but apparently he's decided that he's willing to risk his life, and Rachel's, in order to keep me alive. I'm too weak to keep debating the point with him endlessly, so instead I decide to focus on keeping Rachel entertained. Reaching down to her, I let her wrap her tiny fingers around my hand, and for a moment she stares at me with an expression of wonder. As a faint smile crosses her lips, I find myself feeling more and more certain that my earlier fears about her health were unfounded. There's no way she's been infected by whatever created those creatures last month. She's just a normal little girl who happens to have been put through a lot of trauma.

"It's going to be okay," I whisper to her, even though I'm not certain I believe it anymore. "Whatever happens to me, you're going to be fine."

THOMAS

"I GUTTED A FISH TODAY," Kaylee says as she hurries to catch up to me. "Look," she adds, holding up her bloodied hands and grinning from ear to ear, "see? That's salmon blood. It was kinda gross, but I did it!"

"Cool," I reply, although I'm more impressed by the change in her attitude. Somehow, she seems to have come alive since we arrived here, and it's good to see her getting to work. "You know I helped catch those salmon, right? I was out on the water with Mark as soon as the sun came up. It only took us about half an hour. Mark landed the first one, but the second was all me. That was the biggest one, too."

"It was so interesting," she continues. "It was hard at first, but this woman showed me how to do it properly. In a few minutes, she's gonna show me how to prepare them for the fire, and I'm gonna spend all day learning about the stuff they cook here. There's a guy who's gonna show me a load of other things too. Apparently it's really important to make sure we follow hygiene rules, 'cause otherwise everyone could get sick and we don't really have any way to treat them."

"Sounds like you're really settling in."

"It's amazing how much has changed since a couple of days ago," she points out. "I never would have believed... I mean, look at us!"

I can't help but smile. She's right: suddenly things are looking up.

"It's good to be busy," she continues, keeping pace with me as we make our way toward the forest. "When you're busy, you have less time to think about the past. What about you?"

"I'm off to cut down some trees," I tell her. "Mark's showing me how everything works. I'm gonna try every job that's going and wait to see what I'm good at. So far, I seem to have a hang on fishing, but that might not be where I'm needed the most. I told Mark to think of me as a tool that he needs to apply however he sees fit."

"Huh," she replies with a smile, nudging my arm. "So you're a tool, are you?"

"We're all tools. That's what Mark says, anyway. He says we're all created equal, but that some of us have got a natural affinity for a certain type of work. Like, the way men are often better at physical labor. It doesn't mean that's *always* true, but most of the time women can't go and cut down trees so easily. Mark says that even though women aren't inherently better at things like cooking, that's often the kind of job that's left for them after the men have taken all the physical stuff."

"He seems like he's got lots of ideas about how the world should work," Kaylee replies, not sounding too impressed.

"It's just logic. Men and women are built differently."

"So if I wanted to come and cut down trees -"

"You'd slow us down," I reply. "No doubt about it. I mean, look at your arms. You're not strong enough."

"Your arms aren't exactly covered in muscles."

"They're better than yours," I point out, keen to make sure she understands.

"So I can't come and help with the trees?" she asks. "Come on, please? I'm a good worker."

"It'd be a waste of your time," I explain. "You can be better utilized somewhere else. You'll probably find something you're really good at. It doesn't have to be cooking. You should try a bit of everything."

We walk on for a moment, and it seems as if she's not entirely happy with what I just said. Still, I figure she can't really argue with me, since - as Mark pointed out - the whole thing is based on science. Men and women are different, and that's something that should be embraced, not ignored. Maybe in the old world we were able to smooth over those differences, but now none of us can afford that luxury.

"So have you seen Quinn?" Kaylee asks eventually.

"Earlier. She was pissing me off."

"I saw her just now," she continues. "She looked really sad, like she didn't have anything to do. She was holding her laptop, but she didn't have it on, and she was just staring at it, like she hoped it'd still give her an answer. I offered to let her join me at the cooking site, but she said she didn't have time. It's almost like she doesn't want to join in and help. I kinda feel sorry for her."

"All she cares about is that stupid signal."

"Do you really think it's stupid?"

"I think it's a waste of time," I reply sharply. "So what if someone's sending out a beacon from somewhere? Beacons and signals don't put food on the table or water in people's cups. If there's anything to find, someone'll stumble onto it eventually. It doesn't have to be us."

"She wants me to go with her to keep looking for it," she continues. "She keeps complaining that her laptop doesn't have much more battery power left and that we have to get moving before it runs down completely. She's got it turned off right now, and I think that's eating away at her. You know what she's like, right? She has all these crazy ideas, and she can't put them all in order so she tries to just go for everything at once. I think she's convinced that she's got the location narrowed down, and that all we need to do now is walk about five miles to the east and then we'll find it. I mean... That's what she says, anyway."

"Sure we'll find it," I mutter, "and it'll be something that saves the day and makes us all seem like heroes. She doesn't know what she's on about. I admit, it's good that we ended up coming out here, but it's just a coincidence that we found these survivors. Quinn doesn't want us to join a large group, because she wants to be the center of attention. In her head, she deserves to be regarded by everyone as some kind of leader, but that's not the kind of person she is at all. She's not a natural leader like Mark, she's just someone who wants to be..."

I pause for a moment, feeling as if maybe I shouldn't be too mean. Since I found out about Quinn's son, I've felt that maybe she's a lot more damaged than I'd realized, but I still feel as if she's a disruptive presence.

"So are you gonna go with her?" I ask eventually.

"I was thinking about it," Kaylee replies, "but no. I mean, I'd like to, but I don't think I have time. There's already so much to do here, and -"

"That's good," I say, interrupting her. "All that crap with Quinn is in the past now. If she can't get over it, that's her problem, but we need to focus on what we're doing here. There's no time for running off on a bunch of dumb chases. We can't spare the energy." As we reach the edge of the forest, I turn to her, and I can see that something's on her mind. "Don't you have something you need to be doing?" I ask after a moment. "You said you're going to be shown how to cook the fish."

"Yeah," she replies, but she doesn't turn to walk away. "I was just thinking, though... Do you want to go exploring later? When we're both finished, I mean. We could take a look along the shore, maybe just check out the area. Just the two of us, without Quinn or anyone else."

"Check it out?"

"Well..." She pauses, as if she's a little tongue-tied. "Yeah, I mean, I don't know what's out there. Do you? There might be... something... It's just..."

I wait for her to finish.

"I thought we could go for a walk, that's all. There are so many people here, and sometimes I feel like I'm not very good in crowds. I mean, uh, it'd be good to know the surrounding area a little better, wouldn't it?"

"I don't know," I reply, surprised by the idea. "Maybe. I don't think I'll have time, though. Mark says it's going to take until sundown to get the trees cleared, and then we have to start up again at first light."

"Okay," she says quickly, looking embarrassed as she takes a step back. "It was just an idea, that's all. Don't worry about it." With that, she turns and hurries away, breaking into a run as she heads back toward the main part of the camp.

Watching her for a moment, I try to work out what just happened. It's almost as if she wanted to spend time alone with me, but I guess she's just trying to get a friend. She picked a bad time for it, though; there's so much work to get done, I don't think I'll have a spare moment for the next few weeks. It feels good to have a job, and as much as I like Kaylee, it's time now to focus on the tasks at hand. Mark's right when he says that we need to see ourselves as tools, to be applied to whatever job needs doing. He's also right when he says that egos need to be set aside so we can be more useful to the group. Hell, Mark's right about a lot of things.

Figuring that Kaylee will be fine, I turn and

head through the forest. I can already hear men working up ahead, and I'm keen to join them. This is where I belong now.

ELIZABETH

"DAN HODGE WAS AN old bastard," Toad says as he pushes the door open and leads me into the dark little farmhouse we've finally reached after walking for several hours. "He used to complain about the boundary lines all the time. Sometimes I'd catch him out there, measuring the fences as if he thought I was moving them during the night. I think he was worried other people were trying to take his land."

"It stinks in here," I reply as Toad carries me across the room and sets me down on an old sofa. A huge cloud of dust immediately rises into the air all around me, causing me to start coughing uncontrollably. "What happened to him anyway?"

"He died shortly after all of this started. I came to check on him, and to see if he'd heard anything, but I found his body out front. I buried him next to the gate."

"Don't you have anything for the pain?" I ask, feeling a shooting pain in my knee. "I don't think I can go on like this much longer."

"Keep it raised at all times," Toad says, placing a pillow under my right leg. "This place isn't the cleanest, and another infection is still possible. I'm going to check to see what's in the bathroom. With any luck, Hodge had some kind of medical kit. If there *are* any pills, you can have them, but don't hold your breath."

I look down at Rachel, who's squirming in my arms.

"I can take her," Toad says, reaching down and picking her up. "I'm a fast learner."

"She probably needs a new diaper," I tell him. "You'll have to clean her as well. See if there's any powder here, but if there isn't, you'll need to make sure she's dry before you fasten her back up. In fact -" I try to haul myself up, figuring that I can at least help out, but the effort's too much and I have to ease myself back down. "I hate this," I mutter. "I hate not being able to do anything. There's no point to me!"

"It's not forever," he replies.

"Great, so my leg's gonna grow back, is it?"

"Elizabeth -"

"That's the only way I'm ever going to be myself again," I continue, annoyed at him for trying so hard to sound optimistic. "Unless you can find some way to magically put it back, I'm gonna be like this for the rest of my life!"

Without replying, Toad takes Rachel through to the bathroom, leaving me to look around at the room. It's starting to get dark outside, but I can just about make out a dirty-looking kitchen with a round table next to the stove, while there are a couple of sofas over on this part of the room. I guess the place has been abandoned for the best part of two months now, but it still looks like it wasn't exactly clean and tidy to begin with. Whoever this Dan Hodge guy was, I figure he lived alone and that he didn't really care too much about keeping the place looking good.

"You're in luck!" Toad calls through a few minutes later. "Guess what I've found?"

I turn and watch as he comes into the room with a pair of crutches.

"Hodge broke his leg a few years ago. I thought I remembered him getting about on these things, but I figure it was a long-shot that he'd still have them." He puts them under his arms and leans on them for a moment. "They're sturdy enough. I know they look pretty ancient, but you'll be glad of them soon enough."

"You want me to go around on those like some kind of cripple?" I ask.

"You'd rather stay on the sofa?"

Figuring that he's right, I sit up, taking care not to bump my bandaged knee.

"Not right now," Toad continues, leaning the crutches against a nearby wall. "The risk of you falling and re-opening the wound is too great. I didn't find much else in the bathroom, so we're just gonna have to take care of your leg and hope we have a little luck for once." He steps closer and looks down at the bandage. "There doesn't seem to be too much leakage. That's a good sign. Hopefully you'll be able to get up and about in a week, just for short periods while you develop your muscles and -"

"A week?" I reply, shocked by the idea that I might be on this sofa for so long. "No way! I'm not sitting in this place for a whole week!"

"There's no other option," he continues. "It's not so bad here, Elizabeth, and I'm gonna head out soon and see what kind of food I can find. I know for a fact that there used to be wild rabbits around here, and Hodge kept chickens a little way off to the north. If they're still alive, we could have a pretty damn huge feast tonight."

It's clear that he doesn't really understand the full extent of the hell I'm going through right now, but I guess no-one could know what it's like. The pain in my knee is strong, but it's nothing compared to the pain in my mind. I swear, I can still hear the sound of the saw grinding against my bone.

"I can keep things running while you're out of action," he adds, before sitting on the edge of the sofa. "Remember when I was hurt and you looked after me? I guess I'm just repaying the favor."

"But you got better," I point out. "I'm never gonna get my leg back."

"But you'll be able to move around. You'll be active sooner than you think."

"I still wish..."

He waits for me to finish.

"I still wish you hadn't done it," I continue. "There must have been another way, or if there wasn't..."

"I couldn't just let you die," he replies. "Do you really think I could have gathered Rachel up and just walked away? Would you have been able to do that to me?"

"No, but..." I look down at my bandaged stump. The pain is intense, but it's almost begun to become part of my mind's background noise now, as if I'm getting used to it in some sick way. "It's going to get infected again," I say after a moment, "and I'm going to die, and you'll just end up stuck here. Everyone should just look out for their own needs instead of worrying about other people."

"That doesn't sound like the kind of world I

want to live in," he replies.

"Tough. That's the kind of world we've got now. The days of people helping each other are over. It's every man for himself."

"What about Rachel?"

"That's different. She's a baby. Everyone else has to sink or swim."

He stares at me for a moment, as if he doesn't quite believe that I'm saying these things.

"It's true," I continue. "If you stop to help someone else, you're just going to end up putting yourself in more danger. That's always been the case, but this time even the smallest danger can be fatal. You're sitting here with me when you should be out there on the road, heading for somewhere safe." I pause for a few seconds, hoping that he might reply. "I don't even like you," I add eventually. "You're just someone I met by accident, and now you're the guy who cut off my leg. What do you think's gonna happen here? That we're gonna be friends? That I'm gonna suddenly think you're okay? I hate you. Every time I look at you, I think of the pain you caused me."

"That's only natural, but -"

"Can you just leave me alone?" I add, hoping to cut this conversation short. "I don't want to talk, I just want to sit here and..." My voice trails off as I realize that there's nothing I actually *want* to do. The pain is getting worse and I can still feel my right foot, even though it's gone. The last thing I need is to keep explaining myself to Toad. It's not as if he'd understand, anyway.

"There was no-one," he says suddenly.

"No-one what?" I ask.

"No-one left who I cared about." He pauses. "You asked me earlier if there was anyone I was looking for, but the truth is, there isn't. My parents aren't around, I don't have any siblings, and there was a woman I loved once, her name was Rebecca, but she died long before all of this started. She killed herself. That's when I decided to get the hell out of the city and go to my farm, but even there I couldn't stop thinking about everything that had happened."

"But..." Pausing, I realize that there's nothing I can possibly say that wouldn't sound dumb.

"The worst part," he continues, "is that Rebecca's death was my fault. She talked about suicide so often, I started to think she didn't really mean it. And then one day, when she tried to call me and I was busy, I didn't call her back. I was too tired to deal with any more of her drama. I had so much to do, so I figured I'd just call her back later in the day. And then eventually I just decided to wait until I got back to our apartment, but when I opened the door..."

I stare at him, waiting for him to continue.

"She'd cut her wrists," he says finally. "I don't think she even intended to die. I think she expected me to come and find her, but I didn't. I got home hours later than usual that day, and by then it was far too late. So you see, I've already left one person behind, let one person die... I'm not going to do it again, not ever. If that annoys you, then too bad." Getting to his feet, he heads toward the door, before turning back to me. "Rachel's sleeping. She should be okay. I'm gonna go and take a look at the chickens and see what else Dan Hodge might have left around the place. I'll be back in an hour or two."

Once he's gone, I find myself staring at the door, wondering why I didn't say anything to him after he explained the story about Rebecca. I guess I was just in too much shock. I could always tell there was something dark in Toad's soul, but I assumed it was just that he was missing someone who'd been lost when the crisis started. Now it's clear that he was already hurting a long time ago, and even though I still wish he'd left me behind, I can at least understand why he didn't. I wish there was something I could say that might make him feel better, but I'm not very good at this kind of thing.

Damn it, why did I have to be such a bitch to him?

Leaning back, I stare up at the ceiling. The pain in my knee is bad, but what's worse is the itch on my right foot. It's like a phantom feeling, on a limb that's gone, but the problem is I can't scratch it. It's there but it's not; it's all in my mind, like a ghost I carry around, constantly reminding me of what I've lost and can never, ever get back.

THOMAS

"YOU'RE A GOOD, STRONG WORKER," Mark says as we finish hauling the last of the logs onto the main pile, ready for them to be taken to the site at sunrise. "I can already tell you're going to be an asset to the community."

"I'm just trying to pay my way," I tell him, trying to sound calm even though I'm genuinely pleased that he's so impressed by my efforts. I've worked hard before, of course, back on my family's farm, but back then I was just being forced to help my father; now I feel as if I'm actually contributing, and it's almost as if I've become a man today. I can learn a lot from Mark, but first I need to make sure that he appreciates me.

"Hopefully the chefs will have that fish ready for us by the time we get back," he continues. "After a hard day like this, a man needs good food, and it's even better if he caught it himself."

The other loggers are already heading back through the trees, but Mark seems to be hanging back a little so he can examine the equipment, and I figure I should stick with him. The community doesn't have a leader, as such, but Mark clearly inspires the respect of all the other men here, which means that I'm naturally drawn to work with him. Having seen the mess in Chicago, I'm determined to ensure that I play my part in pushing the people here to do their absolute best.

"Are you capable of making tough decisions?" he asks eventually, as he takes his gloves off. It's getting late, and I can barely see his face, but while the tone of his question was casual, I'm convinced that he's trying to get a better idea of my character.

"Of course."

"Give me an example."

"I killed my brother," I tell him. "I mean, he was dying already, but I finished him off because I didn't want him to suffer anymore. It all happened about a month ago."

"How'd you do it?" he asks.

"I only had a spade, so..."

My voice trails off as I find myself briefly

reliving that moment.

"Sounds like a very admirable approach," Mark says after a moment. "Not a lot of men would be able to do something like that. Human attachment is a weakness these days, at least when it's applied without thought. The new world requires an entirely new perspective."

"It was the right thing to do," I explain, as we turn and make our way through the trees. "He was in agony. I'm not saying it was easy, 'cause it wasn't, but I weighed it up in my mind and I decided it was the best option. Of course, he came back a few days later after he got infected by whatever the hell that thing was, but he was strong enough in the head to break through and still be himself."

"Fascinating. I've got to admit, I still don't understand those zombie creatures. I'm just glad they're gone."

"I saw a few of them up close," I tell him. "They were just, like, rotting cadavers. Most of them, anyway. They all spoke with the same mind, like each of them knew what the others were seeing. There were so many of them, but eventually their bodies just broke down and collapsed."

"Good thing, too," Mark replies. "I can't imagine how we'd have dealt with things if we'd been overrun. We'd have been out-numbered, that's for damn certain. Sometimes, I worry that they might come back, but if -"

Before he can finish, there's a scream from up ahead, followed by another. I turn to Mark, but he's already started to run, and I quickly set off after him. Dodging between the trees and almost losing my footing several times, I eventually drop the bag of tools I've been carrying, and as soon as we get out beyond the edge of the forest I see that a crowd is starting to gather down by one of the cooking sites. Just about managing to keep pace with Mark, I race through a sea of bodies until I come to a halt and see a figure on the ground, with blood flowing freely and soaking into the grass.

"Did you get her?" a voice shouts.

"She got away!"

"Kaylee..." I whisper, as I suddenly realize that I recognize the dress being worn by the injured girl. Hurrying forward, I kneel next to her, but as I reach out to check if she's okay, I'm shocked to see that a thick chunk of flesh and bone has been gouged out of her face, right on her left cheek just a couple of inches above the corner of her mouth. Her eyes are open, staring down at the grass, and even without touching her I can already tell that she's dead.

"Jesus Christ," Mark says, standing behind me. "What the hell happened here?"

"It was that mad-woman," a voice says. "She attacked her without provocation. She just came up and took a swing at her."

"Kaylee?" I say softly, putting a hand on her shoulder and gently nudging her.

No response.

She's gone.

"What mad-woman?" Mark asks. "Who did this?"

"The woman who came with them," the voice continues. "The one who was always waving the laptop around and refusing to work. She was watching for a while, and then she came over, said something to the girl, and then she swing at her with something. I think it was one of the axes from the tool pile. Whatever it was, it only took one strike to knock a chunk of her face away."

"Was there an argument?" Mark asks.

"No," the voice replies. "The girl was working. It all just happened out of nowhere."

"Kaylee?" I whisper, leaning closer to her despite the fact that her wound is wide open. I can see her meat glistening in the low evening light, and the look in her eyes is one of surprise. "Kaylee?"

"She's dead, Thomas," Mark says, reaching down and putting a hand on my shoulder. "Do you have any idea why your friend would have done this?"

"Quinn?" I pause for a moment, before getting to my feet and looking around. "She was never my friend. Where is she?" I ask, feeling a slow fist of anger starting to build in my chest. I swear to God, if I get my hands on her, I'm going to make her suffer.

"She ran that way," one of the other men says, pointing back toward the crest of the hill. "She was sobbing and ranting, but I couldn't make out a word of it."

"She wouldn't..." I pause for a moment as I try to make sense of whatever's happening. "There's no way she'd do this. She's crazy, but she's not a murderer. I mean, I don't really know her very well, but I swear, she's not the kind of person who'd just do this without good reason."

"I think we have evidence to the contrary," Mark replies, grabbing a white sheet from one of the nearby campsites and placing it over Kaylee's body. Blood immediately starts to soak through the fabric, and after a moment I have to turn and look away. My mind is almost completely blank, as if my brain has seized up.

"There was a look in her eyes," says one of the women standing nearby. "It was like she'd been possessed."

"Let's not have that kind of talk," Mark says calmly. "No-one's been possessed. Whatever happened, it was the work of..." He pauses, as if he can't find the right words. "Thomas," he continues eventually, "is there anything you can tell us that might explain why your friend Quinn -"

"She's not my friend," I say darkly. Looking down at my hands, I realize they're trembling. "How many times do I have to tell you?"

"Do you have any idea why she'd want to hurt Kaylee?"

I shake my head.

"Has she ever shown violent tendencies before?"

I shake my head again. Somehow, words seem completely inappropriate.

"We have to go and find her," says a voice nearby. "It was cold-blooded murder. There's no way we can let her get away with it."

"She has to die," says another voice. "She might come back and do it again. We're not safe while she's out there!"

"We can't ignore this," Mark says, turning to me. "You realize, don't you, that -"

"I agree," I say, my voice tense with anger and sorrow. "We have to find her and kill her."

"That's not quite what I said -"

"It's the only answer," I continue, looking back down at the sheet and seeing that one end is almost completely soaked in blood. "All she wanted was a painless death. She talked about it the other day. She said she wanted it to be quick enough that she wouldn't even know it was happening. This can't have been painless."

"She screamed," says one of the women

standing nearby. "She staggered a couple of feet, clutching her face as the blood poured out, and then she collapsed. It probably took a minute, maybe a minute and a half for her to die. She was twitching for a while, almost like a fish when it's been landed. I was starting to think we should try to end her misery, but then she passed."

"She must have been in agony," I reply, still staring at the sheet as I try to work out what must have been going through her mind. For a moment, all I can think about is the last time I spoke to her, when she asked me to go for a walk with her. Maybe if I'd agreed, and come back from the forest a little sooner, she'd still be alive.

"We'll bury her properly," Mark says after a moment. "We've never had something like this happen, not since we got here, but we'll give her a proper resting place. She was one of us, even if it was only for a day, and she deserves our respect and love."

"And then we'll go and find the woman who killed her," says another voice.

"We don't have the resources to launch a witch hunt," Mark replies. "Besides, do you really think she'd come back?"

"I know where she's going," I say, turning to him. "She's following that damn signal."

"Maybe we should just let her go," he says. "If she's on foot, she won't last too long. She'll probably just end up collapsing and dying out there."

"That's not good enough," I say firmly. "I want to *know* she's dead. I want to see her suffer for what she did."

"We'll find her and bring her back," Mark continues. "She'll be given a fair hearing, and witnesses will be able to testify against her. Once that's done, a vote will be taken, and if the majority choose execution, we'll put her to death."

"And if they don't," I continue, "then I'll kill her myself."

DAY 52

ELIZABETH

"OKAY," I WHISPER TO MYSELF, sitting on the arm of the sofa with the crutches in my hands. "You can do this. Toad's wrong. You're not some weak-assed cripple who's gonna sit around for the next week being waited on."

I take a deep breath.

It's time.

Another deep breath.

Damn it, why am I delaying this?

Looking down at my stump, I can see a faint patch of blood showing through the bandage, but no other colors. Toad has repeatedly warned me that although red is okay, anything else might indicate another infection. I didn't sleep last night, instead spending all my time staring up at the ceiling and thinking about everything that's happened over the past few weeks. The pain in my leg was keeping me awake, although Toad gave me some painkillers that helped to make it at least slightly bearable. I've only got enough pills for another day or so, though, which makes me worried about what'll happen when they run out.

Still.

I'm not a cripple. There is no way that I, Elizabeth Marter, am going to let the small matter of an amputated right leg bring me down. I've spent more than enough time wallowing in self-pity. Now's the time to get back up.

I'm fine, and it's time to prove it.

Adjusting my grip on the crutches, I take another pause and try to summon as much strength as possible, before finally hauling myself up. Using my left foot to keep myself more or less balanced, I have little trouble getting upright, and although I feel a little wobbly, I'm finally able to arrange myself more or less comfortably. Once I'm sure I can stay up, I use the crutches to take a faltering step forward, disturbing more dust in this dark, wretched little room. To be honest, this is turning out to be much easier than I'd expected. Toad acted like I wouldn't be able to get about at all, but I guess he underestimated me. Not for the first time.

"What do you think of me now, huh?" I whisper. Damn it, I wish he was here to see this, instead of sleeping upstairs.

Making my way across to the window, I look out at the dull gray morning. Dan Hodge's farmhouse is surrounded by a forest of tall, thin pine trees, resulting in a subtly creepy atmosphere. I can't shake the fear that more of those creatures are going to come marching out of the gloom, at any moment, but so far everything seems fairly peaceful. For a moment, I'm almost able to forget about the fact that I've only got one leg, but the dull, relentless pain soon comes back to bite me. The worst part is, I swear I can feel my right foot resting against the floor, even though my *actual* right foot was left in the clearing before we came down here.

Turning, I carefully make my way back across the room. As I reach the door, I notice a bundle of boxes and wires on a nearby table, and closer inspection reveals what appears to be a radio system. Reaching down, I pick up one of the boxes and find that it's some kind of battery, although I don't really know how any of this stuff works. Still, it's tempting to think that maybe we could get this thing up and running, and then we could try to make contact with the outside world. I don't know what Toad's thinking, but I'm starting to wonder if maybe we might be able to survive after all.

Hell, that's a pretty big change. This time yesterday I wanted him to leave me behind. That was when I thought I was crippled, though. Now I'm starting to think that I can not only get about, but maybe I can even be useful.

Heading through to the hallway, I eventually come to the foot of a flight of stairs. My initial instinct is to turn back, but finally I force myself to start making my way up to the next floor. It's a slow journey, made slower by the fact that I'm determined to do it right, but after a few minutes I'm halfway up. I stop to get my breath back, feeling a little annoyed by the fact that I'm so slow, and then I resume the climb until finally I get to the top. Only one of the doors is open, so I make my way through and find a small, dark room. For a few seconds, I'm vaguely aware of movement nearby, and as my eyes adjust to the gloom I'm finally able to make out a figure on an old mattress. I hobble over to take a closer look, and with a faint smile I watch as Toad turns over and stares up at me.

"Hey," I say, fully aware that he's probably surprised to see me.

"What are you doing up here?" he asks, sitting up with a dazed, barely-awake look on his face.

"Surprising you."

He looks down at my right leg, and it's clear that I've succeeded in giving him a shock. He seems unable to believe that this is really happening, but I guess it's just another example of his tendency to underestimate me.

"It's really not that hard," I continue. "Turns

out I've already got some pretty good upper-arm strength. I'm a bit slow right now, but I figure I'll get that sorted soon enough, and..." I pause, unable to stifle a self-satisfied smile. "Yeah, so here I am. Not bad, huh? It didn't even take too long, either. I kinda just kept it slow, made sure not to take any risks, and got on with it. I know you wanted me to sit around on the sofa for a week, but there's no way I could have done that."

Looking down at his bare chest, I spot the scar from his recent injury. It's larger than I remember, and it's hard to believe that only a month or so has passed since those days. Despite having only known Toad for a short while, and despite the fact that I told him I hated him yesterday, I'm starting to think that I like the guy more than I realized. At the back of my mind, there's even a hint that maybe I'm becoming attached to him in ways that I don't want to admit.

"Do you want to sit down?" he asks, keeping the sheets covering his lower body as he shifts out of the way.

"Nah," I reply. "Once I'm up, I'm up. I'm hungry, though. What kind of food do we have around this place? Please tell me the guy who lived here before had something for us. Even moldy bread would be good right now."

"I found some canned food in the kitchen," he replies. "None of it looks very appetizing, but beggars can't be choosers. Wait a few minutes and I'll -"

"I'll do it," I say, turning and making my way back to the door. "If you can get Rachel up, I'll try to sort out some kind of breakfast. Oh, and I think I found an old radio. We should probably get it working and see if there's anyone out there. You never know, there might be some kind of emergency broadcast that's got information we can use. Either that, or we can get in contact with someone who can help us out."

"Maybe we can -"

"Oh, and I think the weather's going to turn. There are some pretty dark clouds coming this way. That's all the news for now, but I'll keep you posted if there are any more developments."

Without waiting for him to reply, I head out of the room and start the slow process of getting down the stairs. I can't help but feel a little pleased with myself, though, since I've managed to surprise Toad and show him that I'm sure as hell not going to sit around being helpless. The days of feeling sorry for myself are over, and I want to make Toad realize that we might be able to make a go of things here at the farm. More than anything, I feel as if I'm finally done with searching for a new home. With a lot of work, we might be able to make this place habitable.

The first stage of this nightmare might

actually be over.

THOMAS

"I DON'T KNOW WHAT to say," I mutter, standing by the side of the grave. "I didn't really know her very well."

I dug the grave this morning, using just an old shovel that Mark found for me and working through the scorching heat, and now Kaylee's body is down at the bottom, wrapped in a white sheet. Given the nature of her injury, I didn't much feel like seeing her face again, so I just let some of the others prepare her body, and they did a pretty good job. The sheet is covering most of her, except her bare feet which are sticking out at the bottom. There's no blood on the sheet, though, which is good; that's what I was most worried about.

And now...

And now I have no idea what to say.

"There's no right or wrong way to do this," Mark whispers, standing next to me. "I just thought you'd like to say a few words so that the others might get a better idea of who she was."

"But I don't *know* who she was," I reply, glancing over at the handful of people who have come to attend this makeshift funeral, and who are waiting patiently for me to give some kind of speech.

"You knew her better than anyone else here," he replies.

"Yeah, but that's not saying much." I turn to him. "We're wasting time. We should be out there, tracking Quinn down and bringing her back so she can pay for what she did."

"There'll be time for that soon enough," he says, putting a hand on my shoulder. "She's not going to get far, not without food or water. Just take a moment to mourn your friend."

"I don't even know if she *was* my friend," I tell him.

"I saw the way she looked at you," he continues. "Whatever you thought of her, *she* considered *you* to be a friend. I only knew her for a day, but I noticed that she always seemed happier when you were around. I'm sure that has to mean something."

As he takes a step back, I'm left alone by the side of the grave. Part of me is annoyed that everyone seems to want me to somehow take charge of this event, but another part of me feels that there might be some way I can make myself feel a little better. There's been so much death and misery over the past month, first with that Lydia woman, then my parents and Joe, but for some reason Kaylee's death has hit me the hardest. She seemed so sweet and kind, and she seemed to genuinely like me, and then she was cut down not by one of the creatures but by a fellow human being. I can feel a kernel of anger in my soul, and I know there's only one way to deal with it.

First, though, I have to try to say something nice.

"I didn't know her," I say finally, staring at the body but aware that everyone's watching me. "The first time I met her was only, I don't know, less than a week ago. Then she came with us when we left Chicago, and I sorta got talking to her a bit more, which was pretty good. She seemed friendly, but she was in shock 'cause of what had happened to her parents. When we arrived here, though, something changed in her. She was more talkative, and she seemed to want to get to work. I guess we were the same like that."

I pause, wondering if I've said enough. Damn it, I'm not good at this sort of thing.

"I'm gonna kill Quinn," I add finally.

I stand in complete silence for a moment. I

know that was probably the wrong thing to say, but it's the truth, and it's the only thought in my head right now.

"I mean it," I say, turning to the others. There are tears in my eyes, but I refuse to cry. "There's no reason why anyone could have ever wanted to hurt Kaylee. She was so kind and so good, and she never did anything bad to anyone, and I figure that when someone kills someone who's so innocent, there's only one way to deal with them. I know people talk about mercy and justice, but sometimes you just have to say that something isn't right, and you have to -"

"Maybe this isn't the time," Mark says quietly, stepping toward me.

"Hell, it's absolutely the time," I reply, refusing to let him shut me up. "I'm angry. Kaylee shouldn't be down there in that hole. She should be up here with us, helping out and getting to work. I know a lot of stuff has happened lately, but good people should still have a place in the world, and if monsters like Quinn are around, we have to get rid of them, right?" I turn to Mark, and then back to the others. "If we're gonna survive, we have to get rid of people who do things like this. I'm not just talking about Quinn, either. There might be other people here who saw what happened, and who are gonna get the idea that somehow it's acceptable. We need to catch Quinn and kill her so that everyone else can see that we've got some kind of justice around this place. We're not savages!"

"You're right," Mark says, "but this isn't the time for -"

"It's always the time," I reply, interrupting him as I hurry past him. Grabbing a shovel, I start pushing soil back into the grave. Glancing down into the hole, I watch as Kaylee's body is completely covered, and then I keep going, shoveling more and more soil down there until, after a few minutes, the grave has been filled. Breathless now, I take a step back and drop the shovel, and that's when I realize that the small crowd has been watching me this whole time. I guess maybe they think I've gone a little crazy, but I don't care about their opinions. Right now, all I can think about is Quinn, and the fact that she's out there somewhere, probably thinking she got away with this.

"One of the others is going to make a small marker for the grave," Mark says after a moment. "It'll just be something simple, probably a small stone with a few details carved into the face, but it'll withstand the elements. First, he'll need you to provide some information about her. Her date of birth -"

"I don't know it," I reply, wiping sweat from my brow.

"Then at least her last name."

"I don't know that either."

He pauses, clearly a little surprised.

"I don't have time to stand around talking, either," I continue. "I know there's a lot of work to do, but I need to take one day off so I can go and find Quinn. Just one day, that's all it'll take."

"We need to go and collect the wood we chopped yesterday," Mark replies calmly.

"Someone else can do that."

"We can't let this incident affect the work of the entire community," he continues. "We don't have enough resources to allow a group to head off on some kind of revenge mission."

"I don't need a group," I tell him. "I'm not asking for anyone else to come with me. I'll go find her, and I don't even need to bother bringing her back. I'll just go out there, track her down, finish her off and come back. It won't even take me 'til sundown. No-one else has to worry about it. This is my job and mine alone."

As the small crowd starts to dissipate, Mark remains on the other side of the grave, watching me. I can tell that he doesn't approve of my plans, but right now I don't care. The only way I can deal with this knot of anger in my chest is to track Quinn down and make sure she pays for what she did.

"You think it's wrong, don't you?" I ask eventually. "You think I should be all Christian and stuff like that, and forgive and forget. I know that's what a good person would do, and maybe I oughta find it in my heart, but I can't. All the other people who've died, I can kinda see why it happened, but not Kaylee. I'm angry and there's only one thing that's ever gonna set me right. The thought of her getting away with this... I can't handle it."

"No," he replies. "I don't think you should forgive and forget. Actually, I think you're right. That little speech you gave, Thomas, was awfully close to being the speech a leader gives to his people. It was an impressive moment, and I think you've got great potential to really take a powerful role here within the community." He pauses, and it's clear that I've genuinely shocked him. "I was going to say that we should let Quinn go," he continues, "but you've changed my mind. I think you're right, and we have to make sure that not only is justice done, but it's *seen* to be done. And that means bringing Quinn back here for a proper trial."

"I'll bring her," I tell him. "I can't promise she'll be alive, though."

"I'm going to come with you," he replies. "This can't be seen to be the work of one person. We need to establish a system. I'll get someone else to take my place on the work duty this morning, and I'll join you to hunt Quinn down. Two of us have a better chance of capturing her than one. We'll leave immediately."

"Good," I reply, even though there's a part

of me that would have preferred to have done the job myself. "Just don't think you can hold me back," I add, before turning and walking around the grave. "I want her dead. You can have a little trial first if you want, but one way or another, Quinn has to die for what she did here, and there's one other thing." I pause for a moment. "I want to be the one who does it. Whether it's out there in a field or back here after a trial, I want to kill her myself."

ELIZABETH

"THIS IS A TOTAL MESS," Toad says as he fiddles with the radio. "It's as if the old fool took a bunch of different systems, grabbed bits of each, and then tried to fit them together like some kind of Frankenstein's monster."

"So it doesn't work?" I ask as I hobble over to the table and set down two plates of disgusting-looking tinned meat.

"Actually, that's the surprising part," he continues, flicking a couple of switches. "I think it *does* work. I never had Dan Hodge down as an engineering genius, but somehow he managed to rig it up pretty well. I mean, I can't check it right now, 'cause I need to find a way to fit the battery to the main unit, but there seems to be some kind of charge in there. I figure I can work on it later and maybe get it up and running, and then we can give it a try."

"Do you think we can make contact with other people?" I ask.

"Maybe. If there's anyone out there. He's got a booster unit linked in to the system and it looks to be running through to some kind of antenna, so I think the range could be pretty long, maybe as much as a few hundred miles. I've got to admit, I don't really understand all the work he did here, but there's definitely a chance." Getting to his feet, he comes over to the table and takes a seat. "Don't get your hopes up, though," he continues. "Even if I get it working, there still might not be anyone else out there with a similar system. We might get nothing back but static."

"I know," I reply, easing myself into the opposite seat. "I'm not getting my hopes up. I just figure it'd be good if we can try. You never know."

I pause for a moment, watching as he uses his knife to examine the meat.

"So did you find anything we can use?" I ask eventually.

"I found the chicken coop," he replies, "but something had been in and got at them all. Probably a fox. There were a few signs of rabbits, though, so I'm gonna set traps today and see what we can get hold of. Hopefully we can keep ourselves well-fed for the next few days, until we're ready to move on."

"Do we really have to move on at all?" I ask.

He stares at me.

"If we don't have anywhere to go," I continue, "then maybe we should just accept that we need to stay somewhere. Anywhere." I pause for a moment. "Here."

"Here?" he asks incredulously.

"We can fix it up a little," I reply. "We can't be picky, can we? We left your farm because the land was spoiled, but if things are better here, then I don't see why we shouldn't hold out for a bit." I wait for him to say something, but it's clear that he's not very enthusiastic. "I'm tired of always traveling," I tell him. "These constant journeys aren't really getting us anywhere, and I feel like we're slowly slipping further and further until..."

My voice trails off, and I wait for him to say something.

"Just the two of us?" he asks eventually.

"Three of us, counting Rachel."

Again, he seems distinctly unimpressed by the idea.

"It wouldn't necessarily be forever," I continue. "But it wouldn't be *that* bad, would it? I mean, looking after Rachel is hard enough, but doing it on the road, especially when I'm kinda impaired, is going to be almost impossible. At least for a little while, wouldn't the smartest thing be to just stop and try to get ourselves sorted?"

"And act like some happy little family?" he replies, as if the idea is crazy.

"I didn't say that," I mutter, cutting off a slice of meat and slipping it into my mouth, and then having to force myself not to gag as I eventually manage to swallow it. It's quite possibly the foulest thing I've ever eaten in my life.

"I'll think about it," he says, before taking a mouthful from his own plate. I can see from the look in his eyes that he hates the meat too, but he forces himself to swallow.

"It's horrible, huh?" I say with a faint smile.

"It's the most disgusting thing I've ever tasted," he replies.

"There's a lot of it," I continue. "The guy who used to live here, he seems to have stockpiled the stuff. I'm pretty sure it's not gonna go off, either. And if it does, maybe it'll even taste better."

"So this is what you want to do?" he asks. "You want to sit around here, eating this crap, and hoping that things get better?"

"Unless you've got a better idea, I think it's our best option."

He stares at me for a moment, and I can tell that although he doesn't necessarily like my suggestion, he doesn't really have anything to counter it with.

"I'll think about it," he says finally, before cutting off another piece of the foul meat.

As we sit in silence and continue to eat, I can't help thinking that I might have won him around to my way of thinking. The truth is, I feel as if I need to rest, at least for a little while, and it wouldn't be so bad to spend some time here. All I want, for a short period of time, is some stability, at least while my leg starts to heal. If we have to set off again and carry on with our journey right away, I think I might end up collapsing.

A few minutes later, as Toad prepares to head out for another hunting trip, I find myself wanting to ask him what he's thinking, even though I'm too nervous about the answer I might get. I keep myself busy with the dishes, which take a lot longer to clean since I have to balance carefully, and Toad is busy getting his supplies ready. Glancing out the window, I see that the clouds are starting to turn darker, and a cold wind is blowing between the trees. If I didn't know better, I'd say that there's a huge storm coming.

"I'll only be a few hours," Toad says eventually, heading to the door.

"Wait," I reply, hurrying over to him as fast as I can manage. "What I said about us staying here, it was just -"

"I know," he says, looking a little awkward.

"Do you think there's going to be a storm?"

"Looks like it. I'm planning to get enough food for two days, so hopefully I won't need to go out again until it's blown over."

He pauses, as if he wants to say something else, and then to my surprise he leans closer and kisses the side of my face. When he pulls back, there seems to be a hint of tension between us, and almost involuntarily I move toward him and press my lips against his. My heart is racing and I know I should stop, but slowly we start to kiss, and this time neither of us moves away. I can't put my arms around him, since I have to keep hold of the crutches, but I feel a shiver pass through my body as he places his hands on my waist and moves closer, and the kiss becomes more passionate and more intense. Finally, after a few minutes, he pulls back.

"I should get going," he says.

"Do you -"

"I'll be back soon," he adds, before turning and heading out the door.

As I watch him head off through the forest, I realize that I have no idea what that kiss meant. There's a part of me that wants to believe we might actually have a connection, although I'm also worried that we're just doing this because neither of us has anyone else. I wish he'd stayed and told me what he was thinking, but I guess he's a private kind of person and it might be harder to tease out his feelings. Hearing Rachel start to cry in the next room, I turn and start making my way through to comfort her, but all I can think about is Toad and that kiss. Despite all my misgivings, I want to believe that it meant something to him. At the same time, I honestly don't know how he sees me.

"It's okay," I tell Rachel as I pick her up. I feel as if I spend half my life telling her not to worry, but I guess there's not much else I can say to her. "Don't cry. Everything's going to be fine."

THOMAS

"SHE'S BEEN HERE," I say as we reach the truck, a little way off from the lake. The door's hanging open, and I'm damn certain it was shut when we left a couple of days ago. "The bitch probably came to take whatever she could get her hands on."

As soon as I put my hand on the door, I have to pull it away again. It's a cloudless day, and the metal is already hot enough to sear the skin.

Climbing into the driver's seat, I start checking to see if anything's missing. Sure enough, the glove box has been left open, and it's clear that Quinn went rifling through it for anything that might be useful. There wasn't much in there, but I guess she was panicking. As I turn to get back out of the truck, I spot a folded piece of paper on the passenger seat. Reaching down to grab it, I find that it's the stupid drawing she showed me back in Chicago, the one that supposedly came from a dream and convinced her that the three of us should make this journey. Just as I'm about to toss it aside, however, I realize that there's something written on the other side, and I turn it around to reveal a short note:

> *Thomas, I know what they're saying, but I didn't kill her. I'd never do that. It was one of the others. They turned on Kaylee and killed her, and then they blamed me. I'm sorry I ran, but I knew you wouldn't believe me. I've gone to find the signal. Please don't think that I killed her. I'm sure you know in your heart that I could never do that. You have to get out of there. Don't trust them.*

I stare at the note, reading it a couple more times as I try to make sense of the bullshit she expects me to believe. There were fifteen witnesses who all saw her kill Kaylee, and yet she seriously expects me to believe that it's all some kind of big conspiracy against her. I actually feel genuinely insulted that she thinks I'm so goddamn gullible. I'm starting to think that Quinn is seriously wrong in the head, to the extent that she maybe doesn't even recognize reality.

"Lying bitch," I mutter, tossing the note onto the seat before shuffling back out.

"You have a lot of gas here," Mark says as he climbs up onto the back of the truck. "Food, too. I'm impressed, Thomas. You've really got this thing stocked up pretty well."

"I passed a lot of abandoned gas stations," I tell him. "I stopped at them and grabbed what I could. At first I felt like a thief, but then I figured it was just gonna go to waste. I mean, every road was just totally abandoned. My brother taught me that it was okay, and eventually I kinda saw things from his point of view."

"Absolutely," he replies, looking through the bags of food that I got from the gas station where I found George. "You chose wisely, too. A lot of this stuff is going to last for a long time." He pauses, before turning to me. "Thomas, I know I have no right to ask this, but the community -"

"Take it," I tell him.

"Are you sure?"

"We have to share," I reply, before turning to look across the nearby field. To be honest, I'm a little confused by the fact that Quinn didn't take anything else from the truck, but I guess she was in a hurry to get away. She must have taken her laptop and run off through the field, heading toward the spot where she thinks the signal is based. I thought that tracking her down would be easy, but now I'm starting to think that maybe she got a pretty decent headstart. Still, there's no way she's going to escape. By the end of today, I'm going to get hold of her.

"The people are really going to be grateful," Mark says as he sorts through the bags, pulling out candy bars and bags of potato chips. "I know it probably sounds crazy, but stuff like this could give them a real morale boost."

"We have to keep going," I say, keen to make sure that we don't lose focus. "While we're standing here, she's getting further and further away."

"So which way do you think she went?" he asks.

"West," I reply, scanning the horizon in a vain attempt to spot something that might help.

"There's a lot of west out there. Care to narrow it down a little?"

"She's got that stupid laptop," I continue. "She's using it to try to work out the source of the signal, but I think the battery should have run out by now. I don't even know if she was *actually* getting closer or just fooling herself. I could tell there was something wrong with her, but I never thought she was properly insane. She's probably not even going in a straight line. That goddamn laptop'll be leading her in circles."

There's an awkward pause, and when I turn to Mark I can see that he's not convinced.

"So what's the alternative?" I ask. "Should we just let her run off and get away with it? You said yourself that we need to set an example for everyone else. If we let lawlessness rule, there'll be other deaths. People have to be shown the rules sometimes."

"And what exactly are you planning to do if we catch up to her?"

Reaching into the back of the truck, I grab Joe's old toolbox. Once I've got the lid open, it only takes a few seconds for me to find the hunting knife he used to carry for protection. I remember begging him not to ever use it on someone, and at the time I thought he was this dangerous, heavy-drinking thug; now I understand, however, that he simply felt that he had to defend himself. A man shouldn't go out into the world without some kind of protection.

"Thomas -"

"It was my brother's," I reply quickly.

"But still -"

"It's just so we've got something to use in case she turns violent," I tell him, as I hitch the knife to my belt. "You saw what she did to Kaylee. I don't know what's got into her head, but she might have lost her mind. I'm totally prepared to take her back to the lake and let everyone pretend to hold a trial, but if she turns on us, I want to be ready for her. I've killed people before, so I can do it again, especially..." I pause for a moment, surprised to hear these words leaving my mouth. I guess I've changed a lot over the past few weeks. "Don't you think it should be an eye for an eye?" I ask eventually. "You heard what the others said. Kaylee was gasping for air as she died. She knew what was happening. Quinn didn't show Kaylee any mercy, so why should we show *her* any?"

"Because we're not animals," he replies solemnly.

"Yeah, we are. We're humans, and humans are just another type of animal. I'm all for being civilized, but sometimes there's a danger you take it too far. If you don't want to come with me, you can just take the stuff from the truck back to the others and I'll be back as soon as I've tracked Quinn down. I understand that this isn't really your fight."

"I'm coming with you," he replies. "Someone has to -"

I wait for him to finish.

"Someone has to make sure I don't just cut her down in cold blood?" I ask eventually.

"That's not what I was going to say," he replies, obviously lying.

"Really? 'Cause you'd have been right."

He stares at me for a moment.

"Come on," he says eventually, "it's a hot

day. We should try to find some shade as we walk, otherwise we'll end up getting our brains fried."

As he turns and heads west, I take a deep breath and try to stay calm. Mark obviously thinks that I'm some kind of bloodthirsty monster, and he might be right. Still, it's only because I want to make Quinn pay for what she did to Kaylee, and I have to admit that I hope she puts up a fight. Right now, I *want* to use the knife to finish her off, so I hope she gives me an excuse. With the sun burning high and bright above us, I turn and follow Mark. We set out across the field without say another word to one another, each lost in our own thoughts. Somewhere up ahead, Quinn is dancing around with that stupid laptop, but if she thinks she's going to get away with murdering Kaylee, she's wrong.

I'm coming for her.

ELIZABETH

WHEN I HEAR TOAD come back from his hunting trip, I don't immediately rush through to greet him. Instead, I continue to hold Rachel in my arms, lulling her to sleep with a gentle rocking motion.

Toad stays in the kitchen. I can hear him placing various items on the table, which I guess means he managed to find something for us to eat, but he makes no effort to come and find me. I guess that means he's embarrassed, and that he doesn't want to talk about what happened between us earlier.

After a few minutes, my resolve weakens and I set Rachel down before grabbing my crutches and making my way slowly through to the kitchen. I keep expecting to hear Toad going back outside, but finally I find him at the table with two dead rabbits laid out.

"Hey," I say cautiously.

"Hey," he replies, not looking at me but focusing, instead, on the job of skinning the bodies. Back at the other farm, he always used to get me to do this part, so I guess he wants a distraction.

"I can do that," I tell him.

"I know."

"I heard thunder earlier," I add, even though this small-talk is excruciating.

"There's a hell of a storm moving in," he replies, still not making eye contact. "It's a good couple of hours away, but when it hits, it's gonna hit hard. I think tomorrow could be a wash-out, so I'm gonna go back out in a minute and check the land to the south. We've got enough food and water for a couple of days, but I'd like a little extra, just to be safe."

"Sure," I reply, waiting for him to look at me. "While you're gone, I can start making food."

Instead of saying anything, he takes a moment to peel the skin off one of the rabbits before starting work on the second. It's clear that he's not comfortable, and although I'm scared to ask him what he's thinking, I can't help wondering if maybe I should just try to bring up the kiss and discuss what happened. The last thing I want is to come across as some kind of needy idiot who wants to talk about everything, especially since Toad seems to keep his thoughts and feelings to himself, but I need to know the situation here.

"So -"

"Save one of the rabbits for tomorrow," he says, finally glancing at me. "It's one for today and one for tomorrow, okay? I don't know what I'll find to go with them, but the meat alone should be pretty good. Remember to use every part of the animal, though. I noticed you used to throw the heads and guts away, but there are uses for those too. Even the bones can be boiled for stock, and anything we really can't eat can always go into the ground. We can't afford to waste anything. If there are parts you're not sure about, set them aside and I'll come up with something."

"Sure."

"I should get going," he says as he pulls the skin off the second rabbit and then sets it down. "Keep the skin, too. I might be able to use the fur." Grabbing his bag from nearby, he turns toward the door. "I'll be back in a couple of hours. If you get a chance, try to make sure all the windows are securely fastened. This storm is going to be strong and I'm not sure how well-built the place is, so we need to -"

"Was it a mistake?" I ask suddenly, interrupting him.

He turns to me.

"If you kissed me by mistake," I continue, feeling as if I'm drowning right now, "then you should just say it. I mean, I didn't kiss *you* by mistake, but if that's how it was from your point of view, then I'd prefer it if you were honest with me."

He stares at me for what feels like an eternity.

"It wasn't a mistake," he replies eventually.

I nod, although I'm still not sure what he really wants.

"So what was it, then?" I ask.

"I'd..." He pauses again. "It was something I'd been thinking about for a while, that's all."

"Okay," I reply, fully aware that I'm really not doing a very good job here. "It's just that it was kind of a surprise," I continue, "and I'd been thinking about it as well, but I really didn't know whether you were thinking the same thing, and so in my head I was kind of trying to... put things together and..."

My voice trails off as I realize that there's no way I can explain myself.

Setting his bag down, Toad walks around the table and comes over to join me. He stops for a moment, before putting a hand on my waist and gently pulling me closer, and then finally he leans down and kisses me again. This time, all the uncertainty seems to be gone, and the kiss feels as if it really means something. As he pulls me even tighter against his body, I feel for the first time as if he actually wants me, and all the doubts I've been struggling with start to fall away.

"Does that answer your question?" he asks as he pulls back for a moment.

I nod.

"I don't go around kissing people by accident," he continues, keeping his face close to mine. "I have no idea where this is going to go, and I'm pretty sure it's not normal for two people to get involved after one of them had her leg cut off by the other, but I guess we have a little time to work things out. We should probably discuss things and be honest with each other, and make sure we're on the same page."

"You're not just doing this because it's convenient, are you?" I ask.

"Like you're the last girl on the planet and I'm the last boy?" A faint smile crosses his lips. "I really hope that deep down, you know that's not the kind of person I am." He glances over at the window for a moment. "We need to talk, but first I should get out there and find some more food before the worst of the storm kicks in. When I get back, we'll eat, and we'll look after Rachel, and we'll talk and hopefully we can..." He pauses for a moment. "We'll work this out," he adds, before kissing me once more, briefly on the lips, and then turning and heading back over to the door.

I open my mouth to say something, to tell him to be careful or to tell him that I feel the same way, but no words come out. Instead, I just watch as he grabs his bag, smiles at me, and then heads outside.

All I can do is stand here and relive the moment, over and over again, when I had my first proper kiss. Sure, there were a few guys in the old days, but it never felt so passionate before. I know I need to keep my hopes on hold, but at the same time I feel as if Toad and I get on pretty well, and we might actually work together. Heading over to the counter at the far end of the kitchen, I grab the bottle of painkillers and open the top. There's only one pill left, but I figure I really need it, so I swallow it and wash it down with some water.

For a moment, I swear I can hear my heart pounding.

Looking out the window, I realize that the sky is almost black now. There's the sound of thunder in the distance, and a heavy wind is picking up in the yard outside the back door. I can't help worrying that the fury of the natural world is heading straight for this farmhouse.

THOMAS

STOPPING FOR A MOMENT next to a lone apple tree, I stare at the landscape ahead of us. As far as the eye can see, there's nothing but rolling green fields, with the sun's relentless heat beating down. Reaching up to wipe sweat from my brow, I can't help but note that out here, the natural world looks so calm and peaceful. It's almost as if, having managed to extinguish the lives of so many people, the planet is starting to thrive.

"Now where?" Mark asks as he catches up to me, apparently a little out of breath.

"She's out here somewhere," I reply, still scanning the scene in hope of maybe spotting something that'll give us a clue. "She must have come this way. Her laptop would have given out by now, so she'll be trying to guess where to go next."

Pausing, I realize that it's useless to try to understand how Quinn's mind works. She's got her own rules and her own logic, and I don't think there's any way in hell I can ever anticipate her next move. "She's out here," I add helplessly, even though I know this simple fact doesn't really give us much to go on. "She has to be here somewhere."

"I don't doubt you, but unless we can find some kind of trail -"

"She's out here!" I say firmly, annoyed at the implication that he's starting to lose hope. I knew this would happen; right from the start, he's seemed a little reluctant to keep pursuing this murderous bitch, as if he's just here to humor me, and now he's going to try to talk me out of it. "She's insane, but she must have come through here, and there must be some kind of..."

My voice trails off as I look down and see that there's nothing on the ground that might help: no footprints, nothing discarded by Quinn as she continued her journey. For all I know, she might have turned around and headed back toward the lake, in which case we're never going to find her. In my rush to get out here, I guess I assumed that I'd somehow be able to track her movements, but now I realize how easy it is for someone to disappear.

"Thomas," Mark says after a moment, "I know she killed your friend, and I absolutely agree that she should be brought to justice, but right now I don't really see how we can track her down. She's probably gone running off on whatever path she thinks will lead her to this signal, and there's no way we can follow. We could spend a year searching for her, and we probably wouldn't have any luck."

"Why didn't someone stop her?" I shout, turning to him. "Why did they all just let her run off like that?"

"Everyone was in shock -"

"And not one person thought to grab hold of her? Are you serious?"

"She got away in the confusion," he continues, maintaining that frustrating, impeccably calm tone that never quite seems to slip. "I'm sure there are many people who wish they'd acted differently, but their regrets won't help us right now." He pauses. "I think maybe we have to consider a new approach here."

"What are you saying?" I ask, even though I already know. It's almost as if he's been waiting all along to gloat about the fact that we won't find her.

"I'm saying we might have to accept that she's gone. If there was any chance of getting hold of her, I'd take it, but there isn't. She's not coming back, and we can't go out there looking for her. It's like trying to find a needle in a haystack. You need to see sense."

"But -"

"Just think about it," he adds. "Thomas, I

take no pleasure from this, but it's all true. You can't use your anger to magically summon her up from somewhere. Finding her, especially if she's taking even basic steps to remain hidden, is just not going to be possible."

I want to argue with him, but I can't. He's right when he says that she's probably long gone, and although I desperately want to track her down, I know that the odds are stacked heavily against us. I hate admitting defeat, but the alternative would be to waste more time. I just wish that one of those goddamn idiots back at the camp had bothered to stop her running off.

"It's too hot for us to wander around out here," he adds.

"So what are we supposed to do?" I ask. "Just forget about her?"

"Running off on some bloodlust-fueled journey would serve no-one in the long-term," he continues. "We should head back to the site and try to find some other way to deal with the anger that we all feel. For one thing, we need to organize ourselves better. It's crazy that Quinn was able to get away after what she did to your friend, so we should think about establishing some kind of security force, just a few people who can take charge in that kind of situation."

Ignoring him, I keep looking for a clue, but finally I have to admit that there's nothing. In other words, Quinn has managed to get away from us, and she's never going to be made to pay for what she did to Kaylee.

"She'll die," Mark says after a moment. "There's nothing out here. She might survive for a few days, but I doubt she's able to live off the land for too long. In this heat, she'll already be dehydrated, and eventually she'll just pass out and never wake up. I know that doesn't satisfy your need for revenge, but at least it means she won't be able to kill anyone else." He puts a hand on my shoulder. "It's over. We should turn back."

For a moment, all I can do is watch out for any hint of Quinn's presence. I know she's out there somewhere, and all I want is to find her and make her pay for what she did to Kaylee. I also want to know why she did what she did, but I guess it's looking as if I'll never get an answer now. With sweat pouring down my face, I turn and look back the way we came, and I finally realize that we've still got a few hours to go before we can get back to the lake. Unless I want to stay out overnight, I need to accept the fact that Quinn is gone.

"Okay," I say eventually, turning and starting the long walk back. "You're right."

"The heat's too much for us," he replies as he follows. "I'm already running out of water."

"Here," I say, grabbing a bottle from my pocket and passing it to him. "You can have some of mine."

He takes the bottle and drinks from it.

"I swear to God," I continue, "that if by some crazy coincidence I ever end up seeing that woman again, I'm going to make her pay. Screw a trial. I'm not gonna sit around and wait for her to escape again. The second I see her, she's mine."

"She won't be coming back," he replies. "She already seemed to have lost her mind, and now that she's out here in this heat, she won't last much longer. All we can do is try to learn from what happened and make sure that no-one else is ever allowed to kill in our group again. Right now, I'm more worried about this heat. We've got plenty of water, but not everyone is as fit and strong as they could be. At this rate, we might start to lose people to exhaustion."

I know he's right, but I can't shake the feeling that by failing to track Quinn down, I'm dishonoring Kaylee. Mark can put forward calm, logical arguments all day and all night, but nothing's going to cancel out my desire to get hold of Quinn and make her suffer. In fact, I can't imagine anything that can ever take away my frustration, so all I can do is hope that one day, by some miracle, I'm able to find her and give her exactly what she deserves. Until that happens, I'll never be able to rest.

"You've gone very quiet," Mark says

eventually. "Do you want to talk?"

Ignoring him, I reach down and double-check that the hunting knife is still attached to my belt. Not only am I going to find Quinn one day, but this is the knife I'm going to use to cut her throat. Even if it's the last thing I ever do.

ELIZABETH

"PLEASE STOP CRYING," I whisper to Rachel as she continues to bawl in my arms. "Please, it's just a storm. You're perfectly safe."

I'm sitting on the edge of a bed in one of the farmhouse's back rooms. The only light comes from a candle that I found under the sink and managed to get burning thanks to a matchbook next to the stove. Outside, darkness has fallen over the past few hours and the storm has finally hit, smashing into the house with terrifying force. I can hear wind howling past the window, and I can just about make out the trees swaying as they struggle to stay upright. Worse, though, is the sound of thunder overhead, and driving rain is hitting the windows with such force that I'm worried the glass might shatter.

"Come on," I whisper to Rachel, "I know

you're scared, but it's fine. It's your first storm, but trust me, there'll be more and you'll just have to get used to them. This kind of thing just happens sometimes. Nothing can hurt us, not while we're in here."

As if to undermine my point, the roof creaks a little, and as I look up at the ceiling I can't help but wonder just how sturdy this farmhouse is. The previous owner clearly didn't bother to maintain it too well, and I'm terrified that at any moment a tree is going to come crashing down.

"It's okay," I whisper, before looking back down at Rachel. I start singing a song, just some stupid nursery rhyme that my mother used to sing to me when I was a kid, but my voice is cracking and I'm not sure how much longer I can do this.

Ignoring my efforts, Rachel continues to scream. I swear to God, I have no idea where she gets the energy, but right now I kind of wish she'd go back to her earlier, staring self. Then again, wishing that probably just means that I'm a bad person.

"You want your real mother, don't you?" I ask. "You can tell I'm not her. I understand. Don't worry, I'm not offended. It's a natural response."

Realizing that there's no way I'm ever going to be able to calm her down, I settle her on the bed before grabbing my crutches and hauling myself up. Trying to ignore Rachel's cries, I make my way slowly through to the kitchen and then to the door. Staring out through the glass panel, I'm shocked to see that the entire area around the house is being buffeted, and that some of the trees look as if they could come crashing down at any moment. Suddenly a flash of lightning brings a brief moment of light to the scene, followed half a second later by a terrifying, crackling rumble of thunder that sounds as if it's splitting the sky directly above us.

And there's still no sign of Toad.

When the rain started, I was convinced that he'd be back soon. I've known Toad long enough to be certain that he can handle himself, and he said that he'd be back before the storm became too bad. Even when the thunder and lightning started, I was sure he'd only be a few more minutes, but now it's been several hours and he hasn't come back. The thought of him being stuck out there in this weather is horrifying, but I can only hope that somehow he's managed to find shelter, in which case he'll be back in the morning, as soon as the worst of the storm has died down.

"He can look after himself," I mutter, trying to maintain hope. "He's not an idiot. He knows the land."

It's hard to remain optimistic, however, when the storm is so bad. Along with that, the last painkiller is already starting to wear off and I can feel my right leg – or rather, what's left of it –

starting to throb. I have no idea how bad the pain is going to be now that I've got nothing to help take the edge off, but I'm certain it's going to be agony. There's more blood starting to leak through the bandage, and although the stain is red at the moment, I'm terrified that it'll become yellow at some point, which would mean that there's another infection.

"It's okay," I whisper, as Rachel continues to cry. "It's all going to be okay." The problem is, with Toad not around, I no longer believe those words.

DAY 53

AMY CROSS

THOMAS

THE CANDLE'S FLICKERING FLAME provides just enough light for me to see what I'm doing. To be honest, I have no experience with radios, but there's no way I can sleep and at least this is keeping my mind occupied. Mark told me that he'd been trying to get the damn thing working without any luck, and I offered to take a look. It's dumb, but at least it helps keep me calm. Otherwise, I'd be spending the whole night thinking about Quinn.

Sitting in one of the many tents that line the shore, I find that I'm almost able to empty my mind completely. A mass of wires has come bundling out the back of the radio's main unit, and I'm carefully untangling them one by one, hoping that eventually I'll be able to work out how to put them back into the right sockets. It's strange, but this kind of slow, methodical work is actually kind of helpful, and I seem to be doing okay. I know the satisfaction won't last, though. Deep down, I can still feel my anger, and I'm still determined to find Quinn one day and make her pay.

After a few hours, I hear a faint noise outside the tent. At first, I ignore it, but eventually I realize that there are hushed voices talking frantically just a few feet away. Eventually, curious to find out what's happening and worried that something might be wrong, I set the radio aside and climb out of the tent, only to find two girls crouched down nearby, talking quietly to one another. The first rays of sunlight are starting to show over the horizon, providing just enough light for me to be able to make out the tense, worried looks on the girls' faces, and they're in such fevered conversation, they don't even notice me at first.

Suddenly one of them looks over at me, and she immediately hits her friend's shoulder to shut her up. It's almost as if I've stumbled across some kind of secret operation.

"It's okay," I whisper, hoping not to wake anyone else up. "Is something wrong?"

They both stare at me as if they're terrified.

"What is it?" I ask, making my way over to them.

"I told you this was a bad idea," the first girl hisses to her friend. "We should have gone already!

Why do you always say you want to leave and then come up with a reason to stay?"

"It's not the right time, Hannah," the other girl replies. "If we go now, we won't have enough food or water for the journey! We need at least enough for a week, and we can't just grab what we want without raising suspicion!"

"Go where?" I ask, trying to work out what's happening. "What are you talking about?"

"We're getting out of here," says the first girl, whose name seems to be Hannah. "I can't take it anymore. This place... It's not right. If I have to stay here another day, I'll lose my mind!"

I stare at her.

"You're new," she continues. "You haven't seen it yet, but you will. Living here..." Her voice trails off, and it's clear that she's terrified. "There are things here that aren't right. You don't notice them at first, because he makes sure they're hidden from anyone who arrives, but eventually you become one of them and that's when you realize the truth, but by then it's too late!"

"It's never too late," the other girl whispers. "We can handle one more day and get some more provisions before we leave. We have to be logical about this."

"You've been saying that for a week!" Hannah hisses at her.

"Wait," I say, crouching next to them.

"What are you talking about? This place is perfect. I mean, maybe not *perfect*, but it's a good set-up. Trust me, I've been in a city just a few days ago, and it was hell. People were starving, there was disease, and rats... Being out here might seem crazy and hard, but it's so much better than anything else out there."

"You don't know what you're talking about," Hannah whispers. "The worst part is, everyone's in on it. The women who cook, the men who go out logging, they're all involved. It's like all these people have decided to work together so they can..." She pauses, as if she's too scared to even get the words out. After a moment, she turns to the other girl. "If you want to stay, that's your choice, but I can't handle it anymore. I know it's dangerous to set out alone, but I'd rather die on the road than live another day here."

"Wait," I tell her. "When the sun's up, we can talk to Mark. Whatever's happening, you can tell him and I'm sure he'll help to sort it out."

"Tell him?" Hannah stares at me wide-eyed for a moment. "He's part of it! He's the one who controls everything around here! Who do you think punishes people who speak out?"

"What are you talking about?" I ask. "I know I haven't been here for long, but I'd know if there was something being hidden. What exactly do you think is happening?"

"I don't *think*," she replies. "I *know*. I've seen it with my own eyes. I've been there. I've seen them."

"Me too," the other girls says. "Once they know you're stuck here, they don't bother to hide it anymore. They get you to help, and then..." She pauses for a moment. "The worst part is the way the others just accept it. He breaks their spirits, and he twists their minds until they don't think there's anything wrong with that they're doing."

"I won't be like that," Hannah says firmly. "I refuse. I won't help them stay hidden."

"You won't help *what* stay hidden?" I ask. "Will one of you tell me what the hell you're so scared of?"

Hannah opens her mouth to reply, but at that moment there's a sound nearby, followed by a few muffled voices.

"It's further along the shore," the other girl says. "You know the trees on the point, a little way to the east? Never go past them."

"People are starting to wake up," Hannah whispers, her voice filled with panic. "You know what it's like. If we try to leave the main group during daylight, we'll be spotted, and then someone'll come after us. The only chance to get away is when it's dark. If we don't go now, we'll be stuck here for another day! I can't handle that. I'd rather die!"

"We need to be better prepared," the other girl says. "We've talked about this. Just be a little more patient while we gather some more things. With a few more days, we can -"

"You always say that!" Hannah says, leaning around the corner of the tent to make sure that there's no-one too close. "If we do things your way, we'll always be sitting here, talking about leaving but never actually getting out of here, and you know what'll happen." She gets to her feet and grabs a small bag from the ground. "I'm going. Please, come with me."

The other girl pauses for a moment, clearly struggling to decide. "Just one more day," she says eventually. "Please, we're not ready yet."

Hannah shakes her head.

"Please, Hannah. It's easy for you, you don't have to think about anyone else. I've got a child to consider. I need provisions for both of us, and she's going to slow us down."

"And you want to let her grow up here?" Hannah asks. "Do you really think she'll be safe?"

"I just need a few more days to get everything ready," the other girl continues. "Katie's weak and I don't even know if she can handle the journey right now."

"Good luck, then," Hannah replies. "You know which way I'm headed. If you change your mind and you want to catch up... I hope you and

Katie come, but I can't stay here another second. Please, try to understand. I'll try to come back for you, if I get a chance. Maybe I'll meet some people who can help. If that happens, I'll bring them back with me and we'll try to save everyone." She pauses, with tears in her eyes, as if she's giving her friend one last chance to go with her, and then she turns and hurries off between the tents.

"Hannah!" the other girl hisses. "Wait!"

It's too late. Hannah's gone, and her friend sits in stunned silence.

"What the hell's going on here?" I ask, genuinely shocked by the idea that someone would be so keen to get away from this place.

"I can't believe she left without us," she replies, looking lost and forlorn. "I wanted to go, but I wanted to do it properly, and I've got a child to consider. We've been saving rations, just a little bit each day so that no-one would notice. We were going to leave eventually, but we needed a little more time and we needed to maybe get a few more people to come with us." She pauses. "I guess I can't blame her. She's probably right. With Katie to look after, there's no way I can leave this place. I just have to keep my head down and hope no-one notices me. I should have let Hannah take Katie, though. That would have been the best thing."

"Where's she going?"

"Along the shore," she continues. "We were

planning to find somewhere else, somewhere new. Or maybe some other people, people who aren't like this. We hadn't got an exact plan worked out. All we knew was that we had to get away. At first, we were glad just to be alive and to have other people around us, but gradually things changed. We started to notice what was really happening. Not the whole thing, obviously, but little aspects of it here and there." She pauses again. "I can't let Katie grow up here, but she can't travel, not yet. She's hurt, and she needs to rest."

"How did things change?" I ask. "You keep talking about this place as if something bad's happening, but I've been here long enough to know that there's nothing hidden. I've spent a lot of time with Mark and I can tell he's a good leader. He just wants the best for all the people here, and I think he's really got some good plans. You just need to -"

"I have to get to work," the girl says suddenly, getting to her feet. "Please, don't tell anyone about this. There'll be questions when they find out that Hannah left, but you can't tell them that I had anything to do with it. They'll punish me, and then... I still want to go off after her, but I need a little more time. Just one more day and then I'll follow. I swear." With a look of abject terror in her eyes, she pauses for a moment, and then she turns and runs past the tent. Nearby, there are the sounds of people getting up and preparing to start work, and I'm expected soon at the shore so that Mark and I can go fishing.

I want to run after the girl, to ask her what the hell's happening, but I figure this isn't the right moment. Besides, I'm pretty sure that whatever they were talking about, it can't be too bad. People are jumpy and nervous, and as I found out with Quinn, not everyone has managed to stay sane in this brave new world. I guess Hannah and her friend are just two more people who can't see things clearly. This place isn't perfect, but it's a damn sight better than anything else I've found so far, and I can't believe that there are any dark secrets here. It's not like I'm some naive kid who doesn't understand the world.

Making my way back into my tent, I snuff out the candle and find that there's just enough light to keep working on the radio. I want to put Hannah's words out of my mind, but I can't help reliving that conversation over and over again, trying to understand what made her so scared. Whatever it was, she was wrong, she must have been. If there was something bad going on here, I'd know about it by now.

ELIZABETH

I WAS RIGHT. The storm *did* bring down some trees, but fortunately none of them hit the farmhouse. In that respect, at least, we were lucky.

Opening the door, I step out into the yard and stare at the damage. The storm has passed now, leaving behind nothing more than light rain and a cold wind that rustles the remaining trees. Still, the damage inflicted during the night was catastrophic, and most of the yard has been reduced to a muddy bog. The place didn't exactly look great yesterday, but at least it seemed safe and dry; right now, it's as if the end of the world has arrived.

I take a few steps forward, but my crutches almost slip, and I'm forced to inch my way back toward the door. I can't risk falling out here, not with my bandages.

I stop for a moment.

Silence.

I open my mouth to call out, but I'm scared. If I call his name, and if he doesn't come, I'll know that something's seriously wrong. Still, I have to do it. I have to know.

"Toad!" I shout.

Nothing.

"Toad!"

Again, nothing.

I don't know how far from the farmhouse he intended to go yesterday, and it's perfectly possible that he wouldn't be close enough to hear me. Although the morning light has only just arrived, the storm itself has been over for a couple of hours. I guess Toad must have just found somewhere to hide out, and then he had to wait until morning before starting the journey back here. In that case, it's crazy of me to expect him so soon. I have to trust that he's able to take care of himself, and that he'll be back as soon as possible.

Still, the wait is agony.

"Toad!" I shout one more time.

I wait.

No reply.

"Okay," I mutter, trying to give myself a little more confidence, "take your time. I know you're out there somewhere, and I know you're okay. You'll just come back when you can. That's fine."

I wait again, desperately hoping that I'll suddenly see him in the distance, hurrying through the forest. Finally, after a couple of minutes, I force myself to turn and head back into the cold, gloomy kitchen, where the skinned rabbits are still resting on the table. I make my way over to them, and for a moment all I can think about is the sight of Toad skinning them yesterday. Finally, realizing that he's going to be starving after spending the night outside, I decide I should start making some food.

Maneuvering my way around the kitchen isn't easy with the crutches, and I'm much slower than usual, but somehow I manage to find a few old pots and pans in one of the cupboards. Eventually I sit at the table and prop my crutches against the wall, before taking the first rabbit and placing it on a chopping board. Grabbing a knife, I start cutting the carcass, dividing it up just like Toad showed me a few weeks ago. If there's one thing I've learned since this crisis started, it's how to deal with a dead rabbit, and soon I've managed to get it divided up into various separate sections, all ready for the pot.

"My God," I imagine my mother saying. "I barely even recognize you."

I look over at the sofa, where Rachel is sleeping. She cried so much during the night, but then suddenly she stopped, as if she finally got used to the storm.

Continuing my work, I start rooting through the cupboards and eventually I find some salt and pepper. It feels good to be doing something practical, and I'm able to keep my mind from wandering onto the fact that I'm alone here. Working slowly and methodically, I finally get the rabbit ready, with all the pieces arranged on a tray. All that's left to do now is to start cooking, but I figure I should wait until Toad gets back. It won't take long to get the meat cooked, and I want us to have a really good meal. I need to show him that we can survive here.

Grabbing my crutches, I make my way back to the door and stare out once again at the yard. It's as barren and desolate as before, and there's still no sign of movement.

"Toad!" I shout.

Silence.

Taking a deep breath, I try to force myself not to panic. He's coming. He *has* to be coming. There's no way that a guy like Toad would get into trouble out there. Soon he'll walk back into the farmhouse, and he'll laugh at me for being so worried. Forcing myself to get on with other things, I turn and head away from the door.

THOMAS

"SHE MUST HAVE TAKEN off in the middle of the night," says one of the women at the cooking station as she takes delivery of the three salmon Mark and I caught this morning. "I always knew there was something wrong with her."

Keeping my mouth shut, I place the last fish on a wooden board. Glancing to my right, I spot the girl from earlier working with a bowl. We make eye contact briefly, but she immediately looks away. I guess she's worried that I might tell the others what happened earlier. In fact, she looks more than worried: she looks absolutely goddamn terrified.

"That Hannah girl was always flighty," says another woman. "I used to catch her daydreaming all the time. She'd be just staring into space like she had something on her mind."

"What's wrong?" I ask, hoping to get a little more information.

"Just some fool who decided to run away," says the woman closest to me, with a hint of disdain in her voice. "Some people don't know when they've got it good. They're always looking at the horizon and dreaming of being someplace better. Even now, with everything that's happened, some people are never satisfied."

"She must have had a reason for leaving," I continue, glancing at the other girl and seeing that she's studiously avoiding me. "Why would someone run away from a place like this?"

I wait for an answer, but the women suddenly seem to be ignoring me. It's clear that they still see me as an outsider, but I figure I should try to dig a little deeper.

"Was she unhappy?" I ask. "Did she say anything about -"

"Best not to ask too many questions," the closest woman says, forcing a fake smile. "Hannah made her own decision, and she'll have to live with the consequences. If she didn't appreciate things here, there are plenty who do, and we have a few more arrivals turning up every couple of weeks. It's not as if we're desperately in need of people, especially ones who don't really pull their weight. We'll be better off without her. Anyway, I doubt she'll last long out there, not on her own."

"But -"

"Don't ask," she says firmly. "It's none of your concern, anyway." She pauses for a moment, eying me suspiciously. "Why are you asking so many questions, anyway? Did you talk to her?"

"No," I reply. "I didn't know her at all. I was just wondering why someone would run away from this place. It doesn't make sense."

"That's right, it doesn't." Reaching over to a nearby table, the woman grabs a bag of potato chips and holds the open end out to me. "If you're hungry, take a few. It's not often that we get luxuries like this, but Mark managed to find some. He's a good man, always sharing whatever he gets hold of with the rest of us. With people like Hannah gone, there's more for everyone else."

"Mark gave you these?" I ask, reaching into the bag and taking a handful of chips.

"He came through the camp this morning," she continues, "handing them out. He said he'd managed to locate a small supply, and that he wanted the hardest-working people in the whole camp to have a little treat. I don't know where he found them, but it's like a blast from the past. I used to eat these things all day, every day, but I never thought I'd get them again."

"He looks after us," says one of the other women. "Without him, I'm not sure that things would run so smoothly around here."

"The taste reminds me of watching TV," the first woman says, closing her eyes for a moment as she eats one of the chips. "Me and my husband used to watch shows every night, and we'd open a big bag of these things at seven on the dot, and they'd last until nine, which was when we went to bed." Opening her eyes, she seems a little sad. "He's gone now, and I guess there won't be any more shows, but at least I've got the memories."

"Mark cares about us," says another woman. "He wants to share whatever he finds."

"But they came from -" I pause for a moment as I realize that Mark has taken the food from the truck and started giving it out as if it's his own. I told him I didn't mind sharing, but I never expected him to start taking credit for it. For the first time, I feel as if maybe Mark isn't quite as open and honest as I used to think, but then again I know I can't really get too angry. After all, I told him to take things from the truck, and it's not as if I want to have all the credit for myself. I just don't like the way that he seems to be getting built up as some kind of god around this place.

"Haven't you got work to do?" one of the women asks suddenly with a scowl.

Turning and hurrying away, I make my way toward my tent. I'm due to go out to the forest with some of the other men, to chop down some more trees. We're getting through a lot of wood every day, and this is rapidly becoming my main job. It's hard work and my muscles are aching, but I know I have to contribute to the community. Still, as I pass a group of children eating candy from my stash, I can't help but feel a little annoyed as I overhear them talking about how wonderful Mark is for giving them these things. It's as if he's using *my* food to give himself more support among the community.

Hearing voices nearby, I turn and see Mark a little further away. He's talking to a group of women, and after a moment one of them hugs him. As he glances in my direction, he nods a greeting, and I do the same, but I can't help thinking that maybe he's playing a long game here.

"Thomas!" he calls out. "Be ready in twenty minutes, okay? We've got a lot of work to do today!"

I nod, even though right now I'm starting to feel the effects of my sleepless night. I know I can't show any signs of weakness, so I figure I just have to get through the day and hope I have a better night tonight. It might be good to physically exhaust myself and to try to get my brain to shut down for a few hours.

Once I reach the tent, I take a moment to change into a different shirt. I only have two sets of clothes, so as soon as one set is dirty I have to wash it and set it out to dry so that I'll have something to wear tomorrow. These mundane jobs take up so much time, it's hard to remember that in the old days I used to just shove stuff into a laundry basket and let my Mom take care of everything. Still, there's no time to sit around complaining, so I quickly finish changing and then bundle my dirty clothes up, ready to go and wash them down by the lake. I figure I've just about got enough time before I'm due to make my way to the forest.

Just as I'm about to leave the tent, however, I notice a flashing light on the front of the radio. Pausing for a moment, I check the settings, and finally I realize that I must have accidentally left the battery connected, and now I seem to have picked up a signal from somewhere. Grabbing the headphones, I put them on and then try plugging them into the back of the unit. It seems like a crazy long-shot, but at the same time I can't shake the feeling that I might be able to make contact with someone. Right now, I don't even care who I end up talking to. I just want to know for certain that there are other people in the world.

"Hello?" I say as I wait for something to come through. "Is someone there?"

Realizing that I've got the headphones in the wrong socket, I try another, and then another, and suddenly I hear a wall of static, followed by the faintest sound of a female voice. It's not much, and it's impossible to make out what she's saying, but as

I turn a few of the dials I find that I'm able to tune in a little more accurately, and finally I'm able to get rid of most of the static.

"Hello!" I shout, grabbing the microphone. "Who are you?"

"Hello?" the voice replies, sounding garbled and distorted but still human. "Did someone say something?"

"Yeah, I'm here!" I shout, stunned that I've actually managed to make contact. "My name's Thomas Edgewater and I'm right on the shore of Lake Erie! Who am I talking to?"

ELIZABETH

"MY NAME'S ELIZABETH," I say, holding the microphone closer to my mouth. "Elizabeth Marter. I'm... I'm in a farmhouse somewhere in... Pennsylvania, I think. Are you anywhere nearby?"

I wait for an answer, but all I hear is static. Flicking a few switches on the radio unit, I wait for some kind of response, but I'm already starting to worry that I've lost contact. The truth is, when I sat down to fiddle with the radio a few minutes ago, I was just trying to keep myself busy while I wait for Toad. I didn't really expect to hear another human voice, but somehow I've managed to find someone. Then again, they seem to have gone again. Still, I *know* there was someone out there.

"Hello?" the guy's voice says suddenly. "Can you hear me?"

"I'm here!" I shout. "I'm in a farmhouse in Pennsylvania!"

"Are you alone?" he asks.

"Yeah. Well, no. Maybe. I've got a baby with me, but she's not mine. Her mother died. And there's a guy here too, but he went out yesterday and now he hasn't come back." I pause for a moment as I realize how crazy this must all sound. "What did you say your name was again?"

"Thomas," he replies. "Thomas Edgewater."

"It's good to hear your voice, Thomas Edgewater. I'm Elizabeth."

"Have you seen many other people?" he asks. "Are there other survivors down there with you?"

"Not many," I tell him. "I was in New York when this all started. There were only a few people left. My brother and I were in our parents' apartment, but we were alone, and then... We tried to get by for a while, but it was hard and some of the other people weren't very helpful. Eventually my brother died, and I ended up meeting some other people and coming here."

"My brother died too," he replies.

I open my mouth to say something, but the words seem to catch in my throat. It's strange to think that this guy and I are talking, and that even though we don't know each other, we seem to have a few things in common. I'd give anything to meet him face to face, but I guess that's never going to happen. Still, I can't deny that I'm excited by the idea that at least there are other survivors in the world.

"If you're alone," he says after a moment, "you should try to get up here to Lake Erie. Do you have a vehicle you can use?"

"No," I reply. "There's nothing. We've been traveling on foot."

"Find a vehicle. You'll need some gas too, but most cars should still have something in the tank. Then head up to Lake Erie, to the western end of the southern shore. There are people here, not many, but enough to start building a community. Have you seen any sign of the government or anything like that?"

"Nothing," I reply. "It's like everyone's just gone."

"What about..." He pauses. "Did you see creatures? There were these things -"

"There were lots of them in New York," I tell him. "They all had the same voice, but they weren't very mobile. It was like they weren't really able to control themselves properly. Out here in Pennsylvania we saw some too and they seemed to be getting stronger, but lately they've disappeared. There haven't been any for a few weeks."

"Same here," he replies. "It's like they started to rot, so hopefully they're gone. Listen, you should get moving as soon as possible. You need to find other people."

"I can't leave. I have to wait for Toad, the guy I'm with, to come back. He went hunting last night and then there was this huge storm, and I don't know what happened to him."

"How long are you gonna wait?"

I pause for a moment. "What do you mean?"

"How long are you gonna give him before..." His voice trails off for a moment, but I know exactly what he was going to say. "Whether he comes back or not," he continues eventually, "you need to make for somewhere and find a vehicle, and then head up this way. We're managing to find food, and we've got water, and there are a couple of hundred people. Everyone's got a job, and we all work together to make sure that there's enough for everyone. It's actually not so bad, but I don't know what we're going to do when winter comes. I guess we'll just have to make sure we're properly prepared."

"That sounds good," I tell him. "We've been wandering around, not really having anywhere to go. There's no way I ever want to be in New York again. The whole place was just completely ruined. As soon as Toad comes back -"

Suddenly there's a burst of static, and although I can hear Thomas speaking, it's impossible to understand what he's saying since his voice has become distorted and twisted.

"Hello?" I shout, desperately hoping that I won't lose contact with him so soon. "Are you still there?"

"It's not good to be alone," he says suddenly as his voice returns. "We're all much better off if we stick to large groups. How far are you from the nearest town?"

"I don't know."

"Do you have a map?"

"No," I reply, looking across the gloomy kitchen. Suddenly it hits me: if Toad doesn't come back, I'm going to die here. With Rachel to look after, and with only one good leg, there's no way I can keep us alive. "I don't really have anything."

"You need to get organized," he continues. "You need to work out where the nearest town is, and you need to walk there."

"That might be tricky," I mutter, looking down at my bandaged leg. There's still a red stain showing through the bandage, but as I look more closely, I can't help noticing that there might be a hint of yellow.

"You've got no choice!" Thomas says firmly. "There's no point sitting around and hoping that somehow the government's gonna come and save us. All of that's over now, Elizabeth. We've got to look after ourselves. Even if you don't make it to Lake Erie, there are probably other groups. You need to find one and join it, and then maybe you can be part of something that starts rebuilding. Just take my advice and stay away from the cities. I was in Chicago the other day, and it wasn't good there. There's so much disease, and people are dying of starvation."

"I'm going to come up to Lake Erie," I tell him, figuring that I need to stay optimistic. "As soon as Toad gets back, we'll find a way to get there. We'll find a car."

"Is that guy your boyfriend?" he asks.

"My -" I pause for a moment as I try to work out how to answer that particular question. "I guess so," I say eventually, even though I'm not sure whether it's true. "Maybe."

"Whatever he is, you have to get to safety."

"I know," I reply, glancing over at the door but still seeing no sign of Toad. "I can't go yet, though. I have to wait for him to come back. He *will* come. You don't know him, but I do. He's the kind of guy who can take care of himself. He knows the land, and he knows how to stay safe, even when there's a storm. There's no way anything can have happened to him. I just know, deep down that he's okay, and that he's coming back."

Thomas tries to reply, but once again his voice seems to be getting lost in the static. I wait a moment, hoping that he'll come back, but finally I start trying to adjust the dials again.

"Hello?" I shout. "Thomas! Are you still there? Can you -"

Before I can finish, there's a loud bang as the top of the radio unit explodes in a shower of sparks. I lean back and watch as smoke starts to come from the back of the unit, and a brief fire quickly dies down. I have no idea what went wrong, but it's clear that the radio's dead now, and I guess there's no way I can get back in touch with that Thomas guy. Still, at least I know that there are other people out there, and I also know that if we head toward Lake Erie, we'll find other survivors. There's still a part of me that wants to stay here at the farmhouse, but I know deep down that now we've got a destination, we should get moving.

I just need Toad to come back, so I can give him the news.

THOMAS

"ELIZABETH? ARE YOU STILL THERE?"

I wait, but there's nothing. It's as if she suddenly disappeared into the static, and although I make a few adjustments to the system, there doesn't seem to be anything I can do to get her back. Then again, it was just pure luck that I got in touch with her in the first place, so I figure there's no way I can manage it again. Finally, as I'm forced to face the fact that she's gone for good, I remove the headphones and sit back.

There are still people out there. That much, at least, is certain.

Figuring that I'm in danger of running late for work, I grab my bag of tools and climb out of the tent. My mind is still filled with thoughts of Elizabeth, and as I make my way between the other tents I can't help wondering just how many people are left in the world. Since no-one has come to help, it's pretty clear that this catastrophe has hit the whole planet. There were seven billion people in the old days, but I'm starting to think that there might be less than a million now. After all, whole cities seem to have been almost completely wiped out, and people are probably still dying due to malnutrition and thirst.

I just hope that people like Elizabeth are able to get to safety. She seemed nice enough, but she also sounded lost and alone.

"Hey!" a voice hisses suddenly.

Turning, I look around at the nearby tents, but I can't see anyone.

"Over here!" the voice calls out.

Spotting a face staring at me from a few feet away, I hurry over and find that the girl from earlier, Hannah's friend, is crouched behind a tent. She looks scared, but then again that's kind of her default expression these days.

"What do you want?" I ask, keeping my voice down. "I'm going to -"

"Get out of sight," she whispers, grabbing my shirt and trying to pull me down to her level.

Crouching next to her, I realize that she's absolutely terrified.

"I've got a message for you," she continues.

"From who?"

"Amanda Quinn."

"Quinn?" Looking over my shoulder, I almost expect to see her hiding somewhere nearby. "Where is she?"

"That's the message," the girl continues. "She wants you to meet her. She says she's found what she was looking for, but she needs your help. She's -"

"My help?" I stare at her for a moment, stunned by the idea. "Just tell me where she is."

"She said you have to go back to the field you were in yesterday when you were looking for her. She said something about an apple tree you were standing next to, just before you turned back. Does that make any sense?"

"Sure, but..." I pause as I realize what it means. "She was there," I add, stunned by the idea that somehow I missed her. "She was right there, watching us! She must have been hiding somewhere and listening to every word we said!"

"It doesn't matter," the girl continues. "She just asked me to tell you that you have to go and meet her there as soon as possible, and that she wants to show you the source of the signal. I don't really know what she meant by that, but she said you'd understand. She also said that you have to believe that she didn't kill the other girl, Kaylee. She -"

"I don't have time to talk," I tell her, getting

to my feet.

"Wait!" she hisses, pulling me back down. "Quinn *didn't* kill Kaylee. I was there, I saw what happened. It was the other women, the ones who do the cooking for our group. There were five or six of them, and they turned on her. I don't know whether Kaylee provoked it, but Quinn tried to stop them. They chased her away, and then they lied and said that she was the killer. It's not true, though. I saw it with my own eyes."

"Why would all those people lie?" I ask.

"I've told you. This place isn't right. If you don't believe me, go back to your friend's grave."

"Why? What's the point?"

"Dig her up," she continues. "Or try to, anyway. I guarantee you, there won't be a body down there. All you'll find will be an empty sheet. They'll have taken the rest."

"What are you talking about?"

"It's not right what they're doing. They shouldn't take people and hurt them like this, but they don't care. Sometimes I think they just see us as *things* to be used for whatever they're planning. Most people are either part of it, or they don't notice because they're too busy working. The people who do this are careful. They only take a few people every month. You just have to believe me when I promise you that Quinn isn't responsible for what happened. If she hadn't managed to get away, they'd have killed her too. I don't know exactly what they do with the bodies, but there's something going on further along the shore. Mark's involved, he knows about it. I think he might even be in charge. Please, you can't tell anyone that I spoke to you, or we'll both be next." She pauses. "Do you believe me?"

"I don't know," I reply. "I've got to go and find Quinn."

"Maybe she can explain more," the girl continues. "All I know is that I was there two days ago and I saw exactly what happened. Why would I lie to you?"

I stare at her for a moment, and although I find it hard to believe that Quinn could be the victim of some big conspiracy, there's something about this girl that seems very genuine. Then again, she might just be Quinn's latest plaything, someone to be used in an attempt to manipulate me.

"Melissa," she says suddenly, with a faint smile. "That's my name. I just thought... You know, if anything happens to me, at least you'll know my name."

"I'm going to go and find Quinn," I tell her, "and I'm going to finish this for good."

"But -"

"Tell Mark I'll be back soon," I add, before turning and hurrying back toward my tent. As soon as I'm inside, I reach under the flap at the far end and pull out the hunting knife, which I've been keeping hidden in case anyone decides they want to steal it. Once I've hitched the blade to my belt, I turn and make my way between the tents, heading for the crest of the hill. I can feel the fury building in my soul again, urging me forward and making me feel as if the only option is to find Quinn and end her miserable life.

I don't know how she brainwashed that Melissa girl, but I refuse to believe that there's been some big conspiracy. Quinn murdered Kaylee, and now I'm going to make her pay. It's the right thing to do.

ELIZABETH

"STOP CRYING," I WHISPER, staring out the kitchen window as Rachel cries in the next room. "Please, just stop..."

It's late afternoon and I've been standing here by the window for at least an hour. I don't have a watch, but I'm pretty sure it must have been at least twenty-four hours now since Toad set out for his hunting trip, and it must have been eight or nine since the storm died down. Sure, he might have found somewhere to shelter during the worst of the weather, but even so, he should have been able to get back here by now.

"Stop crying," I mutter again, trying not to let my frustration boil over. Rachel has been bawling her eyes out non-stop for so long now, I can barely even hear myself think.

Still, she's just a baby. She must be so scared and confused, and I'm sure she's wondering where her real mother is. She knows I'm an imposter.

"Come on, Toad," I whisper, hoping that maybe in some way he might be able to hear me. I still don't know if I believe in God, but if there's even the slightest chance of my prayer reaching Toad, I'm willing to give it a try. "Please, just come back. I don't care about anything else, but please -"

Suddenly Rachel stops crying.

I turn and look at the door that leads through to the next room.

Silence.

I'm glad she stopped, but there's something strange about the *way* it happened. It almost sounded as if suddenly, with no warning at all, her voice just disappeared. I pause for a moment, almost hoping that she'll at least make some kind of noise so that I know she's okay. Finally, I grab my crutches and make my way slowly across the room, before heading through the door and finding that Rachel's still on the bed where I left her.

"Hey," I say as I get closer, "are you upset about something? When are you supposed to start teething, anyway? I thought it was later, but -"

At that moment, I realize that she's staring at me, almost exactly the same way she was doing earlier in the week. This time, however, there's something different; whereas before she just seemed to be studying me, this time there's a faint smile on her lips, and an undeniable hint of intelligence in her eyes. I want to pick her up and tell her that everything's going to be okay, but at the same time I'm worried about touching her.

"Don't be scared," I tell her. "Everything's going to be fine. We're just waiting for Toad to come home." With that, I turn and make my way back through to the kitchen. I don't want to think the worst, but I can't deny the truth: the way Rachel was looking at me just now wasn't normal. It's almost as if there's another mind in her head, staring out at me through her eyes.

Seconds later, I hear a noise from her room. It almost sounds like she's getting off the bed.

THOMAS

STANDING BY THE APPLE TREE, on the edge of a vast green field, I look around for some sign of Quinn. She's supposed to be here to meet me, but so far there's no sign of her. I guess she might have been too scared. After all, she must know that I won't believe her bullshit story. I doubt she's brave enough to face up to what she did.

"Thomas!" a voice calls out suddenly from the distance. "Over here!"

Turning, I spot someone standing several hundred feet away, at the top of a small hill. It's Quinn, silhouetted against the later afternoon sky as she waves her arms at me. Instinctively, I reach down to check that I've still got the knife.

"Follow me!" she shouts. "Come on! I need your help!"

With that, she turns and hurries down the other side of the hill, disappearing from view.

"Wait!" I call out, before starting to run after her. I swear to God, I should have guessed that this wasn't going to be simple. As I race up the side of the hill, almost losing my footing in the process, all I can think about is the fact that this bitch was able to slip away from me once before. This time, I'm going to make sure she faces the consequences of her actions, but there's no way I'm going to bother dragging her back to face justice in front of the others. I'll deal with her out here, and I'm damn certain my conscience will still be clear by sundown.

"Hurry!" she shouts excitedly.

Getting to the top of the hill, I see that she's already managed to get quite a lot further down into the next valley. She stops and waves at me, before turning and hurrying through the grass. Figuring that I'm going to need to catch up to her and force her to stay still, I set off in the same direction, running as fast as I can until finally I notice that she's stopped up ahead. As I get closer, she turns to me and smiles, but there's a hint of sadness in her eyes.

"Don't worry," she says suddenly, her voice faltering a little. "It's me."

Stopping a few feet away, I stare at her. There's a part of me that wants to kill her right now, but another part of me wants some answers first. The problem is, I don't even know where to start.

"Why did you do it?" I ask eventually, still a little out of breath from the chase.

"Do what?"

"You killed Kaylee. You cut her down in cold blood."

"No," she replies, shaking her head. "I didn't. It was made to seem that way, but I hope you understand that I would never, ever do anything like that. It was those women, Thomas. Other people saw what happened, but most of them are too scared to speak up. There's something very dark happening at that camp, something involving bodies being taken further along the shore. I'd like to investigate a little further, but I haven't had time, not yet. I've been out here tracking down the source of the signal, and I've finally found it. You'll never guess what -"

"You're deluded," I say, interrupting her.

"Why?"

"Because you think I'm going to fall for your bullshit story." Reaching down, I take the knife from my belt, and from the look in her eyes it's clear that Quinn realizes what I'm planning to do. "I don't know how you got that girl Melissa to lie for you," I continue, "but you obviously brainwashed her, the way you brainwashed all those people back in Chicago."

"Brainwashed?" She smiles nervously. "What are you talking about? Thomas, I've never brainwashed anyone in my life. Perhaps I'm a little charismatic, but..." She pauses, and this time there are tears in her eyes. "I'm truly sorry about Kaylee. I tried to stop them, but there was nothing I could do, and then they came after me and I barely escaped. I know this must be difficult for you to accept, but what motive could I possibly have to harm that girl? She was in my dream, Thomas, just like you. She was supposed to be here with us when we found the source of the signal."

"There's no signal," I tell her.

"There is," she says firmly. "We're at the source right now."

"Do you really think I'm going to let you get away with what you did?" I ask, taking a step toward her. "You can't distract me with all this garbage about a signal!"

She immediately steps back, keeping her eyes fixed on the knife.

"Do you want to know why that Melissa girl agreed to help me?" she asks, holding her hands up. "Don't you realize who she is?"

"She's just another impressionable idiot who let you get under her skin," I reply.

"She's George's daughter."

I stare at her, and although I want to believe that this is another of her tricks, I suddenly realize that she might be telling the truth. Not only was the girl named Melissa, but she mentioned a daughter named Katie. It's hard to believe that it could be the same person George and I were looking for last week, but somehow we seem to have found her.

"It was pure coincidence that I made the connection," Quinn continues, "but then I asked her, and I told her that her father was alive and that he was looking for her. I think that helped her to trust me, and then it was only a few hours later that poor Kaylee was killed by those murderous women. I honestly don't know what they're doing with the bodies further along the shore, but you mustn't trust Mark. He's involved in something horrific."

"This is all a lie," I tell her. "That girl, her name probably isn't really Melissa. You just manipulate people and make them -"

"Don't you want to see it?" she asks suddenly.

"See what?"

"If you're going to kill me," she continues, her voice still trembling a little, "then surely you should at least see what I'm going to show you first. I mean, I really *have* found the source of the signal. Why else would I ask you to meet me out here? I've found it, but I can't do anything with it, not yet. I need help. It's so close, Thomas. Won't you at least let me show you? Even if it's the last thing I ever do?"

I hold the knife out toward her, but although I'm determined to punish her for Kaylee's death and for all these lies, I figure I might as well see what she's rambling on about.

"Go on, then," I say eventually. "Show me."

"This way," she replies, turning and making her way a few feet further down the valley until she stops next to what looks like a shallow pit. Her laptop is on the floor nearby, along with a shovel that I immediately recognize as one that was in the back of my truck. I guess she took something after all.

"Well?" I ask, keen not to get too close to her.

"Come and see," she replies, taking a step back.

With the knife still held out toward her, I make my way to the edge of the pit and look down. At first, I'm not even sure what I'm seeing, but finally I realize that somehow she's managed to uncover part of a metal structure, with a door set into the top and what appears to be a small glass window.

"What the hell is this thing?" I ask.

"I think it's some kind of bunker," she replies, sounding pretty pleased with herself. "Before my laptop ran out of power, I traced the source of the signal definitively to this spot. I've tried everything I can think of to get the door open, but it won't budge and I'm running out of options. That's one of the reasons I was hoping you might be able to help."

With the knife still in my hand, I stare at the door and try to make sense of everything. Sure, Quinn's full of bullshit and she's an expert manipulator, and almost certainly a murderer, but there's no way she could have magicked this bunker out of thin air. Somehow, despite her insanity, she's genuinely managed to track down something extraordinary.

"Well?" she asks.

"Well what?" I turn to her. "It's probably just some kind of old Cold War thing."

"Look closer," she continues with a faint smile.

"Why?"

"Because then you'll see the other thing that's caught my attention. And I'm pretty sure you'll realize that whatever this place is, it's most certainly *not* an old Cold War thing, as you so delightfully put it."

Figuring that I can fend her off if she tries anything, I step down into the pit and make my way toward the bunker's metal door. As I get closer, I stare at the small round window at the top of the door, and suddenly I realize that there's something moving on the other side of the glass. Finally, even though I can barely believe what I'm seeing, I get close enough to see the truth.

On the other side of the door, inside the bunker, there's a man. He's staring back at me with wild, startled eyes. Whoever he is, he sure as hell doesn't look very pleased to see us.

ELIZABETH

IT TAKES A LOT OF EFFORT, but I'm finally able to get the back of the radio unit open, only to find a partially-melted bundle of wires and cables. I stare at the ruined remains of the system, and although I try to tell myself that maybe I can find a way to fix it, finally I'm forced to accept that there's no way I can get the damn thing up and running.

From somewhere else in the house, there's a faint creaking sound.

Looking across the gloomy kitchen, I realize that while I've been trying to fix the radio, the evening has begun to get darker. My heart is pounding as I listen to the silence, praying that I won't hear another of the creaks that have been periodically coming from Rachel's room, but moments later I hear it again, followed by a faint knocking sound. I have no idea what's happening in there, but if I didn't know better, I'd start to think that somehow Rachel is moving around.

Hobbling over to the back door, I look out at the forest and see that there's still no sign of Toad. He's been gone for so long now, it's hard to believe that he's okay. Something must have happened to him. Either that, or he's decided he can't hang around and risk his life with a cripple and a baby. I don't want to believe that he'd just abandon us like this, but at the same time, the alternative – that he's been hurt or maybe even killed in the storm – is worse.

"Come back," I mutter, trying to stay calm. "Please, just come back. Don't -"

Hearing a noise nearby, I turn and look back across the kitchen. I swear the noise came from *this* room, much closer than before, but I can't see anything so far. I make my way slowly around the kitchen table, constantly on edge in case I'm not alone, while telling myself that this is all in my head. I'm just being paranoid, and there's no way that there could be anyone else here. Still, I can't help worrying that those creatures might have come back. Even though I'm reluctant to go through to Rachel, I figure I need to make sure that she's okay. I head through as fast as my crutches can carry me, but when I reach the door and look at the bed I pull up short.

Rachel's gone.

From the kitchen, there's another faint creaking sound.

My heart pounding, I stand completely still for a moment before realizing that this is insane. Rachel's a one-month-old child and there's no way she could ever hurt me, even if something was in her mind and controlling her. Still, the way she looked at me earlier reminded me of the way those infected creatures used to look at me, and even though I'd desperate not to admit it, there's a fear in the back of my mind that maybe Rachel has succumbed. Taking a deep breath, I force myself to head back through to the kitchen, but there's still no sign of anyone.

"Rachel?" I call out.

Silence.

"Rachel?"

Slowly, I make my way over toward the back door, constantly looking around for any sign of her. When I get to the middle of the room, I stop for a moment and turn, convinced that I'm going to see her at any moment. The problem is, it's so dark in here, I can barely make out a damn thing. Heading over to one of the cupboards, I reach out to grab a candle, but as I glance over at the window, I spot a reflected flash of movement in one of the cupboard's glass panes. Turning, I almost expect to find Rachel right behind me, but there's nothing.

I open my mouth to call her name.

Seconds later, I hear a noise outside. Someone's coming. Filled with relief that it must be Toad, I run to the back door, but before I can get there it's pushed open and three figures burst into the room, wearing army camouflage clothing and aiming guns straight at my head.

"Put your hands up!" shouts one of the men, his face hidden by a mask. "Drop to your knees! Now!"

I stare at him, barely able to believe that this isn't some kind of horrific dream.

"I won't tell you again!" he shouts. "Drop to your knees!"

I hear a creaking noise nearby. Instinctively, I turn to see whether it's Rachel.

"I -" I start to say.

A fraction of a second later, a gunshot rings out and I feel a sharp pain burst through my shoulder, knocking me off my crutches and sending me crashing to the floor with such force that the side of my head bangs against the wood, knocking me out cold.

DAYS 46 TO 53

Continued in:

Days 54 to 61
(Mass Extinction Event book 5)

Also by Amy Cross

The Devil, the Witch and the Whore
(The Deal book 1)

"Leave the forest alone. Whatever's out there, just let it be. Don't make it angry."

When a horrific discovery is made at the edge of town, Sheriff James Kopperud realizes the answers he seeks might be waiting beyond in the vast forest. But everybody in the town of Deal knows that there's something out there in the forest, something that should never be disturbed. A deal was made long ago, a deal that was supposed to keep the town safe. And if he insists on investigating the murder of a local girl, James is going to have to break that deal and head out into the wilderness.

Meanwhile, James has no idea that his estranged daughter Ramsey has returned to town. Ramsey is running from something, and she thinks she can find safety in the vast tunnel system that runs beneath the forest. Before long, however, Ramsey finds herself coming face to face with creatures that hide in the shadows. One of these creatures is known as the devil, and another is known as the witch. They're both waiting for the whore to arrive, but for very different reasons. And soon Ramsey is offered a terrible deal, one that could save or destroy the entire town, and maybe even the world.

Also by Amy Cross

The Soul Auction

"I saw a woman on the beach. I watched her face a demon."

Thirty years after her mother's death, Alice Ashcroft is drawn back to the coastal English town of Curridge. Somebody in Curridge has been reviewing Alice's novels online, and in those reviews there have been tantalizing hints at a hidden truth. A truth that seems to be linked to her dead mother.

"Thirty years ago, there was a soul auction."

Once she reaches Curridge, Alice finds strange things happening all around her. Something attacks her car. A figure watches her on the beach at night. And when she tries to find the person who has been reviewing her books, she makes a horrific discovery.

What really happened to Alice's mother thirty years ago? Who was she talking to, just moments before dropping dead on the beach? What caused a huge rockfall that nearly tore a nearby cliff-face in half? And what sinister presence is lurking in the grounds of the local church?

Also by Amy Cross

Darper Danver: The Complete First Series

Five years ago, three friends went to a remote cabin in the woods and tried to contact the spirit of a long-dead soldier. They thought they could control whatever happened next. They were wrong...

Newly released from prison, Cassie Briggs returns to Fort Powell, determined to get her life back on track. Soon, however, she begins to suspect that an ancient evil still lurks in the nearby cabin. Was the mysterious Darper Danver really destroyed all those years ago, or does her spirit still linger, waiting for a chance to return?

As Cassie and her ex-boyfriend Fisher are finally forced to face the truth about what happened in the cabin, they realize that Darper isn't ready to let go of their lives just yet. Meanwhile, a vengeful woman plots revenge for her brother's murder, and a New York ghost writer arrives in town to uncover the truth. Before long, strange carvings begin to appear around town and blood starts to flow once again.

Also by Amy Cross

The Ghost of Molly Holt

"Molly Holt is dead. There's nothing to fear in this house."

When three teenagers set out to explore an abandoned house in the middle of a forest, they think they've found the location where the infamous Molly Holt video was filmed.

They've found much more than that...

Tim doesn't believe in ghosts, but he has a crush on a girl who does. That's why he ends up taking her out to the house, and it's also why he lets her take his only flashlight. But as they explore the house together, Tim and Becky start to realize that something else might be lurking in the shadows.

Something that, ten years ago, suffered unimaginable pain.

Something that won't rest until a terrible wrong has been put right.

Also by Amy Cross

American Coven

He kidnapped three women and held them in his basement. He thought they couldn't fight back. He was wrong...

Snatched from the street near her home, Holly Carter is taken to a rural house and thrown down into a stone basement. She meets two other women who have also been kidnapped, and soon Holly learns about the horrific rituals that take place in the house. Eventually, she's called upstairs to take her place in the ice bath.

As her nightmare continues, however, Holly learns about a mysterious power that exists in the basement, and which the three women might be able to harness. When they finally manage to get through the metal door, however, the women have no idea that their fight for freedom is going to stretch out for more than a decade, or that it will culminate in a final, devastating demonstration of their new-found powers.

Also by Amy Cross

The Ash House

Why would anyone ever return to a haunted house?

For Diane Mercer the answer is simple. She's dying of cancer, and she wants to know once and for all whether ghosts are real.

Heading home with her young son, Diane is determined to find out whether the stories are real. After all, everyone else claimed to see and hear strange things in the house over the years. Everyone except Diane had some kind of experience in the house, or in the little ash house in the yard.

As Diane explores the house where she grew up, however, her son is exploring the yard and the forest. And while his mother might be struggling to come to terms with her own impending death, Daniel Mercer is puzzled by fleeting appearances of a strange little girl who seems drawn to the ash house, and by strange, rasping coughs that he keeps hearing at night.

The Ash House is a horror novel about a woman who desperately wants to know what will happen to her when she dies, and about a boy who uncovers the shocking truth about a young girl's murder.

Also by Amy Cross

Haunted

Twenty years ago, the ghost of a dead little girl drove Sheriff Michael Blaine to his death.

Now, that same ghost is coming for his daughter.

Returning to the small town where she grew up, Alex Roberts is determined to live a normal, quiet life. For the residents of Railham, however, she's an unwelcome reminder of the town's darkest hour.

Twenty years ago, nine-year-old Mo Garvey was found brutally murdered in a nearby forest. Everyone thinks that Alex's father was responsible, but if the killer was brought to justice, why is the ghost of Mo Garvey still after revenge?

And how far will the real killer go to protect his secret, when Alex starts getting closer to the truth?

Haunted is a horror novel about a woman who has to face her past, about a town that would rather forget, and about a little girl who refuses to let death stand in her way.

Also by Amy Cross

The Curse of Wetherley House

"If you walk through that door, Evil Mary will get you."

When she agrees to visit a supposedly haunted house with an old friend, Rosie assumes she'll encounter nothing more scary than a few creaks and bumps in the night. Even the legend of Evil Mary doesn't put her off. After all, she knows ghosts aren't real. But when Mary makes her first appearance, Rosie realizes she might already be trapped.

For more than a century, Wetherley House has been cursed. A horrific encounter on a remote road in the late 1800's has already caused a chain of misery and pain for all those who live at the house. Wetherley House was abandoned long ago, after a terrible discovery in the basement, something has remained undetected within its room. And even the local children know that Evil Mary waits in the house for anyone foolish enough to walk through the front door.

Before long, Rosie realizes that her entire life has been defined by the spirit of a woman who died in agony. Can she become the first person to escape Evil Mary, or will she fall victim to the same fate as the house's other occupants?

Also by Amy Cross

The Ghosts of Hexley Airport

Ten years ago, more than two hundred people died in a horrific plane crash at Hexley Airport.

Today, some say their ghosts still haunt the terminal building.

When she starts her new job at the airport, working a night shift as part of the security team, Casey assumes the stories about the place can't be true. Even when she has a strange encounter in a deserted part of the departure hall, she's certain that ghosts aren't real.

Soon, however, she's forced to face the truth. Not only is there something haunting the airport's buildings and tarmac, but a sinister force is working behind the scenes to replicate the circumstances of the original accident. And as a snowstorm moves in, Hexley Airport looks set to witness yet another disaster.

Also by Amy Cross

The Girl Who Never Came Back

Twenty years ago, Charlotte Abernathy vanished while playing near her family's house. Despite a frantic search, no trace of her was found until a year later, when the little girl turned up on the doorstep with no memory of where she'd been.

Today, Charlotte has put her mysterious ordeal behind her, even though she's never learned where she was during that missing year. However, when her eight-year-old niece vanishes in similar circumstances, a fully-grown Charlotte is forced to make a fresh attempt to uncover the truth.

Originally published in 2013, the fully revised and updated version of *The Girl Who Never Came Back* tells the harrowing story of a woman who thought she could forget her past, and of a little girl caught in the tangled web of a dark family secret.

Also by Amy Cross

Asylum
(The Asylum Trilogy book 1)

"No-one ever leaves Lakehurst. The staff, the patients, the ghosts... Once you're here, you're stuck forever."

After shooting her little brother dead, Annie Radford is sent to Lakehurst psychiatric hospital for assessment. Hearing voices in her head, Annie is forced to undergo experimental new treatments devised by a mysterious old man who lives in the hospital's attic. It soon becomes clear that the hospital's staff, led by the vicious Nurse Winter, are hiding something horrific at Lakehurst.

As Annie struggles to survive the hospital, she learns more about Nurse Winter's own story. Once a promising young medical student, Kirsten Winter also heard voices in her head. Voices that traveled a long way to reach her. Voices that have a plan of their own. Voices that will stop at nothing to get what they want.

What kind of signals are being transmitted from the basement of the hospital? Who is the old man in the attic? Why are living human brains kept in jars? And what is the dark secret that lurks at the heart of the hospital?

Also by Amy Cross

The Devil's Hand

"I felt it last night! I was all alone, and suddenly a hand touched my shoulder!"

The year is 1943. Beacon's Ash is a private, remote school in the North of England, and all its pupils are fallen girls. Pregnant and unmarried, they have been sent away by their families. For Ivy Jones, a young girl who arrived at the school several months earlier, Beacon's Ash is a nightmare, and her fears are strengthened when one of her classmates is killed in mysterious circumstances.

Has the ghost of Abigail Cartwright returned to the school? Who or what is responsible for the hand that touches the girls' shoulders in the dead of night? And is the school's headmaster Jeremiah Kane just a madman who seeks to cause misery, or is he in fact on the trail of the Devil himself? Soon ghosts are stalking the dark corridors, and Ivy realizes she has to face the evil that lurks in the school's shadows.

The Devil's Hand is a horror novel about a girl who seeks the truth about her friend's death, and about a madman who believes the Devil stalks the school's corridors in the run-up to Christmas.

For more information, visit:

www. amycross.com

AMY CROSS

Printed in Great Britain
by Amazon